THE ANCASTER DEMONS

Norman Russell

CHIVERS
THORNDIKE

This Large Print book is published by BBC Audiobooks Ltd, Bath, England and by Thorndike Press®, Waterville, Maine, USA.

Published in 2004 in the U.K. by arrangement with Robert Hale, Ltd.

Published in 2004 in the U.S. by arrangement with Robert Hale, Ltd.

U.K. Hardcover   ISBN 1–4056–3021–3 (Chivers Large Print)
U.K. Softcover   ISBN 1–4056–3022–1 (Camden Large Print)
U.S. Softcover   ISBN 0–7862–6731–3 (General)

The text of this Large Print edition is unabridged.
Other aspects of the book may vary from the original edition.

Set in 16 pt. New Times Roman.

Printed in Great Britain on acid-free paper.

British Library Cataloguing in Publication Data available

Library of Congress Cataloging-in-Publication Data

Russell, Norman.
    The Ancaster demons / Norman Russell.
      p.   cm.
    ISBN 0–7862–6731–3 (lg. print : sc : alk. paper)
    1. Deans, Cathedral and collegiate—Crimes against—Fiction.
2. Christian art and symbolism—Fiction. 3. Police—England
—Fiction. 4. Stone carving—Fiction. 5. Iconoclasm—Fiction.
6. Cathedrals—Fiction. 7. England—Fiction. 8. Clergy—Fiction.
9. Large type books. I. Title.
PR6118.U87A83 2004
823'.92—dc22   2004042168

CONTENTS

Contents

PROLOGUE

SUMMER TEMPEST

The air was close and still, the darkness tense and expectant. It had been a sultry day, one of the hottest July days that Nicholas Arkwright could remember, and now the atmosphere seemed as dry as tinder, waiting for the kindling spark.

He wondered how he had come to be where he was, his feet treading softly on the winding stone turret stairs built into the thick north wall of Ancaster Cathedral. Why was he here, in the close darkness of the summer night? Of course! He was stalking his quarry.

He followed Dean Girdlestone up the winding turret stair, stopping when he stopped, moving upward cautiously whenever the Dean continued to climb. The progress of pursuer and pursued seemed effortless, as though they were assisted by a power outside them both. They left the permanency of the stone staircase, and entered a more perilous world of ladders, and the lashed wooden poles of scaffolding.

Lawrence Girdlestone stopped, pushed open a low door, and stepped out on to a narrow ledge, high above the nave roof. Arkwright watched him, and fancied that he

1

could discern dim stars in the sable night sky.

Suddenly, a mesh of brilliant lightning flickered and hissed in the air, and Nicholas Arkwright saw the great tower of the cathedral rising above him, the gilt weather vanes on the four pinnacles shining like lanterns. The four life-sized figures of angels carved into the north flank of the tower seemed to be etched on to his vision by the power of the lightning, and he saw with sudden unease that all four angels now had faces, and that the face of the fourth angel was that of a lifeless skull.

A terrific barrage of thunder followed the lightning. Was this the right moment? Yes! Send him on his way to perdition! Arkwright felt his hands sink into the broadcloth of the Dean's frock coat, and then watched as he plummeted down to his death on the nave roof. It was done. A lifetime of frustration and humiliation was at an end.

Arkwright turned aside—and saw Dean Girdlestone standing once again on the ledge, smiling in amused triumph at the hellish conjuring trick of his resurrection . . .

Nicholas Arkwright jerked up in his bed, and gasped with thankful relief. His bedroom window had blown open, and he could see the gleam of rain on the window sill. Outside, the summer tempest that had helped to conjure up his nightmare was blowing itself out. He lay quite still for a while, reliving the experience of his monstrous dream.

What wicked, iniquitous nonsense! How could he, a clergyman of the Church of England, and Prebendary of Ancaster Cathedral, even envisage such an evil deed?

He swung himself out of bed, and lit his bedside candle. The flame shook and shivered in the draught from the open window. What would Joanna have thought of him, entertaining such impious, crackbrain thoughts? She would have prescribed some noisome medicine from the herbalist, and put him on a low diet . . . Quite right, too!

The words of an old hymn came into his mind, words which could serve very well as a prayer for preservation from such wicked, foolish nonsense as that dream:

From all ill dreams defend our eyes,
From nightly fears and fantasies.

What would Conrad think, if he knew that his father was having such shocking, shaming dreams?

A clock in the room told him that it was ten to three. He crossed to the window, and looked out. Thin, vertical rain was falling into the garden, and a red glow from beyond the wall told him that the workmen on the night shift in the lead works in Pitt Lane were going about their business. What would those honest fellows think, if they knew that Prebendary Arkwright had just murdered Dean

3

Girdlestone—at least, murdered him in a dream?

He pulled on a dressing-gown, took the candle, and went downstairs. He stood for a while on the threshold of the front parlour. He could see the dim outlines of the winged armchairs, the old Queen Anne sofa, and the flat top of Joanna's Broadwood pianoforte.

Joanna had always been the practical one, countering his own tendency to dreaminess. She would have packed him off to the doctor . . . Something from Shakespeare floated into his mind—'More needs he the divine than the physician.' He would go to see Bishop Grandison, and tell him about the dream. Sometimes, the mere recounting of such monstrous things could exorcize them.

*   *   *

Prebendary Arkwright watched old Bishop Grandison as he told him the details of his murderous dream, inwardly wondering why this aged and venerable man had the uncanny ability to read him like a book. The Bishop was a gaunt-featured, silver-haired patriarch of eighty, frail of body, but generally acknowledged to be great in spirit. Arkwright finished his tale, and the bishop sat quite still for what seemed like several minutes. Then he lifted his bright eyes from his desk to Arkwright's face.

'Are you not satisfied with your prebendary's stall? Have you tired of being rector of St Mary in Campo? Your people there speak very highly of you.'

His silvery voice seemed to hold a very faint edge of reproach. Arkwright suddenly felt brash and inept, no fit company for the revered figure sitting behind the desk in the high and airy study of Ancaster Palace. How was he to reply to such an oblique question? The Bishop evidently expected no answer.

'Why did your sleeping mind choose the cathedral roof to play out its wicked drama? And the tower—why was that there, Nicholas? Oh, everybody knows how much you resent Dean Girdlestone—that's no secret! Perhaps it's a human failing, in which case it's probably forgivable. But I don't much care for that face you put on the fourth angel. And why the cathedral tower?'

What an awful man Grandison was! No doubt they'd have burnt him as a witch in olden times. It was as though he already knew what Arkwright would now be forced to confess.

'My Lord, that dream was bound up with an incident that occurred many years ago, and which I'd all but forgotten, until recently. It was something that happened on May Day in 1863. I was still at Oxford, then, and so was Lawrence Girdlestone. You know that we were up at Oxford together?'

'I do. But you were at different colleges. So what did you do to him on May Day, in 1863?'

'*Do* to him? Why, nothing. I . . . There's a charming old custom at Magdalen College, My Lord, for the choir to mount to the top of the tower and sing a hymn on May Day. That year, I resolved to attend. You didn't have to be a Magdalen man to go up there. I climbed up to the roof of the tower, and joined a group of other gentlemen to listen to the choir. Well, Lawrence Girdlestone was there, too, leaning unsteadily against one of the stone parapets. He was still in evening dress, and had evidently come straight to Magdalen from some all-night roistering. I remember feeling shocked that he could contrive to be tipsy in such a place, and at such an early hour—'

'Thus confirming to your own satisfaction, Nicholas, how virtuous and abstemious you were. What a humbug you are! Pray continue.'

'I found myself standing behind Girdlestone. I'd always hated him, you know, ever since our schooldays together—'

'Yes, yes, I know,' said the Bishop testily. 'It's hardly a justification, is it? Just tell me what you did to him.'

'I suddenly decided that I could tip him over the parapet, and that no one would ever know it wasn't an accident. I was only a young fellow, with little judgement of what the consequences would be—'

'The consequences to your precious self, I

suppose you mean? Even a babe in arms would have been able to realize the consequences to poor Girdlestone. But pray continue.'

'Yes, My Lord. I looked down to the bridge below, and saw a sea of faces staring upward. I swear that, but for that crowd of witnesses, I would have sent Girdlestone there and then hurtling over the parapet to his death! I fled the place, My Lord, in fear and horror. But now, you see, the idea's returned to haunt me! I fear that what I dreamed last night is a premonition, and that one of these days, sooner rather than later, I'll translate those dreams into deeds.'

The bishop slowly turned the pages of a large Bible displayed on a reading stand. Nicholas Arkwright watched him. Outside, the rear lawns of the bishop's palace glowed in the summer sun, and the backs of the houses in Dean's Row presented their blank windows to them both through the screen of delicate birch trees.

'You'd have made a good actor, Nicholas,' said the bishop. 'The church's gain was the stage's loss when you chose the road to ordination! What a self-dramatizer you are! But there! You did right to tell me this, even though I suspect that you have not told me all. There's more here than a fantasy arising from injured self-regard.'

Old Bishop Grandison leaned forward in his

chair, and clasped his hands together on the table. When he spoke, the slightly mocking tone that he had used so far in the interview was absent.

'There are two men dwelling in your body, Nicholas,' he said, 'two men who are deadly enemies. One man is the genial and kindly rector of St Mary in Campo, Prebendary of Ancaster, proud father of Conrad Arkwright. The other man—if man he is—reveals himself as a deformed and savage slave, ruthless and without compassion. He's compounded of all the slights, real or imagined, that you fancy you've received from Lawrence Girdlestone. Beware that unregenerate savage, Nicholas! Strive with him until you have overthrown him—or he will overthrow *you*!'

Two men, dwelling in the one body . . . Despite the warm day, Nicholas Arkwright shivered. He would take his Bishop's words to heart, and strive to overcome the creature that his own short-comings had created.

'My Lord,' said Arkwright, rising from his chair, 'I'm sure that I'll benefit greatly, as always, from your advice and counsel. I promise to show more humility where the Dean is concerned.'

The old bishop smiled, and looked fondly at Arkwright.

'More humbug, Nicholas!' he said. 'I suppose I tolerate your ways because it was I who ordained you deacon and then priest, here in our ancient cathedral of the Holy Angels, over a quarter of a century ago. Instead of talking about "humility", it would have been far better for you to have said nothing, and to have gone. But that face that you put on the fourth angel—I don't like that at all. So ponder my "advice and counsel" in your heart, and while you are doing so, reflect upon St Peter's dire warning to us all: "Brethren, be sober, be vigilant; because your adversary, the devil, as a roaring lion, walketh about, seeking whom he may devour".'

CHAPTER ONE

A MAGICAL SORT OF PLACE

Caroline Parrish woke with a start, and looked around the empty compartment. The driver of the little train from Warwick had evidently just sounded the whistle as it emerged from a tunnel. It was now toiling along a great curve on the skirts of a sunlit wood. She had closed her eyes only for a moment, and had found herself drifting off into a light sleep.

The period following her Uncle Alexander's funeral had been hectic and intensely tiring, and had culminated in this, the final stage of her journey to a new life. Warwickshire's lush, elm-bordered fields, hurrying streams and slow, stately rivers were utterly different from the fertile but flat farmland of Lincolnshire.

Caroline had lived beneath her native county's wide skies since babyhood, an orphan cared for by her bachelor uncle with the assistance of various kindly women in the village. She had grown up no stranger to farm work, but had received an excellent education at Miss Barton's Academy for Girls at Wisbech. At the age of 18 she had begun to build up a clientèle of young ladies in need of instruction, and her modest income from teaching, combined with her old uncle's annuity, had enabled them both to live frugally but comfortably at Rose Cottage.

Then, just over three weeks earlier, on Saturday, 8 July, Uncle Alexander, frail and failing at 75, had died quite suddenly of what the doctor from Wisbech had called a seizure, and the death certificate, cardiac spasm. His funeral had taken place on the following Wednesday, the twelfth, in the quiet churchyard of Sutton St Edmund. Rose Cottage, which had been rented, was immediately reclaimed by its owner.

How dreary these second-class carriages were! This one, upholstered in faded green, smelt of stale, sulphurous smoke and musty horsehair. Below the net luggage racks facing her was a small oval mirror. Had she cared to look into it, she would have seen a young woman of 22 looking back at her critically—a young woman with bright blue eyes, a sensible nose and a firm mouth and chin. Nothing much to quarrel with there, she thought, except for the frivolous hat perched on top of her blonde hair. The 1890s, it seemed to her, would go down in history as an era of silly hats!

There were two paintings flanking the mirror. The one on the left showed the proud towers of Warwick Castle. The other was a view of a great cathedral church, rising from a sward of green grass. 'Ancaster Cathedral, from the south', said the legend beneath it. Ancaster . . .

Her uncle's solicitor, Mr Nash, had summoned her to his office in King's Lynn, and told her that Uncle Alexander had left her the total sum of his estate, amounting to £218 6s. 8d. He had spoken for a while about banks and investments, and then had asked her what she proposed to do. The question seemed to have been framed to require only one answer, which she duly gave him.

'What do you advise?' she'd asked.

'Well, Miss Parrish, you have another uncle, you know. If I were you, I'd go and live with him. I took the liberty of writing to him, you know. Your late Uncle Alexander desired me to do so. He thought it was time to think about your future, you see. This other uncle wrote back to me, and said that he'd be more than willing to receive you.'

'Another uncle? I didn't know I had another uncle!'

'No, well, there you are! Families can be very complicated. This other uncle is a married clergyman, and not nearly as old as Mr Alexander Parrish was. He lives at Ancaster—not our Lincolnshire town, you know, but the ancient cathedral town of the same name in Warwickshire. This new uncle, Canon Walter Parrish, is attached to the cathedral there. From the tone of his letter to me, Miss Parrish, I'd say he was a very agreeable man. He said how pleasant it would be to have a young woman in the house again.' The old lawyer had suddenly smiled very engagingly, and observed, 'He never once wrote about his duty, or obligation, or anything of that sort!'

And now here she was, journeying towards the world of Canon Walter Parrish in the cathedral town of Ancaster. What would he be like? She wondered why he had not thought to write to her personally. Perhaps she would find out when she reached her journey's end.

*　　*　　*

'Latchford Halt! Latchford!'

The train had drawn in to a very neat small station, where a smart man in his forties, wearing an immaculate uniform and peaked cap, stood holding a furled green flag in one hand, and a whistle in the other. He had stepped back from the train, and was surveying it with professional pride. Caroline let down the window.

At that moment, a man appeared from the darkness of an archway at the centre of the station building and emerged on to the platform. He was walking with small, careful steps, because he was carrying a wooden crate containing a number of loudly protesting hens. He was a large, homely-looking man with a flushed red face. His mustard-coloured overcoat was unbuttoned, and flapped as he walked. He deposited the crate with a bang on to the platform, and there was a concerted clucking and squawking of protest from the hens. Caroline could see their beady eyes looking with reproachful distaste at their tormentor.

'Whatever possessed you to carry those birds yourself, Mr Bottomley?' asked the station master. 'Here, Edward, bring the trolley, and put these hens on the train!'

A young man appeared from a door trundling a trolley and, with the station master's help, the crate was hoisted into place and wheeled away somewhere out of sight.

Caroline was about to close the window when she saw a little girl in a blue dress emerge from one of a line of brown brick railway cottages and run on to the platform. The man called Bottomley rummaged through the pockets of his overcoat and produced a very shiny red apple, which he gave to the little girl. She promptly thanked him with a wide smile and an uninhibited hug. The big man caught Caroline's amused glance, and smiled.

When it was time for the little train to depart, the man called Bottomley crossed the platform, and raised his hat to Caroline. She saw little bits of straw sticking to his clothes, and there was a scent of juniper berries in the air. Evidently, he was a farmer, or smallholder.

'Asking your pardon, miss,' he said, in a pleasant rural accent, 'but this train has only the one carriage, and the little van. So, if you don't object, I'll join you in your compartment. I'm only going as far as Thornton Heath.'

*   *   *

'So you've come a long way, miss? And you're bound for Ancaster?'

'Yes, Mr—Bottomley, isn't it? I'm going to live with my uncle there. I'm a complete stranger in this part of England. Would you say that Ancaster's a pleasant place in which to live?'

'Ancaster, miss, is a magical sort of place. It's a cathedral town, with a lot of antique buildings, and a history going back to the old Romans, so they say. It's got its surprises, too, but if I tell you what they are, it'll spoil it for you.'

14

Caroline laughed. He spoke to her for all the world as though she was a little girl. Perhaps he'd give her an apple, as he'd done to the child at Latchford Halt! She saw that he had noticed her black mourning garb, and wondered whether he was making an attempt to cheer her up.

'There's two kinds of people at Ancaster, miss,' Bottomley continued, 'town folk, and cathedral folk. Which would your uncle be, if I may make so bold as to ask?'

'Well, I suppose he's "cathedral folk", Mr Bottomley, because he's a canon of the cathedral. Canon Parrish, he's called. My name is Caroline Parrish. I've never met him; but then, I know nobody in Warwickshire.'

Mr Bottomley said nothing for a while. She saw how he looked speculatively at her, and was puzzled at a hint of concern in the man's fine grey eyes.

'I've eight daughters, Miss Parrish,' said Bottomley at length, 'all living. Two are married, two are in service, and the other four are still at home with the wife and me. Maybe it's having that little tribe of girls that's made me presume to talk to you now. I told you that Ancaster's a magical town, and that's true. But it's also a haunted town. I don't mean ghosts and bogies, but you'll find whatever sprites there are abroad up in Cathedral Green, among the cathedral folk. I'll say no more, because you'll think I'm trying to frighten you,

15

as though you were a little girl like Ellie, back at Latchford Halt. But don't worry, miss, I'm not going to give you a shiny red apple.'

He treated her to a humorously mocking smile, and she had the grace to blush.

When the train stopped next, it was at a short timber platform containing little more than a couple of milk churns. The sound of voices and the indignant clucking of hens came from the van. Mr Bottomley lumbered to his feet.

'Well, Miss Parrish,' he said, 'this is where I get off. Thornton Heath's what they call this place. I hope you're very happy at Ancaster, which is the next stop along the line. But if ever you're in need of help and advice—'

He pulled a rather crumpled visiting card from one of his large pockets, and handed it to her.

'If ever you're in need of help, you can come and see me at the address written on the back of that card. Goodbye, miss!'

Caroline watched as Mr Bottomley climbed up from the wooden platform to what was evidently a road behind a hedge, where a horse and cart were waiting. A comely, fair-haired woman in a black dress, presumably Mrs Bottomley, was sitting at the reins. A stooping man in a labourer's smock had put the crate of hens in the cart. Caroline saw Bottomley raise an arm and wave, as though in greeting. At first, she thought he was bidding her goodbye,

16

but as the train moved forward she realized that he had been signalling to the driver that all was well.

What a strange man Mr Bottomley had been, reading her mind, and talking about ghosts and sprites! She looked down at the visiting card that he had given her, and read its inscription.

Detective Sergeant H. Bottomley,
Warwickshire Constabulary.

Fifteen minutes later the train came to a halt at a small bay beyond the main platforms of Ancaster Station, and Caroline saw two clergymen standing beside a brace of porters with their trolleys. Evidently, they had come to meet her. They were both clad in clerical black, and wore shiny silk hats. One of them was a man who looked as though he was well into his fifties, though a certain jauntiness in his manner seemed to belie that possibility. He stooped a little, and peered through gold-framed spectacles. His face was enlivened by an engagingly puckish smile.

The other was a genial, rather heavily built man with greying side whiskers. He, too, stooped slightly, so that the tails of his frock coat billowed out a little behind him; but he was a smart man, Caroline decided, and a man careful enough to have put a rosebud in his button hole. It was this man who stepped

17

forward, and opened the carriage door to hand her out on to the platform.

'Uncle Walter?' Caroline wondered why her voice sounded so timorous.

'Alas, no, Miss Parrish. Merely your uncle's old friend and erstwhile schoolfellow, Nicholas Arkwright. Parrish, come and say "hello" to your niece, will you?'

What a fine, theatrical voice! Caroline glanced at Arkwright's face, and saw the many lines of humour about his eyes. He had taken her hand in greeting, and now made an amusing business of surrendering it unwillingly.

The puckish clergyman stepped forward.

'Welcome to Ancaster, my dear,' he said, and kissed Caroline's cheek. 'I'm your uncle, Walter Parrish. Oh, and this is my colleague, Prebendary Nicholas Arkwright. I know he's already told you who he is—more or less—but let's stick to etiquette, and do the thing properly.'

As they walked out of the station and into the cab yard, Prebendary Arkwright chuckled, and spoke in mock confiding tones to Caroline.

'He's not always like this, Miss Parrish,' he said, 'bringing a fellow up sharpish for no reason at all. It's probably liver, you know. Too much claret. Incidentally, he's told me a bit about you, and said your name was Caroline. It's the female form of Charles, you know. Or maybe you don't. May I call you Caroline, or would you think me terribly forward?'

'Really, Arkwright,' said Uncle Walter, with what was clearly assumed irritation, 'is there any need for you to play the buffoon like this? Take no notice of him, my dear. There's nothing wrong with my liver. He's simply jealous, because you're *my* niece, not his!'

'They have three daughters already, Caroline,' said Arkwright. 'I don't see why they want a niece, as well. It smacks of greed, if you ask me.'

'Pay no attention, Caroline,' said her uncle. 'Here's the cab. While we're going across town, I'll explain what arrangements we've made to receive you. That is, if Prebendary Arkwright will allow me to get a word in edgeways.'

Caroline saw how her uncle tried unsuccessfully to suppress a broad smile. She suddenly realized that these two men were friends of very long standing. That would explain why they were behaving for all the world like two big, exuberant boys.

'I stand corrected, Canon,' said Arkwright. He winked covertly at Caroline, who smiled, and accepted his hand to help her step up into the waiting cab.

*   *   *

The cab passed through an area of small but

19

prosperous factories and workshops, and then laboured gently uphill, leaving the winding streets of the old town behind it. Suddenly, the great pinnacled sandstone tower of Ancaster Cathedral came into view above the rooftops. They passed a long, gabled building that was evidently a set of almshouses, and then turned abruptly right under the weather-worn archway of an ancient gatehouse. It brought them into a wide cobbled court surrounded by fine houses of the seventeenth and eighteenth centuries.

'Abbey Yard,' said Prebendary Arkwright, and something in his voice caused Caroline to look at his face. He was smiling contentedly to himself, as though relieved that he was coming home. And then, for a fleeting moment, she caught an expression of bleak despair. It had gone in a moment, but the memory of it remained lurking at the back of her mind for the rest of the day, and beyond.

'And now, my dear,' said her uncle, 'we're turning into Dean's Row, and Number 7, which is our journey's end!'

Dean's Row, approached through a narrow lane to the left of Abbey Yard, came upon them with dramatic suddenness. It proved to be a range of magnificent eighteenth century residences, which, her uncle told her, housed the Dean and Canons of Ancaster Cathedral. The three-storey houses of mellow red brick glowed in the summer sun. Facing them across an extensive lawn, and now in full view, was the north side of the great cathedral church.

*   *   *

Canon Parrish's wife had been standing on the pavement to greet them, and had immediately banished the two men to her husband's study while she conducted Caroline to a pleasant bedroom on the second floor, facing on to the rear garden.

'The station van will be here presently, and then we'll have all your things brought up. Our maid will bring up hot water in a minute or two. I hope you'll like this room. It was my daughter Helen's, at one time. She was the middle one, you know.'

Caroline had been attracted immediately to Canon Parrish's wife, a handsome woman with elegantly coiled auburn hair. She was dressed with great formality in a beautifully cut beige morning gown, but her natural, friendly manner suggested a very much less formal interior.

Caroline looked out of the window at the tranquil garden. The lawns had evidently received the attention of a mechanical lawnmower, and the sun emphasized the light and dark greens of the straight rows. The garden was surrounded by a rustic wall, against which a number of climbing roses had been trained. Beyond the rear wall, and cloaked by

21

a line of graceful birch trees, stood a grand, castellated mansion. Mrs Parrish joined her at the window.

'That's the Bishop's palace,' she said. 'Old Bishop Grandison lives there. He's a dear old man, well over eighty, but perhaps he's a bit too accommodating to people's freaks and fancies.' She added, rather inconsequentially, 'The Dean, Lawrence Girdlestone, lives next door to us. We're number seven, and I suppose next door's number five, but it's always just called the Deanery.'

Caroline looked across the wall to the left, and saw an even larger garden than the Parrishes'. There were greenhouses, and a loggia, and someone had left a set of croquet mallets lying carelessly on the grass. A woman suddenly appeared from the Deanery, a statuesque, rather haughty but very handsome woman, who was carrying a gardening basket and a pair of secateurs.

'That's Mrs Girdlestone, the Dean's wife,' said Millie Parrish. She moved away from the window, and Caroline heard her murmur to herself the words, 'poor soul'. She suddenly felt it imperative to move their conversation away from the woman in the next-door garden.

'Prebendary Arkwright seems a very pleasant man,' she said. 'Does he also live here, in Dean's Row?'

Mrs Parrish sat down on the edge of the bed.

'Prebendary Arkwright, my dear, has a house that is attached to his position—it's called The Prebendary's House, and it stands at the foot of the town walls. You can't see his house from up here. Mr Arkwright's also rector of St Mary in Campo, an old parish church near the cattle-market. He's a very kind, well-liked man, and a native of Ancaster. He's a widower, with a grown-up son. You'll see a lot of Mr Arkwright now that you're living here with us. He's my husband's closest friend. They were at school together. They've been fast friends for nearly forty years.'

'A widower? Somehow, I didn't think of Prebendary Arkwright as a married man—'

'Well, that's understandable. His wife was only thirty-two when she died, so he's been a widower for—what?—nearly fifteen years. You'll meet him again, tonight, and his son, Conrad. I thought it would be nice for them to have dinner with us. Your uncle has invited Dean Girdlestone, too. We rather think he'll want to inspect you to see if you pass muster!'

Caroline laughed. She was beginning to feel very much at home at Number 7.

'Is Conrad a clergyman, too?' she asked.

'No, my dear. Conrad was an officer in the Cartographic Department of the Engineers. He left the army in February, after five years' service, to accept a post with the Ordnance Survey at Southampton. But there, I can hear Jessie on the stairs with the hot water. I must

23

leave you to settle in.'

'You and Uncle Walter have been so very kind, Mrs Parrish—'

'Nonsense, my dear! It will be lovely to have someone young to talk to, again! And please call me Millie. Not aunty, or anything ghastly like that. You'll find cathedral life rather strange at first. It takes a long time to reconcile yourself to the antics of the higher clergy, and there are times when the affairs of the diocese begin to pall—but there, I'm chattering again! I'll leave you for a while to wash and have a rest.'

*   *   *

Some time later, Caroline Parrish sat in her uncle's small and crowded study, listening to the story of his family. Walter Parrish's voice, she thought, was extraordinarily confiding and comforting, a far cry from the rather strident tones of her late Uncle Alexander.

'So there you have it, Caroline,' he was saying. 'From being a mere man outnumbered by a bunch of lively females, I was, for a brief interval, master in my own house. But now you've arrived, and I'll be outnumbered and outflanked once more!'

Canon Parrish took down a large, unframed photograph from its place on top of a bookshelf, and laid it across his knees. He pretended to examine it critically.

'Here they all are, Caroline,' he said, 'in this photograph, which was taken before they'd fled the nest. The dark one on the left is Emily. She's married to a vicar, and they live in a little village near Norwich. The one in the middle's Helen—she takes after her mother, as you can see. And the third one is Nancy, who's married to a farmer in Cheshire. They're all your cousins, and I expect you'll visit them all eventually.'

'Is Helen married?'

'Oh, didn't I say? Helen married one of those titled actors, a man nearly as old as I am. Sir James Faulkner, a friend of Sir Henry Irving's. So Helen's now Lady Faulkner. They live in London.'

Caroline watched as her uncle carefully balanced the photograph on top of the bookcase. The room seemed to be crammed with photographs, none of them framed. There were a great many well-thumbed books, a good number of them novels.

'I know that the last few weeks have been extremely hectic,' said Parrish, leaning back in his chair, 'but I was wondering whether you had considered the direction of your life here? Or to put it more simply, have you thought about any kind of employment?'

'I was hoping to be able to teach in one of the church schools—'

'Well, that could be arranged, I've no doubt. But I have a proposition to put to you that I think you'll find very interesting. Have you ever heard of Sir Charles Blount? He's what they call a student of the Renaissance, a collector of rare paintings and sculpture—very much a connoisseur of such things.'

'Sir Charles Blount? Yes, Uncle, I've read his introductions to the Adelphi Art Folios. We used those books when we studied the Fine Arts at Miss Barton's Academy at Wisbech. And there was an article about him last year in the *Strand Magazine.*'

Canon Parrish chuckled. He fished an old pipe from his pocket, struck a match, and puffed away thoughtfully for a while.

'You sound very learned, Caroline,' he said at length. 'Much too highbrow for the likes of me. Well, it may surprise you to know that Sir Charles Blount lives here, in Ancaster. He's also got a splendid villa in Taormina, at the foot of Mount Etna. He's looking for an archivist, someone to put his many papers in order, and perhaps produce a catalogue of all the works of art he's crammed into his house here, across the river in Ladymead.'

'Surely he'll want some kind of specially trained person—an experienced archivist?'

'He wants *you.* I was speaking to him last week on cathedral business, and told him all about you. I told him that you were fluent in Latin and Greek, and almost fanatically committed to Classical studies. Don't let me down by pleading ignorance of all these accomplishments!'

'Well, Uncle Walter, it sounds a fascinating proposition. What kind of a man is Sir Charles Blount?'

'Blount? He's a terrible, raving monster, tethered by a long chain to one of the walls of his study. He keeps a museum of living exhibits . . . During the day, he sleeps in a chest of earth, and at night, roams through the chambers of his mansion by torchlight. Apart from those few idiosyncrasies, he's a very pleasant, courteous gentleman.'

Caroline laughed. She looked at the puckish face of her uncle, and saw the mischief endemic to him glinting in his eyes behind the thick lenses. She bent down and gently kissed her uncle's cheek.

'Does that mean that you'll accept Blount's offer? Good. I'll take you over there tomorrow—or, wait! Prebendary Arkwright's going to Ladymead tomorrow afternoon on cathedral business. Would you like to go with him? I promise I won't let him try to poach you!'

'I'd love to go with him, Uncle. I like him very much. Ladymead? What exactly *is* Ladymead?'

'Ladymead is one of Ancaster's surprises. It's the name of Sir Charles's house, and also of the suburb where it stands. But if I tell you more about it, it'll spoil it for you. You'll find out, tomorrow.'

Where had she heard those words before? Yes! The detective-man on the train had used them. 'Ancaster's got its surprises, too,' he'd said, 'but if I tell you what they are, it'll spoil it for you.' What was his name? She had his card, somewhere. Bottomley. Detective Sergeant H. Bottomley, Warwickshire Constabulary.

*   *   *

Detective Inspector Jackson sat in his old cane-backed chair by the fireplace, and thought about that morning's interview with Mr Alfred Markland, Chief Clerk of the Cathedral Treasury at Ancaster. He'd come home to his cottage in Meadow Cross Lane for a lunch of bread and cheese, washed down with strong tea. In a few minutes' time he would walk back down the hill into Warwick. Alfred Markland had described himself as 'a plain man'. He'd meant that he was a straight talker, but he was plain in another sense: his grim, hatchet face, dark, beetling brows and heavy jaw had made him look more like a footpad than a chief clerk.

He and Bottomley had listened in rapt silence while Markland had accused the Dean of Ancaster, the Very Reverend Lawrence Girdlestone, of engineering a massive fraud against his own cathedral. He recalled the prim, rather self-satisfied voice of the clerk as he furnished them with the details of his investigation.

'You see, Inspector, Canon Nicholson, the Cathedral Treasurer, isn't in England at the moment. He's gone to visit his son, who's chaplain to the English colony in . . . I don't remember the name of the place, but it's in Italy somewhere, and that places me in an invidious position. It's a heavy responsibility for a man in my station to bear alone.'

Perhaps, Jackson had thought; but you're enjoying yourself, aren't you, my friend? When the canon's away, the clerk will play—play detective, in this case.

'I've been clerk accountant at Ancaster Cathedral for nigh on twenty years, Inspector,' Markland had told him. 'I've an eagle eye, and a talent for numbers. While Canon Nicholson was away, I thought it would be a good idea to conduct an audit of the cathedral accounts—'

'And you found some discrepancies?'

A little frown of vexation had drawn the beetle brows together.

'Just bear with me, if you please, Mr Jackson. All in good time, as they say. Now, there are twelve accounts in all. Four of them are lodged with trustees, and house the deposits made over the years in government stocks and bonds. There are no irregularities there. But in the other eight accounts—those receiving donations and bequests, and the rents from church lands—I've found irrefutable evidence of fraud. It's not a matter of petty theft. A massive plundering of the cathedral's assets has taken place—something in the region of fifteen thousand pounds. It's fraud on a grand scale, involving payments by cheque and transfers to phantom accounts for expenses and disbursements that were never incurred! I found receipts for the opening deposits on savings accounts with a number of institutions, but no pass books to go with them. I've an eagle eye for irregularities, and I very soon realized what was going on.'

It was then that Markland had openly accused Dean Girdlestone of fraud. He was one of only three people with open access to the cheque books and the transfer registers, the other two being Markland himself, and Sir Charles Blount, Hereditary Steward to the Ancaster Foundation. Markland had kept a secret watch on the Dean's visits to obscure country savings banks. At Mason's Savings Bank in the village of Sedley Vale he had seen him withdraw £150 in gold sovereigns. And there had been other incidents . . .

It was a hot day, and Jackson had opened the back door of the dim, low-ceilinged living-room. He saw a movement among the trees in the orchard, and realized that his friend and neighbour, Sarah Brown, was coming to pay him a call. He hastily put on his coat, so that he would appear to her in his familiar garb of brown, three-piece suit, the waistcoat adorned with a gold watch chain with pendant medals.

Sarah appeared at the open door. She was holding an earthenware bowl in her left hand.

'Saul! I'm glad I've caught you before you went back to work. I've brought you some fresh eggs. The hens are laying well today.'

She stepped over the threshold, and Jackson watched her as she went unbidden into the adjacent kitchen. She was a slim, graceful woman with fair skin, and rich brown hair. It had become evident to Jackson over the past two years that Sarah Brown liked him, though why, would always be a mystery. He was a widower of 47, solidly built and, according to the police surgeon, Dr Venner, in danger of 'running to fat'. True, there were already incipient signs of a double chin. For all that, Sarah Brown liked him. She was a widow, just turned 39.

'Sarah,' said Jackson, as his neighbour emerged from the kitchen, 'a man came into the Police-Office this morning, and said that the Very Reverend Lawrence Girdlestone, Dean of Ancaster, had defrauded the Cathedral of fifteen thousand pounds.'

Sarah Brown stood transfixed, looking at Jackson with indignant disbelief.

'What wicked nonsense, Saul! Who was this man? No—don't tell me: I don't think I want to know! You know how closely my life was bound up with the Reverend Mr Girdlestone. I'll not stay silent, Saul, when I hear him so cruelly slandered.'

'I'm sorry, Sarah. I didn't mean to revive painful memories—'

Sarah Brown seemed not to hear him. She was reliving her tragic story.

'It was in the early spring of 1880, Saul, that Tom and I left here with the children, and went to farm a couple of acres at Sedley Vale, which isn't very far away from Ancaster. The soil was good, and the crops promised well. But the water—the water in the village wells— was tainted, and the cholera broke out. It raged like the plague. There were over eighty folk living in that village, but only twelve survived. When it was all over, I came back here to Meadow Cross, and buried my husband and my three little boys in our parish burial ground.'

Sarah's normally placid face suddenly flushed with anger.

'And it was the Reverend Mr Girdlestone, Saul, who stood out in that village as a true hero, and his heroism mustn't be forgotten. Our doctor laboured on for a week, with his pills and permanganate water, and then he, too, fell to the scourge. He died within the day. It was the Rector who laboured without rest to bring what comfort he could to us all. He'd feed the dying himself, with no thought for his own safety. He seemed to know all about cholera, and had a store of special medicines— opium was one of them, and . . . yes, bismuth. He brought things most village folk had never seen before, things like port wine jelly, smoked ham, brandy—and all around him so many people were dying that the sexton from Walton Devereaux had been called in to help dig the graves.'

Sarah wiped away a tear with the edge of her apron.

'That was the last great visitation of the cholera in Warwickshire, Saul. It was Mr Girdlestone who gave me the money to bring Tom and the children back for burial here, in their own village. I said I'd pay him back over a year, but he wouldn't hear of it. "Faith without works is dead". Those were the words he said. I've never forgotten them.'

'That man is now the Dean of Ancaster—'

'Yes, so you've told me. And a Very Reverend, into the bargain. But he'll always be the Rector of Sedley Vale to me, Saul. He wasn't a doctor, but he saved lives! He saved mine. He told me that he'd worked with cholera in India as a young man.'

'Did the Rector ever say where he'd ministered before he came to Sedley Vale?'

'No. I don't know where Mr Girdlestone came from, but a few years later, he left for a position in London. I've not seen him since the days in Sedley Vale, but I'll never forget him.'

Sarah Brown put the lunch things on a tray, and moved towards the kitchen. She paused on the threshold, and said with a note of subdued, almost tearful defiance, 'If ever you see that slandering man again, Saul, you can tell him from me that Mr Lawrence Girdlestone, in the eyes of some folk, is by way of being a saint!'

*   *   *

'There's a note come for you, Miss Caroline. From next door.'

'A note, for me?'

'Yes, miss. From the Deanery.'

Caroline had only glimpsed the Parrishes' maid when she had brought up hot water to her room earlier in the afternoon. She was a comfortable-looking countrywoman approaching middle age, dressed neatly in black, with a stiffly starched white cap and apron. She handed the note to Caroline, who broke the little round paper seal, and unfolded the single sheet of paper. A quick glance at the signature showed her that it was from the Dean's wife, Mrs Girdlestone.

'Mrs Girdlestone says that she's not coming to dinner this evening,' said Caroline. The maid had stood comfortably beside her, as though expecting some comment on the note. Caroline, utterly unused to servants, was content to tell her what the Dean's wife had written.

'No, miss, she's having one of her indispositions again, poor soul. But Mr Girdlestone will be here. He's another of Canon Parrish's old school friends. Funny, how

34

they've ended up living next door to each other.'

'Mrs Girdlestone wants me to call on her tomorrow morning, at eleven o'clock.'

'Well, that'll be nice, miss. I think the poor lady would welcome some genteel female company. She's got her maid, Ballard, with her, but that's not quite the same.'

Caroline wondered how to address the Parrishes' maid. The woman seemed to sense her uncertainty, and supplied the elusive answer.

'I'm Jessie, miss. There's only me, and cook, and William, who's supposed to be the boot boy. We manage the house between us. Us, and Mrs Parrish, who's never been a lady to sit around sewing samplers.'

Caroline laughed. There was a fresh directness about Jessie that immediately appealed to her.

'I was brought up in a country cottage, Jessie, where we had to break the ice on the well in the winter mornings, and learn to chop kindling wood in the yard. I know what you mean about sewing samplers! But these are lovely houses, aren't they?'

'Well, Miss Caroline, they are, and they aren't, in a manner of speaking. You see, when all's said and done, they're only tied cottages, like what farm labourers have.'

'Tied cottages?'

'Well, yes. They go with the position, you

35

see, and then, when the reverend gentlemen retire, they're turned out to grass. These houses belong to the church, you see, miss. I mentioned the fact to Canon Parrish on one occasion, but he said that as he was a labourer in the Lord's vineyard, it was only right that he should have a tied cottage!'

Jessie gave vent to a peal of laughter, and opened the door.

'He's very funny, is master. Well, I must go. If ever you want anything, miss, just pull the bell by the fireplace. There's one in each room, you'll find. That'll bring me, or Daft William, to see to you.'

'Daft, is he, Jessie? This William?'

Jessie drew the door to, without closing it. Caroline saw her glance briefly at a clock on the mantelpiece. Evidently, she had work to do, but gossip was about to take precedence.

'I'm not one to gossip, miss, but I've heard in the town that William's mother went down on her bended knees to Mrs Parrish to get her boy this post as boots. He'd been tried in shops, and in the timber yard, but he could never do anything properly. Prebendary Arkwright—you've met him, I think, miss?— he's Rector of St Mary's, in the cattle-market—what was I going to say? Yes, Prebendary Arkwright got him a very nice job in the lead works, but it didn't last. And so he came here.'

'He's not lacking mentally, is he?'

'Oh, no, miss, he's just daft. I must go. I'm needed downstairs. Lovely to meet you, miss, and I hope you'll be very happy with us at Number 7.'

CHAPTER TWO

THE RENAISSANCE MAN

'Well, well,' said Dean Girdlestone, 'this is very nice!'

Caroline Parrish wondered what these words were meant to convey. She had quietly observed Dean Girdlestone throughout dinner, and had noted that he sometimes spoke as though his words were simply an automatic reaction to his surroundings, or to a sudden awareness that he was not, in fact, alone in the Parrishes' dining-room.

He had been given the place of honour at the top of the long table, facing Caroline. The dinner had been a pleasant one, with pea soup followed by baked ham and spinach, a rice souffle, and a savoury of anchovies on toast. It had been served very nicely by Jessie, who felt it necessary to give no sign that she had ever met Caroline before.

'When you say "nice", Mr Dean,' said Walter Parrish, 'are you referring to the food, or to the company?'

'What's that? Oh, I meant having your charming niece here.'

The Dean bowed elegantly to Caroline. She smiled, but thought it best to say nothing. She looked at the Dean's healthy pink face, his heavy jaw, the firm line of his mouth, his slightly protuberant blue eyes, and thought to herself, this is a strong-willed man, accustomed to getting his own way in everything, but he's vulnerable, too. Despite his powerful presence, Dean Girdlestone seemed almost unconsciously on the defensive.

'I hope, Miss Parrish,' the Dean continued, 'that you'll interest yourself in the affairs of our diocese. I'm sure that one or other of the church schools would welcome you with open arms.'

'As a matter of fact, Mr Dean,' said Parrish, 'Sir Charles Blount has already laid claim to Caroline's services. He wants her to catalogue his papers and antiquities.' Dean Girdlestone paused in the act of lifting a glass of wine to his lips. His eyes assumed a strangely disturbed expression, and he slowly put down the glass again on the table.

'Blount? Does he really? Well, perhaps it's a good idea. I'd suggest that you give the post a try, Miss Parrish, but if you find that it doesn't suit, then we'll see what can be done for you in the schools.'

Caroline watched the Dean as he set the matter of her employment aside, and turned to the young man on his right. All through the meal she had managed not to glance too obviously in the direction of Prebendary Arkwright's son, Conrad. Had she done so, her admiration for him would have become embarrassingly apparent.

'You're very quiet this evening, Mr Conrad,' said the Dean. 'What are you thinking about? Are you, perhaps, pining for the magical cities of India?'

Conrad Arkwright turned his long-lashed dark eyes on the Dean, and smiled. That smile, thought Caroline, lights up his rather haggard face. How handsome he is! Perhaps his father, the Prebendary, had looked like him once, long ago? She mustn't stare. Young Mr Arkwright would think she was very forward—if, of course, he thought of her at all.

'You're right, sir,' Conrad Arkwright replied. 'I *was* thinking of India. I enjoyed my two-year tour with the Engineers there, and now that I'm a civilian again, I'm experiencing a certain nostalgia for that great sub-continent.'

'I thought as much,' said the Dean. 'I was out in India as a young man, as I think you know, but I've never entirely forgotten its allure.'

'I know what you mean, sir,' said Conrad. 'India is a marvellous place. It's . . . well, it's almost impossible to describe its magic if you've never been there. It's something to do with the quality of the light, the intense colours of everything, the gorgeous majesty of the native princes and their courts—'

'Talking of light,' said Prebendary Arkwright, cutting off his son's paean for India in mid-flight, 'talking of light, Mr Dean, I wonder whether I could ask you to look into the business of ancient lights? With respect to the great west window, you know?'

The effect of these words seemed to be quite extraordinary to Caroline. She felt the sudden tenseness in the atmosphere. The Dean winced as though he had been stung. Uncle Walter moved restlessly in his chair. Prebendary Arkwright, who was seated on the Dean's left, looked dangerously innocent. What could all this mean?

'Ancient lights? In what context, Prebendary? I don't quite understand—'

Instead of replying to the Dean, Nicholas Arkwright addressed himself to Caroline.

'You see, Caroline,' he said, 'the Dean—and the chapter, of course—have concocted a scheme for building a new choir school on part of the cathedral precinct. Now, if that choir school is built where the Dean has decided, it will effectively block the light of day from passing through the west window, which happens to be one of the ancient glories of England. Ancient lights, as the Dean will bear me out, is the legal right to receive, in perpetuity, through certain windows, a

40

reasonable amount of daylight.'

Nicholas Arkwright suddenly abandoned Caroline, and turned once again to the Dean.

'I do hope I'm not speaking out of place, Mr Dean,' he said, in studiously friendly tones. 'I was simply wondering whether you had given any thought to the matter? It could, perhaps, prove to be a nuisance if a formal plea of ancient lights were entered.'

'Entered? Entered by whom?'

'Well, by interested parties, you know.'

'Oh, interested parties! Oh, quite.'

Dean Girdlestone smiled, and Caroline heard her uncle give vent to a suppressed sigh of relief. For some reason not apparent to her, Dean Girdlestone seemed to have recovered his equanimity.

'Well, Prebendary,' said the Dean, 'thank you for raising the matter. I must confess that I'd not even considered it, but I'll most certainly look into it. I'll seek an opinion, you know. Of course, you'll agree with me that we do need a new choir school? The present buildings in Salter's Lane are decidedly insanitary.'

'Oh, quite,' said Nicholas Arkwright.

Canon Parrish stood up. 'It's starting to get dark,' he said. 'Shall we adjourn to the drawing-room for coffee? Jessie will have lit the lamps by now.'

'I wonder, Canon Parrish—and you, Millie—whether you'd both excuse me? I'm just a little anxious about Laura. She's not feeling quite herself today. I'd better be getting back. Thank you for a wonderful meal. It was a . . . a haven from the cares of the world, if only for a little while. Good night, Prebendary. I'll look into that matter of ancient lights immediately. Good night, Miss Parrish. It's been a great pleasure to make your acquaintance.'

They congregated briefly in the high, narrow hallway of the house to make their farewells to Dean Girdlestone. He was limping slightly, and Caroline remarked on the fact.

'He acquired that limp last week,' said Parrish, 'when he tried to run up the organ loft stairs after Dr Beckford. He should have known how fast our organist moves. The Dean tried to emulate him, and came slithering down the steps. But come on, Nicky, and you, Conrad, come into the study for a while, and smoke a pipe.'

*　　*　　*

'Oh, Millie, is it possible to fall for somebody at first sight? He's wonderful, isn't he? He makes me think of maharajahs, and elephants, and those things on top of them, that the princes ride in—what do you call them?'

'Howdahs. As for love at first sight, well, there's no rule-book to follow in these matters, as far as I know. It certainly didn't happen to me. Your Uncle Walter's the kind of man who grows upon one, becomes a settled habit, and then an absolute necessity. But love at first sight has a distinguished pedigree. I'm thinking of Romeo and Juliet.'

When the men had disappeared into the study, Millie had taken her niece upstairs to her private sitting-room, where Jessie had served them coffee.

'Do you think it would be terribly trying, living in India?' asked Caroline.

Millie treated her to an amused glance.

'Why, my dear, are you thinking of going out there? No, of course you're not! You're lining up Conrad Arkwright as a potential beau, aren't you? Well, young Conrad's finished with India, now. But wait until tomorrow, after you've met Sir Charles Blount, over at Ladymead. Then, Caroline, you might change your mind!'

*   *   *

Just before eleven o'clock next morning, Caroline knocked at the door of the Deanery. It was opened by a young woman in the neat dress of a house parlour maid.

'I'm Ballard, miss,' she said. 'Mrs Girdlestone is upstairs in her boudoir. Would you please follow me?'

This young woman has been crying, thought Caroline, and if she was not mistaken, she's

43

only just dried her tears. She was, Caroline judged, about thirty years old.

They reached the landing, and the maid opened a white-painted door that gave on to a short passage. A second door led into a light, well-furnished room, containing, among other things, a combined bookcase and bureau in walnut, a *chaise-longue,* and a small round table, flanked by two tapestry-covered chairs.

Mrs Girdlestone was sitting in one of the chairs. She was wearing a fawn morning dress, and her golden hair was coiled and pulled back from the ears in Grecian fashion. She still preserved the hauteur and conscious poise that Caroline had observed on the previous day. Her features, she noticed, were regular and unlined.

'Miss Parrish has called, ma'am,' said the maid.

'Very well, Ballard. You can go now.'

Mrs Girdlestone's dark, unblinking eyes followed the maid as she left the room, and closed the door. Then she turned her glance to Caroline.

'Miss Parrish,' she said, 'I'm very pleased to meet you. I was indisposed last night, and confined to my room. Or rather, rooms. This is my boudoir. Through that door there, behind the curtain, is my bedroom. I was indisposed, so he confined me here.'

Caroline had sat down in the other chair. Her hostess seemed for the moment to have forgotten her. She sat with her hands clasped beneath her chin, her elbows resting on the table. She was gazing at the half-open window, where a light summer breeze was stirring the lace curtains.

'May I call you Caroline?' Mrs Girdlestone's voice came harshly and unsteadily, and for a moment Caroline wondered if she was ill. 'It seems fitting, somehow. Anything young in this mausoleum is a rarity, and you're young, God knows. You can call me Laura, if you like.'

Laura Girdlestone fumbled in a pochette that hung from the narrow belt of her dress, and produced a small key, which she used to open the glazed bookcase in the walnut bureau. She reached into a space behind the books, and Caroline heard the clink of bottle against glass.

'Do you know what they call this, Caroline?' asked Mrs Girdlestone, as she poured a clear liquid from the bottle into the glass. 'Mother's ruin. That's what they call it in the tracts. Well, I'm not a mother. I've never been a mother. I've—why are you staring at me, girl? Don't stare, it's rude. Gin, that's what it is. Dean's Row is also Gin Lane. No, I've never been a mother. Not like Millie Parrish.'

Laura sipped steadily from the glass of gin. Her voice became increasingly slurred.

'Did you see Ballard? Of course you did: she brought you up here. She's my personal maid. I had her in London, you know, and brought her down here to this backwater when the Dean was preferred to this living. She was my confidante—still is, I suppose. Who else have I to talk to? But she's also the Dean's spy! She keeps all the keys of the house at his behest, including the key of that cabinet. But I got that off her, this morning! I twisted her arm until she gave it back to me. All the keys in this house should belong to me. I'm the mistress here. That's what I am, Caroline. I'm the Dean's wife. No, I'm not a mother. I was a vicar's wife first, when he was a vicar. Then I was an archdeacon's wife, when he was an archdeacon. And now I'm a dean's wife, because he's a dean.'

Caroline rose from her chair, and firmly took away the glass from Laura Girdlestone's hand. The Dean's wife looked up at her in surprise, but made no protest. Caroline put the glass back into the bookcase, and closed its door. Mrs Girdlestone glanced out of the window, and shuddered with some kind of disgust.

'It's stifling today,' she said. 'This house— am I to be entombed here forever? Every day, the rooms seem to be smaller, the air more choking . . . I was brought up in the country, Caroline, on a spacious estate, where one could breathe. There were horses in the paddock, and dogs in the house. But this! This gaol, and that ogre of a cathedral over there, squatting like a brute beast in the sun—it's an idol of stone, demanding human sacrifice. We're all victims of that juggernaut. How I hate the whole place! And I detest all the cathedral folk, except for Walter and Millie. And Nicky, of course. You've met him, haven't you?'

'Nicky? I don't think—'

'Nicholas. Prebendary Nicholas Arkwright. Don't be so obtuse, girl. He was going to propose to me, you know. Nicky, I mean. Just think of that! It was at Vaux Hall, back in the sixties, on a terrace, by moonlight. Or maybe it wasn't moonlight. I'd already had one proposal that evening.'

'Another proposal? I don't really understand what you're telling me—'

'Then you should listen more closely. I'd already had another proposal earlier that evening. It was from the Dean. Only he wasn't the Dean, then. He was just a bumptious young man with money. He'd asked me to marry him, and I said I'd give him my answer next morning. Then poor Nicholas took me out on to the terrace—Prebendary Arkwright, I mean, only he wasn't that, then, he was just Nicky—and I waited for him to propose. I thought he was going to, you see. Someone had seen him earlier that day in the local town, at a jeweller's, buying a diamond ring . . . So I waited. But he said nothing. He just stood there, in the moonlight. I thought I'd spur him on a bit by arousing his jealousy. I told him that I'd accepted Lawrence's proposal, and waited to see what he'd say.'

'And what *did* he say?' asked Caroline, fascinated by Laura's reminiscence.

'Say? He said he hoped we'd be very happy!'

Laura laughed, but the laugh assailed Caroline's ear like the tolling of a funeral bell. Then Mrs Girdlestone suddenly took command of herself. Caroline saw a new, determined light kindle in her dark eyes. She stood up.

'Caroline,' she said, 'you've seen me at my worse, today. Can I hope that you'll not be afraid of visiting me again, in the future?'

Poor soul! What could Caroline say? Why shouldn't she visit this unfortunate woman? Perhaps she could do her some good.

'I'll look forward to that, Laura. And please—don't speak of yourself as being "confined" to your own home. You make it sound as though the Deanery is a prison!'

For answer, Laura Girdlestone took Caroline by the hand, and led her back along the short corridor to the outer door, which she opened. She pointed to the lock.

'You see?' she whispered. 'The key is on the outside of the door. When I'm—when I'm not feeling myself, the Dean orders that this door should be locked. Until I am well again, I remain a prisoner in my own home!'

The lumbering four-wheeler that had called at
7 Dean's Row to convey Arkwright and
Caroline to the prosperous suburb of
Ladymead had threaded its way through the
twisting streets of the old town, leaving the
heights of Cathedral Green behind them, and
had finally turned into a cab yard hidden
behind an old church. Arkwright paid the
driver, and led Caroline down a short alley
that brought them out on to a wide, paved
esplanade. Riverside, as it was called,
belonged firmly to the Victorian age. Caroline
immediately appreciated the lightness and
airiness, and the sense of modernity, that was
lacking in the ancient cathedral town.

'What a delightful place, Mr Arkwright! It's
quite a summer resort!'

Caroline watched a constant procession of
pleasure boats moving in stately fashion both
up and down the river. There were many
green-painted iron park seats arranged along
the wide terraces. Nicholas Arkwright pointed
to an elegant, white-painted footbridge,
gracefully suspended across the river.

'In a moment, Caroline,' he said, 'we'll walk
over that bridge into the suburb of Ladymead,
where all the wealthy folk live, including Sir
Charles Blount. You see that fine, square,
three-storey mansion rising just above the far
end of the bridge? That's where Blount lives.

Did your Uncle Walter tell you about him?'

'He said he's a vampire, who has to be chained to the wall. By day, he sleeps in a chest of earth.'

Prebendary Arkwright laughed.

'Sir Charles Blount, Caroline, is a beacon of culture and enlightenment shining out from his hilltop mansion up there across a world of philistines, mired in darkness. That's what he is. He's a big man in every way—big in stature, in breadth of mind, in human sympathy—but there, if I stop talking, and take you across the bridge into Ladymead, you'll see the man himself.'

*   *   *

'Arkwright! Sit down! It's good to see you. And you've brought Miss Parrish with you. My dear young lady, I'm delighted to meet you. I wonder, now, whether you'd step into the picture gallery for a while? I'll be two minutes with Prebendary Arkwright, and then you and I will be able to talk at leisure.'

Sir Charles Blount's ringing tones matched his ebullient character. He had received Arkwright and Caroline in the long, high drawing-room of his house, a room that served as a gallery for his collection of Italian Renaissance sculpture. It was not an exotic room, but its character had been formed by the sunlit salons of Sir Charles's villa at

50

Taormina, on the Sicilian coast, where he spent six months of every year.

Caroline murmured a suitable response to the baronet's flow of words, and walked into the next room. It lay through an open arch of moulded stucco, and contained three rectangular windows, through which the strong summer light fell on a number of clearly priceless paintings displayed on easels, and upon one which was tantalizingly hidden by a green cloth dust cover.

The walls between the windows were occupied by fitted bookshelves containing hundreds of ancient vellum-bound books. On the wall immediately facing her, Caroline saw two immensely powerful portraits in oils, executed in one of the typical styles of the fifteenth century.

The wall facing the windows was almost entirely filled by a massive carved and gilded piece of furniture which seemed to combine endless sets of shallow drawers with an elaborate writing desk. She judged it to be French, dating, perhaps, from the later years of Louis XIV.

What an overpowering room! What an overpowering man! He seemed to prowl rather than walk, a sign of physical power and restless energy. His features had the chiselled quality of a Greek statue. Perhaps his olive complexion came from his long residence in Italy? The man had the power to draw, and, perhaps, subdue.

Caroline sat down on an elegant upholstered bench placed near the opening into Sir Charles's drawing-room. She half listened to Prebendary Arkwright's voice, and noted with some surprise that, divorced from his cheerful physical presence, it held an edge of hesitancy that she would not normally have associated with him.

'It's good of you to see me, Sir Charles,' he was saying. 'I expect you know what's brought me here. I dined with the Parrishes yesterday, and the Dean was there. I'd unearthed the business of ancient lights, as you suggested, and made a present of it to him. He masked his surprise as well as he could, but I saw that he was vexed, for all that. He said he'd look into the matter. But you know, I fear he'll find some cunning way around the problem. He's utterly determined to execute his plan to block the light from Master Geoffrey's window——'

Sir Charles Blount's voice cut Nicholas Arkwright's narrative short.

'Not quite that, you know, Prebendary. If he's successful, it will be in his desire to site that new choir school of his on vacant ground in the cathedral precinct. A different matter altogether, I think? But there, I know what you meant, and I sympathize. Girdlestone's a philistine! Art means nothing to him.'

Caroline heard chairs being pushed back, and knew that Sir Charles must have unwound his great frame from the carved chair in which he had been sitting. In a moment he burst into the gallery, accompanied by Nicholas Arkwright. Caroline stayed where she was, content to watch the two men as they walked among the easels in the sunlit chamber. Sir Charles's face had assumed a look of what she thought of as angered sympathy. Caroline watched him as he looked thoughtfully at Arkwright. Evidently, he was wondering whether or not to take the Prebendary into his confidence.

'Arkwright,' he said, at last, 'in this matter of the choir school, and any similar business that may arise, I'd advise you very strongly to stay your hand. In my position as Hereditary Steward I hear things—things that may or may not be true. The Ancaster Foundation at certain times considers hypothetical situations, and plans accordingly. Discretion has its uses. I wonder whether you understand what I mean? I'll not ask you to compromise your private integrity. All that I'm advising you, is this: be very careful what you say or do at the moment with respect to Dean Girdlestone. *Stay your hand.'*

*   *   *

'And now, Miss Parrish,' said Sir Charles Blount, 'let you and me talk business! Prebendary Arkwright has settled himself in the window seat next door to read *The Times.* He'll be quite happy there. Now, Miss Parrish, I'm in urgent need of someone with flair, and an ability to classify and categorize. You see that great cabinet-desk against the wall? It contains a mass of documents, all thrust—by me!—higgledy-piggledy into all those drawers. When I say documents, I don't mean letters, and so on. I have a very capable secretary who deals with all that.'

Sir Charles suddenly raised his voice, and called out, 'Hayden!'

Caroline had not noticed that the gallery had an extension. It turned sharply left at the end of the main room, and from the hidden portion a man of thirty or so suddenly appeared. He was dressed formally in a frock coat, and was holding a letter in his hand. He had a handsome, rather lined face, and a strong moustache.

'You called, sir?'

'I did. This lady is Miss Caroline Parrish, whom I hope to engage as archivist. Say hello, won't you?'

'Hello, Miss Parrish,' said Hayden. She saw the amused smile on the secretary's face. He bowed slightly, and disappeared from sight into the extension.

'These documents, Miss Parrish,' Sir Charles continued, 'are things that I've picked up on my travels—pages of old manuscripts, collections of letters from the archives of defunct Italian noble families, manuscript tales and poems from the pens of medieval scribes—all sorts of things. And all these books—these vellum-bound things on the shelves between the windows—they were acquired in much the same fashion. I want all these things catalogued, and the catalogue made into a descriptive card index. There may be treasures hidden in all that paper, and I need someone who will subdue it into some sort of order.'

'I'll be delighted to undertake the work, Sir Charles—'

'Very good! I thought you would. I don't want a professional librarian fussing around here, you see. Hayden and I get on very well together, and we both want someone who'll fit in here without a lot of arch primness and fuss. As to your remuneration, I'll discuss that with your uncle, Canon Parrish. Come any time, morning or afternoon—come all day, if you feel so inclined! You can work up here, and there are reading desks around the corner in the extension.'

Sir Charles suddenly checked his flow of words, and subjected Caroline to an unabashed survey. She stood her ground, and eventually he threw back his head and laughed.

'You'll do, Miss Parrish! You see, I'm a man who's very fond of beauty. Art is my consuming passion—painting of all kinds, and sculpture. Those dusty old papers in the drawers, and the books on the walls hold no intrinsic appeal to me. But I've a shrewd eye for a bargain, and I rather think there are a number of gems there among the dross.'

Sir Charles Blount suddenly seized the green cloth hiding one of the paintings, and pulled it up over the top of the frame. Caroline gasped in awed surprise. Surely, she had seen an engraving of this painting before? And now, here it was, in the light upstairs gallery of Sir Charles Blount's mansion in Ladymead.

'Isn't it magnificent?' cried Sir Charles. 'I've only just acquired it. It's Bellini's *Madonna and Child with Lilies,* done in 1478. He'd forsaken tempera by then, and was working wonders in oil. What do you think of it?'

'It's rather overwhelming, isn't it, Sir Charles? He's painted a real woman, a woman who's proud and shy at the same time, but full of strength . . . And the Child accepts her protection, but looks out warily at the world. Yes, "strength" is the word that springs to my mind when I look at that painting.'

'That's a very interesting reaction, Miss Caroline. And over there, on the end wall of the gallery, are my two Titians. What do you think of them? A far cry, I think, from Bellini. There's nothing very spiritual about Titian, but he's grand, Caroline, and he's sumptuous! Look at those colours!'

'I don't recognize the sitters, Sir Charles,

but they're both rather haunting portraits, aren't they?'

'They are. They follow you around with their eyes, summing you up, and passing judgement . . . The one on the left's Pope Paul III. The other one's Philip II of Spain. Wondrous works. And then the plague caught him, and the wonders ceased on 27 August, 1576.'

Sir Charles Blount reached up, and drew down the green dust cover.

*   *   *

The same creaking four-wheeler that had conveyed them to Riverside deposited Nicholas and Caroline at the door of 7 Dean's Row. The driver executed a necessarily clumsy turn on the cobbles, and lumbered off towards Abbey Yard.

'Now, Caroline,' said Prebendary Arkwright, 'you've seen the mansions of the rich, over in Ladymead. You've seen the dwellings of the righteous, here in Dean's Row. Would you care to venture down among the plebeians, and visit the Prebendary's House? There'll be plenty of time, before Millie misses you.'

Caroline gladly accepted the Prebendary's invitation, and fell into step beside him as he set off along Dean's Row. As they walked in comfortable silence, she stole a glance at

Arkwright, noticing the firm, rather stubborn, set of his mouth, the whiteness of his curled side whiskers, and the curious stoop that he had adopted, his hands clasped behind his back, his silk hat tipped a little forward over his brow. She suddenly realized that each trusted the other to the extent of not being disturbed by silences.

At the end of Dean's Row was a stretch of ancient wall, with a simple opening made in it.

'The town wall,' Arkwright declared, suddenly breaking the silence. 'Some people say it's Roman, others that it's medieval. The latter, I think, have the advantage. I've known these steps all my life, Caroline! I used to play hide and seek with the other children round these steps when I was a little boy. They represented a kind of promotion in those days—steps up to heaven, you know. But now—well, now they take me down from the lofty residences of the Dean and Canons to the mundane reality of Friary Street!'

Nicholas Arkwright chuckled, but Caroline had seen for the second time the fleeting expression of bleak despair that had disfigured her new friend's genial face. She wondered very much what it could portend.

They descended the steps together, waited for the stream of horse-traffic in Friary Street to pass, then stepped out through the dust, horse-droppings and discarded orange peel to reach the farther pavement. There, between an optician's shop, and the premises of a wholesale draper, rose The Prebendary's House, a massive sandstone building with a rectangular Tudor window on either side of the front door.

Arkwright produced a key to open the front door, and they entered a narrow hallway, the walls of which were covered in Tudor linen fold panelling. Caroline noticed a number of candle sconces with little tin reflectors fixed to the panels, and realized that this house, unlike those in Dean's Row, was not yet lit by gas.

'This place,' said Arkwright, as he struggled out of his topcoat, 'was built in 1574.' He seemed quite irascible when he mentioned the date, as though it constituted a personal affront. Perhaps he resented not being able to live in one of the fine eighteenth-century houses in Dean's Row?

Arkwright preceded her into his study, a wide, low-ceilinged chamber at the end of the hall passage, its walls lined with open bookshelves. A stately old grandfather clock ticked away gently in one corner. There were framed photographs fixed to the wall above an occasional table, upon which had been displayed a row of demure little silver cups, which looked like sports trophies. Nicholas Arkwright relaxed with a sigh in a big leather armchair beside the empty fireplace, and motioned to Caroline to take a chair opposite him.

'Well, Caroline,' Arkwright said, 'what did you think of Sir Charles Blount? Rather an impressive man, wouldn't you say?'

'Very impressive, Mr Arkwright. And very handsome, in a foreign sort of way. I shall enjoy working in his picture gallery. You do realize, don't you, that I could hear you both talking? Especially Sir Charles. Talking about the Dean, you know.'

'Well, there was nothing specially secret about what we were discussing. Everyone knows that the Dean and I are at odds over Master Geoffrey's window. I don't suppose you've seen it, yet? Ask your uncle to show it to you tomorrow. It's one of the glories of Ancaster.'

Prebendary Arkwright began to gnaw the flesh near the nail of his right thumb. His brows drew together in a frown.

'That school of his could be built elsewhere, you know. There are three or four ideal places in town where it could be sited. But that's the Dean all over! Stubborn as the proverbial mule, always right, never wrong. He was just the same at school. Pigheaded.'

Arkwright laughed, in spite of himself. He looked slightly abashed at his outburst. Caroline took no notice. Her new friend was beginning to talk as though she wasn't there. That was a good sign!

'If you look at that old photograph up there,' Arkwright continued, 'you'll see the

60

three of us as boys in a school group. See if you can pick out your Uncle Walter and me!'

Caroline left her chair and peered at the photograph. It was very faded, but she could make out the individual fresh faces of a number of serious-looking boys sitting on benches, with a large silver trophy standing on a little table in front of them. One boy held a board, upon which had been chalked, 'Canons Athletics Week, 1860'.

'There you are, Mr Arkwright. Third from the right on the back row. Oh, don't you look young! About fifteen I suppose? Now, let me see . . . Oh! There's Uncle Walter, long and lanky, and wearing spectacles. Well, not long and lanky really . . . And which one is the Dean? He must have changed a lot: I can't pick him out.'

'Look for a big, strong, smug, self-satisfied boy, the king of the castle. He's there, somewhere. That's Lawrence Girdlestone.'

'Second from the right, on the second row? Yes, of course . . . But you know, Mr Arkwright, he doesn't look smug to me. I'd say he was uncertain of himself, shy——'

Nicholas Arkwright laughed, and shook his head.

'Uncertain of himself? Lawrence Girdlestone? Not he, my girl. The king of the castle, that's what he was. And is, come to that. But let's not talk about him for the moment. I must tell you about Conrad. He's been staying here with me for a few days, but now he's gone back to Southampton. Before he went, he said to me: "Father, please convey my choicest sentiments to Miss Parrish, and say that I trust to meet her again in the very near future".'

Caroline clasped her hands together in delight.

'Oh, Mr Arkwright, did he really say that?'

'Well, as a matter of fact, he didn't. But he would have done so, had the opportunity arisen! There, I've made you laugh. But now I'll be serious for a moment, Caroline, if I may. Conrad was very smitten with you last night. I hope you and he will become friends. He's a fine young fellow, you know. He hasn't inherited my—Yes, he's very well thought of by all kinds of people.'

'Does he come down to Ancaster often?'

'Oh, yes. I expect we'll see much more of him now that he's left the army.'

Caroline glanced around the comfortable but untidy study. It had a French window, which looked out on to a rather neglected garden.

'Mr Arkwright,' she asked, 'who looks after you here? Are there any servants?'

'Well, Caroline, I've not felt the need for a staff of servants, but I have the help of a very faithful married couple, who manage things well between them. And there are a few young girls who come in to help.'

Prebendary Arkwright glanced at a clock on

the mantelpiece.

'Is that the time? I must bestir myself and get down to St Mary's. I've a meeting of the Workhouse Board of Guardians scheduled for half-past four. Don't forget what I said: get your Uncle Walter to show you the Master Geoffrey window tomorrow. It's the most beautiful thing imaginable, and it may not be revealed to the light of day for much longer, if Dean Girdlestone gets his way.'

CHAPTER THREE

SERMONS AND STONES

Just after ten o'clock the next morning, Caroline Parrish had her first sight of the great west window of Ancaster Cathedral. She and Uncle Walter had crossed Dean's Row and entered the precinct through a wicket gate in the iron railings. The sun had been in their eyes, and the gloom had increased when Canon Parrish had led her through the north porch into the cool and cavernous interior of the cathedral church.

And then, as they had turned a corner from the dimly seen transept, the glories of the window had burst upon her sight in such a way as to make her catch her breath in awe. The whole west wall of the ancient cathedral seemed to have yielded to the power of the sun, leaving only the heavenly vision of Master Geoffrey's glowing window, soaring nearly forty feet above a long blocked-up door.

'It's wonderful!' Caroline whispered, and her uncle murmured his agreement.

'It is, rather. It was made in 1438, in the seventeenth year of the reign of King Henry VI, by a great artist in glass, called Master Geoffrey of Coventry. There are over a thousand separate pieces, apparently. It remained untouched throughout the Reformation, through the influence of the Beaufort family.'

Caroline only half heard her uncle's words. She was enthralled by the hundreds of painted figures—the apostles, the martyrs, and the great doctors of the church. She allowed herself to be dazzled by the reds, the golds, the blues, the subtle greens, and the sudden flaring darts of pure white glass. She understood Nicholas Arkwright's despairing anger at the thought of all that celestial light being blotted out.

'If you look in the left-hand corner,' said Uncle Walter, 'you'll see the likeness of Bishop Arnulf, who founded the first cathedral on the site, in 904. Then there comes a line of bishops and patrons. They're actually genuine portraits of the monks who were here in Master Geoffrey's day. He made them sit for him as models.'

'And right at the end, Uncle Walter—surely that's Henry VII? You can tell from his pinched, mean little face.'

'Yes, that's old Henry. They inserted that little extra pane after he gave us the St Catherine Chapel in thanksgiving for the birth of Prince Arthur, in 1486.'

From somewhere in the dim recesses of the cathedral someone rang a silvery little hand-bell. Walter Parrish took out his watch, opened it, and scowled at the dial.

'I thought I'd have had more time to show you round, Caroline. But that's the robing bell for the clergy. Well, they can do without me this morning. You and I will sit in the nave, and enjoy choral matins as spectators.'

It was with considerable reluctance that Caroline turned her back on the glowing window, and followed her uncle into a pew in the vast nave of Ancaster Cathedral. At eleven o'clock precisely, the organ began to play, and the clergy of the Chapter, preceded by a robed choir of men and boys, came down the aisle and took their places in the stalls for choral matins, which was sung daily. Two tall candles had been lit on the high altar, throwing little pools of yellow light on to the huge alabaster reredos with its dim niches full of carved and gilded saints.

Caroline watched, fascinated, as her friend Nicholas Arkwright, now gravely robed in white surplice, scarf, and Oxford MA hood, took his place in a richly carved and pinnacled stall, with a hooded canopy that gave it the appearance of a sentry box. He looked incredibly dignified. The organ, for some reason, continued to play. Then a second procession appeared from some hidden place to the right. It consisted of two robed beadles carrying staves, followed by the Dean. The beadles conducted Lawrence Girdlestone to his own highly decorated stall, bowed low, and quickly retired. The morning service commenced.

The Dean was to preach that day. The two robed beadles reappeared, and preceded him to the towering stone pulpit. The Dean announced his text: 'Little children, keep yourselves from idols'. There was an urgency in his voice that made Caroline sit up straight in the pew.

The Dean's condemnation of idolatry was delivered with persuasive zeal. He thundered against graven images, and the ever-present dangers of paganism. It was a powerful sermon, and when he had finished, there was a kind of awed hush before the organ played a brief recessional, and the busy beadles appeared with their staves to conduct the Dean of Ancaster back to his stall.

*   *   *

After the service, the Dean emerged from the

vestry. His face was flushed a healthy red. His white preaching bands had slipped on their hidden tape, so that they seemed to be heading for his left ear. Caroline received once again the impression of a man who held both power and vulnerability in balance as part of his nature.

'Ah! Canon Parrish!' Girdlestone exclaimed. 'I *must* have a word with you about Syme. He's drinking heavily again, and a word from you, I'm sure, will put him right.'

'I'm at your service, Mr Dean,' said Uncle Walter. He lowered his voice, and whispered to Caroline, 'Syme is our resident hobgoblin. He's the porter, and lives in a dim lair above the gatehouse. He's addicted to the demon drink.' He added aloud, 'Caroline, why don't you ask Prebendary Arkwright to show you round the chapels? Here he is, now.'

Nicholas Arkwright had just emerged from the canons' vestry. He looked grave and sombre, but his face lit up when he saw Caroline. The Dean walked away down the nave, talking in loud tones to Walter Parrish. Arkwright watched him until he disappeared with Parrish into the north choir aisle.

'"Little children, keep yourselves from idols",' Arkwright muttered, as though to himself. 'The First Epistle of John, Chapter 5, and verse 21. Why did he treat us to that particular gem of oratory this morning? Well, we'll see. The Dean never does anything, you

67

know, without a reason.'

As Nicholas Arkwright spoke, Caroline became conscious of the fact that they were both being observed by a powerful, tall man in a sober black suit and open frock coat, both of which were permeated with a powder of fine grey stone-dust. The man stood perfectly motionless beside a pillar of the nave crossing, watching them. He carried a dusty silk hat in his right hand. Nicholas Arkwright suddenly caught sight of the man, and smiled.

'Mr Solomon!' he said. 'I was hoping you'd be here this morning. I want you to meet Canon Parrish's niece, Miss Caroline Parrish, who's come to live at Number 7.'

'I'm very pleased to meet you, miss,' said the big, dusty man. 'I hope as you'll be very happy here with us at Ancaster.'

He spoke with a warm, Warwickshire accent, though a certain measure of huskiness suggested that some of the dust with which he was surrounded had got permanently into his throat.

'Mr Solomon is Clerk of the Works, Caroline, which means he's responsible for the maintenance of this great building, and a good deal more besides.'

As the three of them stood at the crossing, they were bathed in the many-coloured lights thrown upon them by Master Geoffrey's great west window. Mr Solomon turned to face it, so that his deep-set eyes were dazzled by its glory.

'Now, Mr Arkwright,' he said, 'you heard the Dean's sermon, just now, the sermon about idols. Would you and Miss Caroline care to step into the works office? I'd like to have a word or two with you about that sermon, if I may.'

Mr Solomon's dark eyes seemed to grow darker. He had a massive, heavy face, bronzed with long years of working out of doors. The man exuded an earthy, almost chemical smell, a smell that put Caroline in mind of damp stone. When he smiled, it reminded her of a satyr carved in oak.

Solomon moved away from the window and into the south aisle. Arkwright and Caroline followed him. Solomon produced a massive key from the pocket of his frock coat, and opened a stout door, half-hidden by a monument to an eighteenth-century landowner, forever writhing in white marble garments, as he sought to escape a skeletal image of Death, dart raised, ready to strike.

The door led directly into a lofty chamber lit by four tall Gothic windows filled with plain glass. There were a number of stout benches covered in the tools of a mason's trade. Massive pieces of hewn stone stood on wooden trestles, each marked roughly with a painted number. In one corner of the room, a modern roll-top desk stood incongruously next to an ancient stone coffin, which contained an assortment of chisels and adzes.

'I've known this secret place since childhood, Caroline,' said Nicholas Arkwright. 'Josiah—Mr Solomon—and I sang in the choir for years, ever since we were little boys of seven. Life's taken us down different paths since those palmy days, but we still share the same set of values, don't we, Mr Solomon?'

'We do, sir. I often think of your late father, God rest him, and his wire works in Speedwell Lane. And my father was Clerk of the Works before me, and taught me to love this old place . . . Of course, that was in the days before Dean Buckley, and the cathedral was a drab and dusty hole, wasn't it, sir? Its only glory was Master Geoffrey of Coventry's magical window.'

Mr Solomon pushed the heavy door of the works office shut. He leaned against it, his arms folded, and observed his visitors. Nicholas Arkwright had sat down uninvited in the Clerk's swivel chair. Caroline had settled herself on a wooden bench near the door.

'You've not changed one jot, Mr Arkwright,' said Solomon, 'in all the years I've known you. You feel things keenly, sir—too keenly, some folk would say. You were just the same when you were a little chap. So, if I tell you something about the Dean and his idols, will you promise me not to take on so? You know what I mean, sir.'

'Of course I promise, Mr Solomon.'

'Very well, sir. Now, as to idols, and such—

he went up on to the tower with me early this morning—'

'What? Dean Girdlestone, do you mean?'

'Yes, sir. He's limping a bit, as you know, because he twisted his ankle last week, when he tumbled down the stairs from the organ loft. But he insisted on climbing up the spiral stairs to the roof space above the nave. "Are you sure, now, Mr Dean?" I asked him. "Oh, stop fussing, Solomon", he said, and I helped him up the ladders and on to the masons' platform.'

Caroline was startled at her friend's agonized look. It was as though he was suffering an acute physical pain.

'What did he want? He's never gone up there since you raised the scaffolding over the St Catherine Chapel.'

'The Dean just stood there, sir, looking down at the roof of the chapel. My men have already loosened the slates for removal, and covered them with canvas sheets against the weather. They're good slates, early eighteenth century. Then he turned round on the little gallery just under the clock dial, and pointed to one of the four angels. The Ancaster Guardians—'

'Gabriel, Raphael, Michael, and the one whose face had been chiselled off, presumably by some Reformation zealot.'

'That was the one the Dean pointed to. "Who do you suppose that fellow is,

Solomon?" he asked. "Azrael, sir", I said, "the Angel of Death. That's what the old rumours say".'

'And what did the Dean say to that? Azrael, you know, is a Muhammadan angel. Not one of ours at all.'

'So the Dean told me, sir. "This place, Solomon," he said, "is supposedly the house of God, but it's in imminent danger of turning into a cesspit of superstition. These angels— idols, for that's what they are when unlettered folk start ignorantly worshipping them—they should be taken down. Guardians, indeed!" Then he said something about hill-altars—I wasn't listening too closely by that time—and then I guided him down from the roof to the nave pavement.'

'For a man who wasn't listening closely, you seem to have remembered every word! And the bit about hill-altars would have been from psalm 78. "They grieved him with their hill-altars, and provoked him to displeasure with their images." Verse 59. So the Dean doesn't like our Guardians?'

'He does not, sir. He thinks they should be taken down. He thinks—'

Josiah Solomon seemed to choke on his words. Caroline saw that he was making a heroic effort to master some kind of growing resentment. Presently, he regained his composure.

'And that's why he preached about idols

today. To my way of thinking, it's not just the Master Geoffrey window that's in peril. It's the Angels, as well. To Dean Girdlestone, sir, Ancaster Cathedral is nothing more than a great heap of stone! He's no feeling for it, sir. But I often pause in my work about this great church, and in the stillness, maybe up in the triforium, or in the crypts, I fancy I can hear the place breathing; and if I rest my hand against a pillar, or a wall, I can feel the beating of its heart.'

*   *   *

Would the choking heat of summer never abate? It was almost impossible to breathe, and Nicholas was afraid that Girdlestone would hear his panting as he followed him up the ladders. This time, there would be no mistake. He would slay the serpent lurking in their bosom. He moved further upward, conscious of the black looming shape of Dean Girdlestone going before him.

But now—surely he was on the leads of Magdalen tower? The choir boys were singing some kind of tuneless dirge. Girdlestone was looking down over the parapet. Now! Send him plummeting down to the road below! Lawrence Girdlestone turned, and smiled. His eyes shone like stars, and his teeth were bared in a demonic smile of triumph.

No; he was not on Magdalen tower. That

was merely an old dream. He was above the clerestory of Ancaster Cathedral, where Dean Girdlestone was standing motionless on the ledge above the nave roof. Nicholas surged forward, and sent the dark figure reeling off the ledge. His enemy turned as he fell, and cried out: 'Arkwright!' Then he had gone. At last! The burden of a lifetime had lifted from Nicholas Arkwright's shoulders.

The four Guardians carved into the north flank of the tower turned their faces towards him, and smiled their approval. Then, suddenly, they crumbled to dust, sliding down with a thunderous shriek on to the roof below. Nicholas turned away in fear—and saw Lawrence Girdlestone standing safe and well on the platform by the ladders. 'Nicholas,' he said, and his voice was both mocking and menacing, 'keep yourself from idols. From idols. From—'

Nicholas Arkwright sprang from his bed in terror, and knelt on the floor, his head clasped in his hands. Were these wicked dreams portents of what was to come? Were his wrongs, and the slights he had suffered, to end in murder? This devilish night-torment could only be exorcized by ghostly counsel. He would go again to Bishop Grandison, and tell him all.

*   *   *

Bishop Grandison listened to Nicholas

Arkwright's account of his dream. His gaunt face betrayed little of what he might have been feeling, and at one moment in his narrative, Arkwright wondered whether the aged prelate had not fallen asleep. However, when the Bishop spoke, the Prebendary realized that he must have pondered over every word of his murderous tale.

'Nicholas,' he asked, in his quiet, silvery tones, 'are you confiding or confessing? A confession binds me to canonical silence. A confidence, however, can be legitimately shared with others.'

Nicholas was silent for a while. What a dreadful old man he was! He was saying, in effect, that his fantasies of murder were indeed preludes to the thing itself.

'I am confiding in you, My Lord,' Arkwright replied. 'I have nothing to confess, because in this business of the Dean, I have done nothing that could conceivably harm him.'

Bishop Grandison sighed. He glanced at Arkwright, who dropped his eyes.

'Very well. Now, Nicholas, in this dream you actually saw Dean Girdlestone fall, and you heard him utter your name. Why was that?'

'My Lord, that part of my dream was a recollection of something that occurred to Lawrence Girdlestone and me when we were both boys together, at school. It was in the summer of 1857. A group of us had been tackling a fairly gruelling hike along one of the

75

narrow, leafy paths along Yarnton Edge, three hundred feet above the Warwickshire countryside. It's a splendid spot for a hike, but a dangerous one. Well, Girdlestone was walking in front of me—'

The Bishop held up his hand to stem the flow of words. Nicholas saw the sunlight reflected from his episcopal ring as he did so.

'Is this the story that Dean Girdlestone loves to tell us? The story of how you saved his life when he clumsily slipped on the wet grass, and almost fell to his death? If so, then I have already heard it.'

'No, My Lord, you have not! Far from saving him, I tried to murder him! Of course, I was only fourteen at the time—'

'How careful you are to excuse yourself before you have even told me what you did! It's just as well that you're confiding, not confessing! Pray, continue. What did you do to him?'

'Girdlestone was always careless about where he put his feet. It had rained heavily on the night before our hike, and the way underfoot was treacherous. One little push, and I would be delivered from my old enemy.'

Arkwright laboured to control the tremor in his voice as he continued his tale.

'I clutched Girdlestone's sleeve—I can still remember the rough texture of the serge as my fingers closed on it. I cried out, as though I had slipped and fallen against him—and then I

76

used my whole weight to send him hurtling over the precipice.'

'What did you do then?'

'I threw myself to the ground, and looked over the edge. Girdlestone was desperately clutching at the tangle of ivy and monstrous weeds covering the overhanging rocky outcrop. His feet were beating the air. I saw the pleading in his eyes, but a demon whispered in my ear: "Let him fall!" And then he called my name. "Arkwright!" he cried. My Lord, I was overcome with revulsion at what I'd done. I dug the toecaps of my boots firmly in the soil of the path, stretched myself over the drop, and seized Girdlestone's wrists. I called for help, but it was I alone who hauled him back to safety on the path.'

When Nicholas had finished his tale, he was surprised to feel a sudden surge of resentment against the saintly old man sitting behind the desk. Why could he not have offered a few words of encouragement? Nicholas was a grown man, who had long ago forgiven his own fourteen-year-old self, burdened with a boy's untamed animosities. Besides, he'd sometimes wondered whether, at the moment when he had surged towards Girdlestone, he had not suffered a sudden seizure. It could have happened like that.

The Bishop spoke, and his words came to Nicholas like a stab to the heart.

'I very much fear, Nicholas,' he said, 'that

77

you are hovering on the brink of mental and moral dissolution. These dreams, mingled with half-remembered recollections of your youth, are the signs of worse to come. You said, last time you came here, that you feared your dreams were premonitions. Who am I, to say you nay? So you had better tell me why you resent Lawrence Girdlestone so much.'

'Mental and moral dissolution? How can that be, My Lord? I have confessed to you the wretched sins of my youth—'

The old Bishop rapped his knuckles sharply on the desk. His face was suddenly angry and forbidding.

'Enough! Do not prevaricate! If you do not tell me the whole story, I cannot help you. That demon you are harbouring will destroy you.'

Nicholas remained silent, conscious of the quiet ticking of a clock, and the movement of light thrown on the ceiling by the stirring foliage of the birch trees in the garden of the Bishop's palace. He would have to speak. There was no escaping from this awful old man.

'You know, My Lord, that Girdlestone and I read Greats at Oxford. We met socially on a number of occasions, though our respective ways of life were rather different. He was in with what they termed a "fast set"; though he was clever enough never to let himself be carried further than he chose to go.

Girdlestone managed his vices judiciously.'

'You have some wonderfully wicked turns of phrase, Nicholas,' the Bishop observed coolly. 'Under normal circumstances, I would enjoy them, but not now. Give me a plain, unvarnished tale.'

'Yes, My Lord. Well, in the summer of 1865, at a weekend party at Vaux Hall, in Essex, I made the acquaintance of a young lady, to whom I was much attracted. She had the welcome ability to converse easily and with thoughtful understanding on the raging topics of the day.'

'Talking? I see. And was that what attracted her to you, Nicholas?'

In spite of his mental turmoil, Nicholas found himself smiling.

'Well, partly. She liked talking with me, and from that moment at Vaux Hall she added me to her bevy of admirers. Well, My Lord, you'll appreciate that ours was a small world, and that we were forever crossing each other's paths. That summer party at Vaux Hall was the first of many, and it was inevitable, I suppose, that Lawrence Girdlestone should have turned up at one or other of them. The upshot of all this is that at one such weekend party, in 1868, Girdlestone was much in the company of the young lady, and I could see immediately that she was impressed with him.'

'Or perhaps, Nicholas,' observed the Bishop drily, 'she had decided to play one admirer off against the other.'

'Perhaps so, My Lord. But whatever her purpose, my jealousy was roused to fever pitch. What fools young fellows are! I was twenty-three years old, and the time had come for me to settle down. I'd known the young lady since 1865. She was twenty, and still unmarried. I determined that, for once, Lawrence Girdlestone was not going to win the prize.'

The Bishop smiled, and looked at Nicholas with detached amusement.

'So what did you do? Did you challenge him to a duel? Purchase a brace of pistols?'

'I did neither of those things, My Lord. There's a large market town near to Vaux Hall, and from a jeweller there I obtained a fine silver betrothal ring, set with small diamonds. That very evening, when dinner was ended, I invited the young lady to walk with me on the moonlit terrace. To my joy, she readily assented. I saw Girdlestone glance sharply after us as we left the drawing-room, and felt a surge of triumph that sent my pulses racing!'

'Very natural. What happened next?'

'It was a quiet, warm evening, and Laura— Oh, drat it!'

Bishop Grandison permitted himself a little silvery laugh.

'Don't worry, Nicholas! You were never very good at dissembling. All the dates and places told me that you were talking about Laura

Taverner—Mrs Girdlestone, as she is now. Continue your tale.'

'Laura seemed particularly radiant that evening, but I could sense that her manner towards me had become timid—even apprehensive.'

'She would have sensed that you were about to propose marriage to her.'

'Yes. My fingers clasped the little jewel box in the pocket of my evening coat. For nearly a minute I was tongue-tied with anxiety. Eventually, I opened my mouth to speak; but it was Laura who broke the unbearable silence. "Nicholas", she said, "I'm so glad that you wanted to stroll out here with me. You and I have been good friends for a long time now, and I've come to regard you as a very special confidant. So I want you to be the first to know that, just before dinner tonight, your old friend Lawrence Girdlestone offered me his hand in marriage".'

'And what did you say to that?'

'I was crushed, My Lord. Once again, he had triumphed over me. I managed to observe the decencies, though. "I hope that you will both be very happy", I said, and Laura replied: "I hope so, too". We parted there on the terrace at Vaux Hall, and went our different ways. It was not a great romantic story, of course, but—I wonder whether you can understand this?—its very inevitability seared into my soul. Seared . . . I kept the betrothal ring, you know. I have it to this day.'

Both men sat in silence for a while. Then the Bishop sighed.

'Nicholas,' he said, 'you must leave Ancaster as soon as possible. I wondered all along whether there wasn't an element of old-fashioned jealousy in this problem of yours. You need time for rest and contemplation. Your senior curate will cope perfectly well with St Mary's in your absence. I will send you to look after the parish of St Elphin's, Arden Leigh, which is vacant at the moment. If anyone should ask you why you are going there, you may say that it is at my request.'

'Very well, My Lord,' said Arkwright.

'There is something else.'

'My Lord?'

'Before you go to Arden Leigh, you must consult your physician, Dr Savage. Go to see him, and tell him all that you have told me. You have come to me with spiritual problems, and I have addressed them. But you know as well as I do that these terrible dreams are part and parcel of your prevailing physical condition—epilepsy.'

'My Lord, I beg you not to mention that matter—'

'I must mention it, because it is part of your perilous sickness, and must not remain untreated. Go to see Dr Savage. He will know what to do.'

                    *   *   *

'I think it's going to be essential, Jackson,' said Superintendent Mays, 'that we clear up this business of Dean Girdlestone quickly and discreetly. You did right, of course, to seek my help in the matter, and I've done some delving for you. The Very Reverend Lawrence Girdlestone, Dean of Ancaster, banks with a London private bank, Messrs Cooper and Partners, in Lothbury. I've made enquiries, as you requested, and I can confirm that his balances at Cooper's are nothing out of the ordinary, though they are very substantial.'

Inspector Jackson had been summoned to visit his superior officer at Peel House, the headquarters of the constabulary in the thriving town of Copton Vale. Mr Mays, a grey-haired man in immaculate uniform, always reminded Jackson of a distinguished physician or surgeon. He was a man totally dedicated to his work.

'But he has other bank accounts, Jackson, which require some explanation. I've made a list of them here. They include an account with Morgan's Saving Bank at Sedley Vale, where he has over eighteen thousand pounds on deposit. These savings banks are designed for modest country folk to deposit their spare silver, and the occasional sovereign. That account, with its colossal deposit, needs urgent explanation. There's another similar account in the savings bank at Fort Hill. There's five thousand in that. Find out about these accounts, Jackson, when you confront Dean Girdlestone.'

'When do you think that I should move in the matter, sir?'

'Well, it's Monday today, Jackson, and the last day in July. There's the August Bank Holiday due on the seventh, which is the day when the Ancaster Revel begins. There'll be three days of junketing and jollification. Try to conclude your business before the start of the Revel. Then, if you have to do something unpleasant, people will forget about it when the ox-roasting, and the games, and all the rest of it, begin.'

'I thought of calling on the Dean this coming Thursday, sir,' said Jackson. 'I agree that some kind of discretion is necessary, because Dean Girdlestone is regarded as a hero in some quarters—'

Superintendent Mays rapped sharply on his desk. His face flushed a little, but his voice remained steady.

'Let's have less of this "calling on the Dean" business, Jackson! You're going there to initiate an enquiry into serious fraud and theft. The man you're supposedly "calling on" could end up doing twelve years' penal servitude. Do you understand what I'm saying?'

'Yes, sir.'

'Very well. Go on Thursday, by all means.

Take Sergeant Bottomley with you. Let's get it over with before the county starts to interfere. I've already had a letter from Sir Charles Blount, offering his help and advice. Very decent of him, and very precipitous! Incidentally, I've seen that man Markland myself. I asked him to come here, to Peel House, and he was more than happy to do so. He's a mean-spirited little man, Jackson, very proud of his own cleverness, and very eager to do whatever damage he can to Girdlestone. I don't think he's quite as clever as he makes himself out to be, but he's as honest as the day, and he proved to my satisfaction that the sum of fifteen thousand pounds has undoubtedly been embezzled from the cathedral treasury. So get out to Ancaster on Thursday, Jackson, and confront the Dean with your suspicions. I want the truth of this matter brought out into the light of day.'

*   *   *

It was quiet in the brown-painted back room of Warwick Police-Office. The strong afternoon sunlight poured in through the single uncurtained window, casting long shadows from the iron bars on to the scrubbed floorboards.

Detective Inspector Jackson looked at the big railway clock hanging above the fire grate. Half past three. Sergeant Bottomley would be back from Sedley Vale soon, and they'd be able to compare notes. Things looked black for this Dean Girdlestone, despite Sarah Brown's passionate advocacy. In cases of this sort, there was no smoke without fire.

He and Bottomley would go over unannounced to Ancaster Deanery on Thursday, which was the third of August. He'd write a note to Inspector Traynor at Ancaster, letting him know that he and Bottomley would be stepping on to his patch. No need to say more than that. Bob Traynor had no detectives at Primrose Street, and knew better than to ask questions before there were any acceptable answers.

Jackson got up from his desk as Sergeant Bottomley clattered past the window on a grey pony. He watched in detached interest as his sergeant, who was wearing his usual flapping yellow greatcoat, came to an abrupt halt at the entrance to the stable yard, and slid with casual elegance out of the saddle. He came to rest in a neat heap on the cobbles.

Jackson sighed, and made an unconscious effort to stifle a smile. What was the use of making a fuss? Evidently, Herbert Bottomley had stopped for a nip of something reviving on his way back from Sedley Vale, probably at the Beehive, or the Volunteer at Thornton Heath. It wasn't the first time he'd done it, and it wouldn't be the last. Gin was never a problem. It was gin followed by a quick beer that wrought havoc with Bottomley's balance.

'You'll do yourself an injury one of these days, Sergeant,' said Jackson, as Bottomley came into the office, 'You'll fall off your horse once too often, break your neck, and leave me short-handed. That is, if you don't drink yourself to death before that happens.'

'Sir,' said Bottomley in a suitably melancholy tone, 'on this inauspicious occasion, with the dereliction of duty, and gross disrespect . . . disregard . . .'

'Yes, well never mind all that, Sergeant. You can repent at leisure in private, to your heart's content. But for the moment, just sit there quietly, and while you're gathering your wits, you can listen to what Superintendent Mays wants us both to do.'

When Jackson had finished the account of his visit to Copton Vale, Sergeant Bottomley stirred in his chair, and pulled a dog-eared notebook from the inside pocket of his yellow greatcoat. He moistened a finger, and slowly turned over a couple of pages.

'I spoke to the manager of Mason's Savings Bank at Sedley Vale, sir. He was a bit huffy at first, standing on his dignity, and so forth. So I showed him my warrant, and told him how serious it was to obstruct the police. After that, he was all smiles. Dean Girdlestone, he told me, has had a deposit account with the bank since 1878. He makes irregular withdrawals of large sums, and also deposits large sums from time to time. He has a pass book, and all the transactions are in cash. Sovereigns in, and sovereigns out.'

'That's where the funny business is going on, Sergeant, always supposing that our Dean is anything other than pure as the driven snow. Peculiar transactions at Mason's Savings Bank, and at a similar establishment over at Fort Hill. Did you find out anything else?'

'Yes, sir. I talked to quite a few people in Sedley Vale, and the general opinion there was that Mr Girdlestone was a saint. But I was told something else, that may be of importance. There's a Mrs Girdlestone, sir, as perhaps you already know. Our man married her in the '70s. Well, all the time that Girdlestone was Rector of Sedley Vale, Mrs Girdlestone wasn't there. He lived a bachelor existence in the big old rectory there until he left for his next post.'

'Not there? I wonder where she was? Perhaps we'll find out, Sergeant, when we call on the Dean on Thursday. Let's wait and see.'

*   *   *

Caroline Parrish looked down from the farther window of the picture gallery, watching Sir Charles Blount, and his secretary, Mr Hayden, walking purposefully across the elegant white suspension bridge spanning the River Best. Sir Charles was sporting an ebony walking stick; Mr Hayden carried a black leather valise. They had told her that they had urgent business in the old town, and had left the house as the many clocks in the saloons and on the landings had struck or chimed one o'clock.

Caroline left the gallery, and made her way up the bright, wide staircases to the floors above. She paused on the first-floor landing, and looked at a gilded ormolu table set in an alcove between two doors. On the table stood a fantastic clock, wrought in ebony and silver gilt, which Sir Charles told her had been made for an eighteenth-century Egyptian Pasha. Its little ivory dial told not only the time, but the date, and the day of the week.

The clock was lovingly cared for by a talented horologist from Coventry, who had adapted its mechanisms as far as was possible to function successfully in the nineteenth century. However, Sir Charles had forbidden any tampering with the revolving plaques of silver and lapis lazuli that displayed the day and the date. Accordingly, the clock told Caroline that it was now twenty past one, on Thursday, 3 August, 1793.

Arrayed behind the clock, like soldiers mounting guard, were four heavy basalt figures of the jackal-headed Egyptian god Anubis, each about a foot high. They were covered in carved hieroglyphs, and looked strangely crude in comparison with the fantastic clock. She had noticed them a few days earlier, though she had imagined then that there were five of them. Both clock and basalt figures, she thought, had probably found their way to Europe, and so to England, in Napoleon's baggage-trains.

The second-floor landing was dominated by a huge oil painting in a heavy gilt frame. It depicted Sir Charles Blount's villa in Taormina, a romantic seventeenth-century mansion set in a grove of cypresses. There were some fanciful depictions of fauns and satyrs disporting themselves in the darker corners of the canvas.

A steep staircase behind a narrow door took Caroline up to an empty, echoing chamber in a tower rising above the roof line. It had once been used as an observatory. The house, she had learned, had been built in 1838 for Dr James McArthur, the noted astronomer. Sir Charles had bought it on McArthur's death in 1882.

The room was glazed on all sides, and afforded magnificent views of the Warwickshire countryside. Caroline looked across the river at the ancient town, where the cathedral rose above the roofs of the houses, establishing its right of seniority. From that height, Ancaster seemed to contain more trees than she had noticed, beeches, venerable oaks, and lines of stately elms. She wondered why Sir Charles and his secretary had been so gravely subdued that morning. Where had they gone? They would be down there, somewhere, in Dean's Row, perhaps, or in Foregate.

She looked beyond the town, and saw the modest hills and gleaming cornfields of Warwickshire stretching to the horizon. This was the world to which she really belonged, the world of Canon Parrish and Millie, the world of her enigmatic new friend, Nicholas Arkwright, and his son Conrad. Standing there in the silent chamber, and looking beyond the confines of the house in Ladymead, Caroline suddenly realized that the romantic villa in Sicily, half-hidden in its grove of cypresses, was something essentially alien to her own native spirit.

CHAPTER FOUR

THROUGH A GLASS, DARKLY

Nicholas Arkwright left his house in Friary Street a little before two o'clock, after having fortified himself with a solitary luncheon of bread and cheese. He had obeyed the Bishop, and consulted his physician, Dr Savage, who had scolded him for neglecting his constitution, and then prescribed a special preparation of bromide mixture. That morning, he had taken a carefully measured dose of Dr Savage's medicine, and had almost immediately experienced a feeling of overpowering drowsiness which at some moments bordered upon stupor.

Confound Girdlestone! These wicked dreams would not have happened if the Dean had shown more sympathy for Ancaster, its ancient treasures, and its popular customs.

Nicholas dragged himself up the thirty steps into Dean's Row. He was just in time to see Sir Charles Blount knocking at the door of the Deanery. He wondered idly what the Hereditary Steward's business was with the Dean. Nothing to do with him, of course. Blount had his secretary with him—he'd forgotten the man's name. He was carrying a valise, no doubt crammed with official papers.

Nicholas had no wish to meet them that afternoon. If he looked as sickly as he felt, they'd start to ask him intrusive questions. He turned aside into the cathedral gardens in order to avoid greeting them.

He made his way through a little-used side door into the dim north transept of the cathedral, from which he entered the St Catherine Chapel, an awkward kind of place architecturally, dominated by a modern tomb, exuberantly carved in the Gothic style by Sir Arthur Blomfield. Beneath it lay the remains of Edward Parr, a seventeenth-century bishop. From niches capped by heavily foliated arches the heads of the Twelve Apostles looked out suspiciously on the nineteenth-century world. A figure representing

Bishop Parr lay in majestic sleep on top of the tomb, a mitre on his head, and two approving angels at his feet.

The St Catherine Chapel was the only part of Ancaster Cathedral that had not yet been restored. Money had become tight towards the end of the '70s, but new funds established then had now matured, and the work was at last about to commence. The low plaster ceiling was to be replaced with a soaring hammer-beam roof of English oak, with many gilt figures of angels, wings crossed, and coloured heraldic shields.

It was pleasingly cool in the shady chapel, and Nicholas found his eyes closing almost as soon as he sat down in one of the old twisted elm pews. From time to time he jerked awake, with an indefinable feeling of alarm. The open marble eyes of Bishop Parr stared sightlessly at the claustrophobically low ceiling. Nicholas Arkwright found himself staring at the rows of gleaming red garnets with which the sculptor had adorned Bishop Parr's fanciful medieval vestments. The garnets, and the whole monument, became a blur between flickering eyelids . . .

He was walking unsteadily through the north transept, his only audience the marble plaques and chaste stone urns fixed high on the sandstone walls. Suddenly, he could hear the booming tones of the Dean. Where was he? Over there, by the baptistery. His powerful tenor accents echoed from the vaulted nave roof like the assertions of a giant. Who was that rock-like, impassive figure, standing beside him?

'When your men have finished on the chapel roof, Solomon, they can go up on to the leads above the nave, and make some preliminary experiments in detaching those idols from the tower. If all goes well, they can be taken down, and lowered by winch into the old burial ground below the south wall—'

'Mr Dean,' said Solomon, 'those angels are very dear to Ancaster folk. They've stood guard over the town since the days of the Old Religion, through times of plague, war and tempest—'

'That may well be, Solomon, but I have decided that they must go, and go they shall! They are rags and remnants of superstition, and misleaders of simple faith. See to it, will you?'

Arkwright opened his eyes. Yes, he was still in the St Catherine Chapel, so that threat to the angels must have been a dream. But had he really been sitting in this pew? Surely not. Perhaps he'd changed his seat in the manner of a sleepwalker. It wasn't worth thinking about it. His eyelids closed once more.

*   *   *

It was almost impossible to breathe in this

stifling summer heat. Would Girdlestone hear him, as he stumbled behind him up the ladders? Not just the great west window was threatened: the ancient carved angels, the town's guardians, were to be thrown down. There must be no mistake this time. Nicholas clambered further up the ladders, conscious of the black looming shape of Dean Girdlestone going before him.

Or was it Magdalen tower? Or Yarnton Edge? No. Those things had been mere dreams, but this was now reality. He was above the clerestory of Ancaster Cathedral, and the Dean was standing motionless on the ledge above the nave roof. Nicholas surged forward, arms outstretched, to send the dark figure reeling off the ledge.

Such wicked, wicked thoughts! When was all this nightmare going to end? How foolish this animosity seemed, when the cursed dreams had receded! Arkwright sensed that he was awake. He opened his eyes.

He found that he was sitting hunched against one of the rough stone walls in the roof space above the clerestory. Sunlight found its way into the space, from the perilous walkways at either end. What had he done? There was the sound of thunder in his ears, a thunder of his own making. He looked at the hands which had pushed his old enemy to his death, and saw that they were covered in blood.

Blood? Was this, then, another dream? He

wiped the blood off his hands, and threw his handkerchief away from him in disgust. Once more, inner darkness welled up, drowning him in its velvet blackness.

*   *   *

Would he ever wake again to the wholesome, everyday world? Although his eyes were tight shut, he sensed that he was huddled in his great carved Prebendary's stall in the choir. He had no idea why he should be there, but the world that he now inhabited was essentially unreal. He opened his eyes, and almost cried aloud in gleeful relief.

The whole cathedral seemed ablaze with festal light. Master Geoffrey's window glowed as though each separate colour carried its own blazing fire. The ancient stonework had taken on a vibrant honey colour. The black and white tessellated paving of the choir had all the deep contrasts of a picture newly pulled from an inked press. Footsteps rang in the nave, and Arkwright leaned forward cautiously.

It was Dean Girdlestone. He walked with the slight limp that had plagued him for the last week, but otherwise he seemed his usual self. He strode up to the great brass lectern, and rapidly turned over the pages of the Bible with his characteristic impatient worrying of the silk markers as he sought for that evening's readings.

Arkwright felt a welling up of relief so overpowering that he almost fainted. The dreams had been Divine punishment for his festering jealousy and selfish resentment. He half rose in his stall and, at that moment, a heavy door banged somewhere in the cathedral. Instantly, the illusory image of the Dean vanished from the lectern, and the unnatural light faded from windows and fabric. Ancaster Cathedral was itself again.

*　　　*　　　*

The next time Arkwright opened his eyes, he found that he was sitting in the same pew that he had chosen when he had first slipped into the St Catherine Chapel. Mr Solomon was standing in the doorway, observing him. The Clerk of the Works held a pewter tea jug in one hand, and two enamel mugs in the other. He chuckled, and shook his head, at the same time depositing his burdens on one of the stone window ledges of the chapel.

'You and I are getting old, sir,' said Mr Solomon. 'You came in here just after two o'clock, and you've been here, fast asleep, ever since! I looked in once or twice, but you looked so far gone, sir, that I thought to myself, "Leave him be". So I did.'

'What time is it now?'

'Four o'clock, sir. I've made so bold as to

bring a ready-made brew from the works office. It's not the first time you've partaken of my special tea, and I think it'll buck you up a bit.'

Arkwright watched Josiah Solomon as he carefully decanted the steaming contents of the pewter jug into the two mugs. Was he really awake, this time? Yes. This was the real world, and here was his old and trusted friend. He often accepted a mug of Solomon's brew, especially in the winter, when he'd stand leaning forward delicately to avoid spilling tea down his well-cut and expensive clerical frock coat. Josiah's tea came ready mixed with milk and sugar. One learned first to tolerate it, then to like it.

'Didn't I hear you talking to the Dean, earlier this afternoon? Somewhere near the baptistery—'

'The Dean? No, sir. The Dean's not been over here this afternoon. Not as far as I know, anyway. I gather he had an interview arranged with Sir Charles Blount. I expect he'll be across for evensong though, unless his business with Sir Charles detains him.'

Mr Solomon handed Arkwright his mug, and he sipped the hot tea gratefully. The Clerk of the Works stood against the wall near the door, watching him. It was very quiet in the chapel, and there was no sound from the deserted north transept beyond.

'You've been bad today, haven't you, sir?

With the epilepsy.'

Josiah was one of the very few who were allowed to share Nicholas Arkwright's secret. As a young boy in the parish school, Josiah Solomon had watched over Nicholas whenever he suffered a sudden fit. He had simply accepted the role of protector, sitting patiently on the ground until Nicholas regained consciousness. Both boys had attended the parish school, until Nicholas had left for Canons at the age of ten.

'Yes, Josiah,' said Arkwright, 'it's been very bad of late. I've had disturbing dreams, and one or two attacks, mercifully while I was at home. I've felt wretched today, because of some strong medicine given to me by my physician. Perhaps that's why I've slept here so long this afternoon.'

'I expect you're right, sir. You could do with a change of scene, and a rest from your parish for a while. I gather you're going out to Arden Leigh. Mr Leggatt told me, the Bishop's chaplain. I think that's a very good idea, sir. It'll get you away from Dean Girdlestone for a while.'

Nicholas Arkwright laughed, and finished his mug of tea. He felt enormously refreshed, and encouraged by his old schoolfellow's unobtrusive concern and kindness. It was time now to give thanks for his deliverance from his inner demon; time to go home and rest.

He thanked Josiah Solomon, and left the

cathedral precinct by the iron wicket gate. He noted, as he walked down Dean's Row towards the steps, that two men were calling at the Deanery. One, a stout person in a brown suit, looked rather like a seed merchant he'd once met at an agricultural fair. His companion was a rather vulgar-looking fellow, dressed in a lurid yellow topcoat, and clutching a battered brown bowler hat. Whoever they were, their presence suggested that Lawrence Girdlestone had finished his business with Sir Charles Blount.

Prebendary Arkwright descended the thirty steps, let himself into his house, and went straight to bed. He slept without dreaming until six o'clock the following morning.

*   *   *

Saul Jackson paused in his perusal of Dean Girdlestone's appointments diary, and glanced thoughtfully at the clergyman who had shown him into the library of Ancaster Deanery. Apparently, he had been hurriedly summoned from his house next door. He stood like a sentinel near the window, a man of fifty, slightly stooping, and peering at him and Bottomley through round, gold-framed spectacles.

'I'd be grateful, Canon Parrish,' said Jackson, 'if you'd tell me a little more about Mrs Girdlestone. I don't really understand why she's unable to see me. A lady is usually curious at the presence of detectives in her house, particularly if their business is connected with her husband.'

Jackson studied Canon Parrish's reaction, and was pleased to see his face break into a good-humoured, patient smile. Evidently, this gentleman was not given to standing on his dignity.

'I take your point, Inspector! But you'll appreciate, I think, that people can't time their illnesses to suit their visitors. Mrs Girdlestone has episodes of indisposition, when she's not fit for company. I will undertake to tell her about your visit, once she has roused herself. But is it in order, Mr Jackson, to ask you the purpose of this visit? You've shown me a search warrant, and have already begun to examine the Dean's private papers.'

'I have come here this afternoon, Canon, to confront Dean Girdlestone with a very serious accusation of fraud against the Treasury of Ancaster Cathedral. Evidently, the Dean is not to be found, which is why I'm looking at his appointments book. There's only one entry for today, and it reads: "Thursday, 3 August. Charles Blount, two o'clock." Does that convey anything special to you, Canon Parrish?'

'Fraud?' Parrish's voice held disbelief. 'Nonsense! I've known Lawrence Girdlestone for most of my life, and I tell you, Inspector, the idea's preposterous. You'll realize that yourself, as soon as you meet him. He's a man of almost tiresomely high principles. Besides, he's very well-to-do—'

'I grant you all that, Canon,' said Jackson, 'but I happen to know that information against the Dean has already been laid by Mr Markland, the Chief Clerk, and that Sir Charles Blount, as Hereditary Steward to the Ancaster Foundation, knew of it. I need hardly remind you, that professions of rectitude and high-mindedness are often a cloak for something else.'

Jackson was aware of the sumptuousness of Dean Girdlestone's library. It was a long room to the left of the spacious hallway, and it had been fitted up with a line of free-standing bookcases, each crowned with a white marble bust of a Roman emperor. The room was thickly carpeted, and furnished in mid-Victorian style with heavy mahogany furniture.

'You asked me about Sir Charles Blount, Inspector. I can confirm that he called here at the Deanery at two o'clock this afternoon. Millie—my wife—happened to be adjusting the curtains in the front parlour, and saw him arrive. He had his secretary with him. A man called Hayden.'

'Did you happen to notice when Sir Charles left the Deanery?'

'I'm afraid not, Inspector. Sir Charles is a very busy man, and I expect he returned to his house in Ladymead when he'd finished his business here—'

'Sir Charles Blount will keep, as they say, Canon Parrish,' said Jackson. 'At the moment, I'm more interested in the contents of this desk. Perhaps we can talk again, later.'

It was a clear dismissal, which Walter Parrish received with good grace. As soon as he had left the room, Jackson began a thorough inspection of Girdlestone's desk. He worked systematically and quietly, glancing through each document that he found before replacing it exactly where he had found it. Eventually, rummaging through the confused contents of a deep pigeon-hole, he drew out a small black notebook bound with faded tape. He turned the pages of the book slowly, then shook his head in disbelief.

'What do you think of that, Sergeant Bottomley?' he asked. 'You'll see that it's in the Dean's handwriting—you can check it against any of these letters and papers. It beggars belief that a man could be as foolish as that. It's a confession in all but name.'

'"A List of the Sums Removed from the Cathedral Accounts",' Bottomley read. '"Compiled by me, Lawrence Girdlestone, Dean, 24 July, 1893."' There followed a kind of balance sheet, showing the many sums that had been embezzled from the cathedral accounts, and their destinations. The money had been secretly deposited with banks in twelve different English towns, and under as many aliases. The list concluded with two neatly drawn lines in black ink, between which the Dean had recorded the total: £15,000.

'As you say, sir,' said Bottomley, 'it beggars belief. And Sir Charles Blount knew about this. I expect that's why he called on the Dean this afternoon, after which, seeing that the game was up, the Dean decamped—But, hello, sir, what's this?'

Bottomley had found a single sheet of notepaper, which had been folded, and slipped between two blank pages of the notebook. The page bore a curt message, written in a bold, flowing hand. It was dated 28 July. *Dear Girdlestone,* it ran, *you have asked for time to make these depredations good. I cannot jeopardize my own standing as Hereditary Steward by conceding to your request. I will call upon you, as planned, next Thursday, when I expect you to offer me your resignation.* It was signed *Charles Blount.*

*   *   *

'Detective Inspector Jackson? I can guess why you've come out here to see me. It's about Dean Girdlestone, isn't it? Sit down, won't you? This is a terrible business.'

Sir Charles Blount's ringing tones seemed to fill the long, high drawing-room of his house in Ladymead. Jackson had heard of Blount, but had never met him. He looked at him now, a big, powerful man, handsome in a foreign sort of way, with black ringlets falling over his forehead, like in those old engravings of Disraeli as a young man. His face, though, was pale, and the look of disquiet in his eyes belied the ebullience of his voice.

'You're quite right, sir. Acting upon information received, I conducted a search of the Dean's private desk this afternoon. I found evidence there of a massive and impudent fraud against Ancaster Cathedral. I also found a note from you, sir, which told me that you knew about Dean Girdlestone's culpability.'

'He kept it, did he?' Sir Charles Blount sighed, and shook his head. 'Even a devious fellow like Girdlestone will make the most ill-advised blunders. I told Girdlestone that I would do what I could to avoid scandal, but that he would have to make full reparation. I also told him that he would have to resign. I went to the Deanery this afternoon to receive that resignation in writing.'

'And did you receive it, sir?'

'No. Girdlestone begged me once more for a week's grace and, like a fool, I agreed. I left him, and came back here with my secretary. We'd taken some of the books with us, books from the Cathedral Treasury, you know. I don't know whether you'll find anything of direct relevance in Girdlestone's house—'

'Oh, but I did, sir. Enough, certainly, to

apply for a warrant of arrest. I intend to wait until after the Bank Holiday. If he's not turned up by Tuesday morning, I'll go after him with my warrant. I take it, sir, that you'll volunteer evidence at any trial or enquiry?'

'Of course. Meanwhile, Inspector, I wish you God speed.'

*　　*　　*

Herbert Bottomley peered up at the Roman emperor standing on top of one of the Dean's polished mahogany book-stacks. 'Vitellius', he muttered, 'I expect he was a right beauty, like the rest of them.' Nero had played the violin while Rome burned, so he'd heard. And Plato—hadn't he drunk hemlock? Or was that Cato? And did it matter?

Bottomley sat down at the Dean's desk. It was neat and tidy, apart from the wide central pigeon hole, which had been crammed haphazardly with papers. That was where the guvnor had found the damning notebook— there, in among the confusion, as though thrust hastily out of sight.

He could hear the sound of female voices upstairs. Perhaps Mrs Girdlestone had recovered from her episode of indisposition. He wondered what particular beverage caused it. He understood that the ladies were very fond of gin, and he could sympathize with that.

There was something decidedly odd about

Dean Girdlestone's desk. It was tidy and ordered, and no doubt reflected its owner's tidy mind. You didn't get to be dean unless you had a tidy mind. And yet . . . That untidy central pigeon hole looked as though it belonged to a different man.

At the back of the desk Bottomley found a leather-bound quarto book, fastened with brass clips. When he opened it, he saw that it was a journal, and he could see at once that it was in Dean Girdlestone's handwriting. The earlier pages were faded, and the ink had turned brown, but towards the end of the journal the entries were bright and of recent date. One page was headed with the ominous words: *My Burden.*

No one seeing my present success, and, perhaps envying my high social position as Dean of Ancaster, would believe that I was afflicted with the burden of feeling at all times inferior to a man who has been a friend and companion throughout a lifetime, a man who, as a mere boy of 14, saved my life by an act of instinctive bravery. Prebendary Nicholas Arkwright is that man. He seems quite unaware of my lack of self-worth, of my striving to model myself upon him, in order to win that gift that he has of attracting the love and respect of all who know him.

Only recently, he drew my attention to a

foolish lack of foresight on my part with respect to the possibility of a public objection to my plan for the new choir school. Why had I not foreseen it? And how kind of him to bring the topic up during an informal dinner!

Sergeant Bottomley closed the book, and slipped it carefully into his pocket. Prebendary Arkwright . . . He'd heard that name somewhere. Whoever he was, he sounded like a paragon of virtue. Arkwright . . . Suddenly, the Dean's library seemed to be harbouring an unseen presence, a kind of silent voice striving to impart an unheard secret. There was something wrong here, Bottomley thought, something that would not be brought to the light of day by sitting alone in this quiet and enigmatic room. He went out into the hall.

A young woman in the cap and apron of a house parlour maid was coming down the stairs. She started in surprise when she saw Bottomley, and her face assumed a look of wary defensiveness, as though she was about to be accused of some misdeed. She reminded Bottomley of his second eldest daughter, Nan. She had the same wary way with her when she was nervous.

'Good day, miss,' said Bottomley. 'I'm the detective sergeant who came here with Inspector Jackson to see the Dean. There seem to be a lot of servants in this house, and

108

I'm trying to work out who you might be?'

'I'm Ballard, sir, the house parlour maid. I am also Mrs Girdlestone's personal maid. She's much better now, and ready to see you. Shall I take you upstairs to her boudoir?'

'If you don't mind, Miss Ballard, I'd like to have a little word with you in private. Come into the Dean's study for a moment. We won't be disturbed there.'

Bottomley, the father of eight daughters, thought of all young women as girls. Ballard, he saw, must have been about thirty years old.

'Sit down, Miss Ballard. That's right. I'll not keep you for long. I believe that Sir Charles Blount came here this afternoon, at about two o'clock.'

'Yes, sir. He came with Mr Hayden, his secretary. It was I who let him in. I was coming down the stairs, and opened the door to him.'

'And how did Sir Charles seem to you? Would you say that he was happy, or sad?'

'Well, sir, he was more serious than he usually is. And Mr Hayden was quiet, too. There's usually a lot of fuss and booming voices when Sir Charles comes here, but not this time.'

'How long did he stay?'

'They weren't here more than half an hour. Sir Charles and Mr Hayden, I mean. They came by appointment. I was at the entrance to the back parlour at the end of the hall passage when they left. The Dean and Sir Charles came out of the library into the hall. They were talking quietly. Sir Charles looked very grave. I thought the Dean looked cross, as though something had upset him.'

Ballard was quiet for a while, and Bottomley was content to wait for her to speak. Somebody clattered past the door, someone who seemed to be humming very tunelessly, and snuffling at the same time. He saw Ballard glance angrily at the door.

'What happened then?' he prompted.

'Mr Hayden came out of the study, and he and Sir Charles left the house. The Dean opened the door for them himself. When they'd gone, the Dean stood in the hall, thinking. At least, I suppose that's what he did. And then he opened the front door, and went out into Dean's Row. I assumed he was going over to the cathedral, or next door to Canon Parrish's. I've not seen him since.'

Bottomley leaned forward in his chair, and clasped his big hands on his knee.

'Now, miss,' he said, in a quiet, earnest voice, 'I've heard about your mistress's episodes of indisposition. I don't suppose you'd find that vague description in a doctor's vade-mecum. Would I be right in thinking that it's something to do with the contents of a bottle? I don't mean medicine—not in the ordinary sense, at any rate.'

He saw the faint smile hovering around the maid's mouth.

'It may not be in the book, sir,' she replied, 'but "episodes of indisposition" is what we call it in this house. The mistress can be a bit of a handful, as they say, but then, it's not always easy to be the wife of a senior clergyman.'

'I'm sure it isn't, Miss Ballard, and I ask your pardon if you think I've spoken out of place. Where does she keep the gin?'

'In the bookcase— Oh!'

'Well, never mind, Miss Ballard. It was bound to come out, sooner or later. It's just a little detail in a wider picture, you see. Something that the guvnor and I need to know as we try to find out what's happened to the Dean, what he's done, and why he did it.'

Bottomley made a show of glancing at the clock.

'I wonder when he's coming back?' he asked.

'May I go about my duties, now, sir?' Ballard's voice had become respectfully frigid and aloof. This awful, shambling man had tricked her into betraying the mistress's secret, and he was implying that Dean Girdlestone had run away! Impudence!

'Certainly, miss. But what was that peculiar snuffling noise that passed the door? You haven't got a singing dog in the house, have you? You see them, sometimes, on the music hall. Terrible din, they make.'

Ballard's haughty features broke into a brilliant smile. There was no point in being hoity-toity with this man.

'That was William, sir, Canon Parrish's boots. He can't do much more than use a blacking brush, and he's recently taken to coming here in the afternoon, to do our footwear, too. He does that work well, but he's an awful fool. A great lolloping lad. Half cracked, he is. He works in the space under the stairs. Daft William.'

'Daft William, hey? Well, I think I'll have a little word with him before I go. You go about your work now, my dear. I'll find this William for myself.'

*   *   *

Bottomley found William, the Parrishes' boots, sitting on a stool in a cubby-hole beneath the staircase. It was a gloomy place, but the boy seemed happy enough, totally absorbed in painting a gentleman's leather boot with blacking, which was contained in an earthenware jar on the floor. William turned a round, rather vacant face to look at Bottomley.

'Be you the policeman, master?' he asked. His high voice held the hint of an incipient giggle, which was compounded with a tendency to snuffle and sniff. His untidy fair hair stood up in slender little tufts all over his head, rather like pipe cleaners.

'Yes, William, I'm the policeman. One of them, at any rate. The other one's gone off to visit Sir Charles Blount at Ladymead. You've seen Sir Charles Blount, haven't you?'

William slowly deposited his blacking brush in the jar, and wiped his mouth on his sleeve. He looked at Bottomley for half a minute without flinching, and then scratched his head.

'Sir Charles Blount come here today,' he said. 'He come to see the Dean. That's what Mr Girdlestone's called. My master, next door, is called a Canon. Canon Parrish. You can't move for clergymen in Dean's Row.'

'I don't suppose you heard anything that Sir Charles Blount and the Dean said to each other? You being here, hidden like, under the stairs? You look a bright sort of lad, to me!'

William laughed. He looked at one of his blacking-stained hands, and wiped it on his coat.

'They speak so funny, those two, that you can't understand what they say. You speak proper English, though. You're the policeman, aren't you? "I'll give you a week", he said, and then they went away. Him and the other man. They didn't know I was here, doing the boots. Missus lets me come here from next door. He gives me sixpence a week when I come here. The Dean does.'

Sergeant Bottomley looked at the boy sitting huddled on the stool in the gloom of the little space under the stairs. Daft William, they called him. But was he as daft as he looked?

'How long have you been working for

113

Canon Parrish, William?' he asked. 'You're making a very good job of all those boots and shoes. Fair gleaming, they are.'

'Thanks, master. I been with Canon Parrish for . . . for a long time. Way back in winter. Very nice she is to me. Missus, I mean. Jessie laughs at me, and says I'm daft. I used to be at the lead works, but it was too heavy for me. Mr Arkwright got that job for me. He's the Rector, down where I live, in the cattle-market. Mr Arkwright's a very nice man. "You're not daft, William", he said to me once, "you're just dense". That was very nice of him. So you're the policeman. What's he done?'

'I don't rightly know that he's done anything yet, William. I'm trying to find out. Me and my guvnor. I've been looking at your own shoes for the last minute or two. They're covered in dust and mud. Not very smart, are they? Why don't you clean them, as well?'

William thought about this for a while, frowning, and moistening his lips. At last his puzzled face cleared, and he treated Bottomley to a smile of triumph.

'I know! It's because this is the Dean's blacking. And back there, it's Canon Parrish's blacking. So I've no right to be using it.'

Bottomley produced a penny coin from one of his trouser pockets, and held it up in front of the boy.

'If I pay you this penny, then you'll be able to polish your shoes as well. That penny will make it all right. What do you think?'

'Thanks very much, mister. You're very kind. I'll do that straight away.'

Herbert Bottomley left the boy pulling off his shoes, and picking up the blacking brush prior to making himself presentable. Arkwright . . . The name of William's kindly rector made Bottomley recall the strange feeling that had overcome him in Dean Girdlestone's library. As yet, he knew nothing of this Prebendary Arkwright. Perhaps the time had come for him to find out who he was.

*   *   *

Arkwright's breakfast was always prepared for him by one of a number of young girls known to the married couple who came in to look after his house. They were trusted with a key to the house left with Mr Worden, the neighbouring optician.

It was Friday morning, so Amy Dale, a gentle, good-tempered girl of fourteen, had cooked breakfast for him. She was a favourite of his, slender and dark-haired, with hazel eyes and a quiet way of speaking. Amy placed a dish of sizzling eggs and bacon in front of him, and cast a critical eye over the table.

'Got everything you need, Mr Arkwright? There's your toast, there's your butter, and there's your marmalade. There's more hot coffee on the kitchen range.'

'Thank you, Amy. I think that's all.'

Nicholas Arkwright had arisen from his long sleep more refreshed than he had been in years. The fantasy of lurid dreams had been presented to him now for what they had actually been—the product of a disordered mind, brought on by his refusal to confront the practical realities of epilepsy. Dr Savage's bromide mixture would be the making of him.

Amy Dale seemed disinclined to leave the little dining-room, which led directly off the kitchen. She surveyed the master of the house with particular attention, as though there was something about him that needed explanation.

'You don't know about it, do you, sir?' she asked.

'Know about what, my dear?'

'About what's happened to Dean Girdlestone—'

'Not dead?' Arkwright was shocked to hear the harshness of his own voice. Why should he have thought that about Girdlestone?

'Why, of course not, sir! Look how pale you've turned . . . There's no need to take on like that. No, he's not dead, but yesterday, the police came for him, to arrest him for fraud, and they found that he'd fled. He's gone, sir.'

'Gone? You're not . . . you're not making this up are you, Amy?'

'No, sir, it's true. I'm sorry if I frightened you. That comes of you being all alone here, when Mr Conrad's not staying. You'd have known right enough, sir, if this house was run as a gentleman's house should be, with proper servants, and a lady of the house to see that all was done right.'

Arkwright's mind dwelt upon what the girl had told him. Fraud? Ridiculous! He'd go straight away after breakfast and see Walter Parrish. Amy must have got the wrong end of the stick. Amy Dale was developing her domestic theme. Apparently, she'd forgotten all about Dean Girdlestone.

'You see, sir, if you'd only marry again, and settle down properly, your wife would see that you had proper curtains, and proper decoration. This house is too dark, for one thing—there are too many panels, and not enough wallpaper. You're a very nice gentleman, sir, and deserve better than you've got.'

'Is that all, Amy?' he asked. 'Have you finished planning out my life for me? Or—I say! You're not proposing marriage, are you?'

Amy Dale laughed shyly, and shook her head.

'Oh, go on, sir! Get on with your breakfast, or it'll go cold. And when you've done here, go and talk to Canon Parrish. He'll tell you all about the Dean.'

*   *   *

Nicholas Arkwright turned the corner of

Dean's Row, and crossed the great cobbled court of Abbey Yard. For a moment a cloud obscured the sun, and a rogue breeze darted out of nowhere to blow down smoke from the chimneys above the gate house in an acrid swathe across the pavements.

Amy Dale had told him the sober and shocking truth. Lawrence Girdlestone had walked out of the Deanery just after 2.30 on the previous day, and had disappeared. Where on earth could he be? What about the next Chapter meeting? And next week the Fabric Committee was due to meet at the Deanery. How could the Chapter function properly without the Dean? Still musing on the affairs of the Diocese, he stepped out into the throng of traffic in St Michael Street.

When Arkwright returned late in the afternoon to the Prebendary's House, he found that three letters had arrived for him in the afternoon post. One was a courteous note from Lawrence Girdlestone. He had consulted an eminent counsel concerning ancient lights, and had been assured that, as Dean, he held property rights over the whole of the cathedral and its contents. He could not be accused of depriving himself of light by his own action, so that any plea of ancient lights would fail.

So much for that. He'd not expected anything to come of it, but it had been worth a try. What was this second letter? A summons from Sir Charles Blount. He was to attend a specially convened meeting of the Queen's Commissioners of the Ancaster Foundation, to be held at Ladymead, at three o'clock in the afternoon on Sunday, 6 August, 1893. Almost certainly, that would be to comment formally on whatever it was that Lawrence Girdlestone had done.

He opened the third letter, which had been addressed in the familiar spiky handwriting of Josiah Solomon. It contained a linen handkerchief, freshly laundered, and carefully ironed.

*   *   *

When Arkwright called at Ladymead on Sunday morning, he was ushered into the impressive drawing-room, where Sir Charles sat at the long polished table, flanked by six solemn ladies and gentlemen. Sir Charles looked pale and worried.

'Prebendary Arkwright,' Sir Charles began, 'this is an emergency session of the Ancaster Foundation. I think you know the other commissioners?' He did. They were familiar figures to Arkwright: an earl, two titled ladies, and three gentlemen from influential Warwickshire families. Sir Charles had evidently summoned a quorum at very short notice.

'Of the charges laid against Dean Girdlestone, I can say nothing,' Sir Charles continued. 'But we feel that you should be told that Lawrence Girdlestone was about to be offered the new Bishopric of Bury, in Lancashire, and had privately indicated to me that he would accept it.'

'It is that fact,' said the earl, 'that makes his present disappearance so sinister. Men don't usually run away from preferment.'

'In my view,' observed one of the titled ladies, 'it confirms his guilt—'

'Perhaps, madam,' said Blount, 'but we must be careful not to prejudge the issue. Now, Prebendary, whatever may have happened to Mr Girdlestone, the cathedral cannot be left incapable of action through the lack of a Dean.'

(A bishopric? The wily fox! Why hadn't he said so?)

Sir Charles pushed a large sheet of parchment across the table. It had three red wax seals hanging from it, attached to silken tapes.

'This is our writ of appointment, which I now deliver to you, Nicholas Arkwright, Clerk in Holy Orders, confirming that from the date of this writ, which is today, you are, by common consent of us all, affirmed as Acting Dean of Ancaster, and that you are herewith endowed with all the privileges and benefits consequent upon that office.'

'Including,' added the second titled lady, 'the title of Very Reverend, as is both right and proper.'

Sir Charles waited for the lady to finish, and then asked, with an edge of amusement to his voice, 'Do you accept this appointment?'

Nicholas's reply came firm and sure.

'I do.'

Some half-hour later, the Very Reverend Nicholas Arkwright, Acting Dean of Ancaster, began his return across the suspension bridge to the old town.

CHAPTER FIVE

THE TRIUMPH OF THE IDOLS

Conrad Arkwright sprang from the punt on to the small landing-stage at Willow Reach, and secured the boat to a mooring post. He hauled a wickerwork picnic hamper out of the punt, then offered a hand to Caroline Parrish. He thought she looked very fetching in her patterned summer dress and demure straw boater.

It was Bank Holiday Monday, and Ancaster had been thronging with people, all bent on enjoying the day to the full. The weather was hot, but not close. Conrad had taken Caroline down to Riverside, where he had hired a punt. They were to picnic at the hamlet of Willow Reach.

'I wonder what's happened to Dean Girdlestone?' asked Caroline without preamble, when they had settled themselves on the grass, and opened the hamper.

'I don't know. Nobody's going to believe this incredible accusation against him. Quite frankly, I think it's tosh. Someone's got hold of the wrong end of the stick. Still, it's odd . . . Someone like Dean Girdlestone doesn't simply disappear.'

Caroline thought: how handsome he looks! He's wearing a white linen suit and a rakish wide-awake hat, and has contrived to look not only older than his twenty-three years, but desperately piratical into the bargain.

'Father doesn't believe this fraud business— at least, he doesn't want to believe it,' said Conrad. 'But I can tell that's he delighted at being appointed Acting Dean. All those ghastly things that Girdlestone was going to do, won't be done, now—unless, of course, Girdlestone turns up. But I don't think he will. I was talking to Canon Hall earlier today, and he says the Foundation knows more about the Girdlestone business than it will admit in public. He thinks that Father will very soon be confirmed as Dean by the Crown, which will make his appointment permanent. Eat up your chicken. You're not eating anything.'

Caroline obediently attacked a chicken leg, carefully wiping her fingers on one of the napkins that Jessie had packed. She thought

122

about Laura Girdlestone, who had asked her to go to the Deanery as soon as the police had left the house. She had talked wildly to Caroline about her husband's lack of concern for her, but had dismissed the accusations of fraud with vehement contempt. Caroline was suddenly aware that Conrad was talking to her.

'I'm sorry, I wasn't paying attention—'

'I was just saying that Father was considered for the post of Dean six years ago, after old Dean Cunningham died. Everybody thought that Father would be successful, but the Prime Minister of the time didn't like him. That, as they say, did the trick. Have a salad roll.'

Caroline looked up towards the hills in the distance. Faintly through the haze, towards the horizon, she thought she could discern the tower of Ancaster Cathedral. She saw Conrad's eyes following hers.

'Yes,' he said, 'that's the old girl herself, shimmering in the haze. You can't get away from Ancaster Cathedral in this corner of Warwickshire. Have you seen the Guardians yet? You can't see them from this distance away. They're our talismans.'

'Dean Girdlestone says that they're idols.'

'Well, yes; poor man, he's obsessed with the dangers of idolatry. I believe he'd told Solomon to take the figures down—so Father told me, anyway. But everyone in Ancaster likes those images. Hello, what's this! A half bottle of claret, and two glasses. Your Jessie will give us ideas beyond our station if she goes on feeding us like this.'

'This Ancaster Revel—what is it exactly, Conrad?'

'It's an old celebration connected with those figures on the tower, or rather, the beings that they represent. It's a three-day holiday, and it's very much for Ancaster folk. People from round about tend to keep out of the way during the Revel.'

'It sounds rather thrilling—and slightly sinister, the way you recount it.'

'I suppose it is, in a way. Father used to take me to all the Revels when I was a boy. It's really quite a spectacle, you know. There's a concert given in the Assembly Hall for the Mayor and Town Council, and two or three country bands are licensed to play in the streets for the three days. Oh, and there are mummers who go through the streets, acting scenes from the old miracle plays.'

Conrad handed Caroline a glass of claret. He seemed lost in thought for a while. A warm breeze was stirring the grass. Far off, the cathedral tower was emerging from the failing mist into strong sunlight.

'Some folk reckon it has its origin in pagan times. Maybe they're right. The Revel proper really starts this evening, just after dark, when a great bonfire is lit in St Michael's Square, just south of the cathedral. Until Dean Girdlestone's time, a group of men used to present themselves with tarred poles, and ask the Dean to light one of them from the bonfire. Then they'd shin up a little turret staircase, and emerge on top of the tower. There's an iron brazier up there, and they'd kindle what they called the "Angel Fire". It lit up the four figures, everybody cheered, and the Revel began. Girdlestone put paid to that ceremony, though.'

Conrad drained his glass of claret, and began packing away the remains of the picnic. Caroline handed him her empty glass.

'I've never seen a bonfire,' said Caroline. 'We had nothing like that at Sutton St Edmund.'

'Well, you must let me take you to St Michael's Square. The men will be preparing it now for the great blaze tonight.'

*   *   *

St Michael's Square proved to be a small enclave of old brick houses arranged on three sides of a tired-looking garden enclosed by railings. A pedant would have denied it the title of 'square', because the fourth side was merely a simple grass slope leading gently up into the old cemetery on the south side of the cathedral.

The square was filled with a crowd of men and excited boys, who were adding heaped armfuls of kindling wood to an enormous bonfire, which was well over six feet in height. Two or three men were balancing rather precariously on ladders, weaving ribbons of tarred rag and paper in and out of the stiff, dry branches that had been tossed on top of the great pyre.

Mr Solomon, who had been busy directing operations, caught sight of Caroline and Conrad, who had been admiring the scene of good-humoured activity, and raised his hat in greeting. He wore his usual formal dress of open frock coat, and, as always, seemed to be covered in fine stone dust.

'Mr Conrad, sir! I heard as how you were coming down for the Revel. Nice to see you, sir. And you, Miss Caroline. This will be your first Ancaster Revel. I hope that Mr Conrad will squire you around, this evening. Things can get a bit lively, miss, once dusk's fallen.'

Caroline Parrish turned aside for a moment to hide a sudden blush. What a quaint expression: 'squire you around'! But it *would* be nice to have Conrad's company. Uncle Walter had declared firmly that she was not to go out unaccompanied.

Mr Solomon gave a few parting words of advice to the men working on the bonfire, and then turned his way towards the cathedral. Conrad and Caroline joined him. They soon found themselves in the old graveyard, at the foot of the south wall. It was a quiet spot, where half-effaced stones from the previous two centuries were gradually sinking from sight under a burgeoning screen of weeds and summer plants. Mr Solomon paused, and looked about him with a professional interest.

'Dean Girdlestone, sir,' he said, 'had prepared a scheme to bury all these stones beneath the soil, and create a tidy lawn, with laurel beds. I don't know whether that'll go ahead now, all things considered.'

'But there's nothing wrong with this peaceful old spot, Mr Solomon,' Caroline protested. 'Surely, not everything in life has to be tidied up?'

Mr Solomon glanced briefly at Conrad Arkwright.

'You're right, miss. There can be too much tidying up, as you so rightly observe. When old Dean Buckley came here, in the sixties, he found this cathedral of ours in a sorry state. There were empty windows, boarded up, whole sections of stone arcading missing in the cloisters—it was a sad ruin, in many ways, and there was much work waiting for him to do. But he was a man who knew when to stop. There were parts that he left untouched, like this old burial ground, and the two medieval chapels in the crypt. So did Dean Cunningham, God rest him. But Dean Girdlestone—Nothing was sacred, with him. He'd have thrown it all down, tower and tile, if he thought that was the right thing to do.'

'What do you mean by that, Solomon? The

right thing?' asked Conrad.

'Right according to his lights. He was dead against idolatry, and saw idols everywhere. I think he disliked Master Geoffrey's Window because it's so beautiful! With people like Dean Girdlestone, sir, anything that causes pleasure is an idol!'

Mr Solomon's eyes suddenly narrowed, and his heavy brows drew together in a frown. He glanced up at the tower, and Caroline saw his face flush with sudden anger.

'Still, least said, soonest mended. I was talking just now about Dean Buckley. Would you care to see a picture of him, Miss Parrish?'

They entered the cathedral through a side door, and Solomon preceded them into the lofty chamber that housed the works office. The Clerk of the Works beckoned them to his roll-top desk in the corner, above which hung an old framed photograph.

'This photograph was taken in 1869,' said Solomon. 'That's Dean Buckley, seated in the armchair. The other men, standing around him, are the craftsmen who worked with him to restore Ancaster Cathedral to its ancient glory.'

They looked at the small, rather stubby figure in the armchair, a round-faced man with white mutton-chop whiskers and a very tall top hat.

'Looks fierce, doesn't he? And he was, when he had to be. But he was very patient with us

128

boys. I'm talking about myself, sir, and your father, when we were both little fellows of six or seven. I remember one winter, when the snow was on the ground, I dared your father to throw a snowball at Dean Buckley as he crossed the cloister garth—'

'And did he?' demanded Conrad Arkwright. Mr Solomon chuckled.

'He did, sir. And it knocked Dean Buckley's tall topper off into the bargain! Well, we stood there, petrified. We just looked at him, and wished that the earth would open to swallow us up.'

'What did he do?'

'Do, sir? He stooped down and made a big snowball, which he lobbed at your father. It was a corker, sir! Fair knocked your father off his feet. Then he did the same thing to me. He seemed to like it, sir, because he didn't stop until he'd left the two of us rolling round, plastered with snow, and crying our eyes out. We heard him laughing as he disappeared into the north transept.'

Caroline looked at the still, faded image of Dean Buckley, sitting stern and proud in his armchair, and tried to imagine him pelting two small boys with snow. Mr Solomon pointed with a broken-nailed finger at a stern, bearded man in working garb standing to Dean Buckley's right.

'That's my father, Miss Caroline,' he said. 'He was Clerk of the Works before me. And that's Thomas Bates, and next to him, George Pearson. There's Albert Plummer, who carved the stone flowers around the reredos of the High Altar. They're all dead now, Miss Caroline, but they've left behind them a magnificent legacy.'

*   *   *

Inspector Jackson sat in his old cane-backed chair, and looked down at a sheaf of papers arranged rather precariously across his knees. He puffed away at a short briar pipe, and slender wisps of fragrant smoke rose up to the rafters of the cottage living-room. He glanced across the hearth at Sergeant Bottomley. He had brought him up here to Meadow Cross Lane so that they could speak privately, and perhaps voice their fears. Because this affair of Dean Girdlestone didn't ring true.

'He was born in 1845, Sergeant, which makes him forty-eight years old. He came from a very wealthy family, who owned an engineering works. They were Guildford folk, originally. He was up at Oxford in the sixties, and married a lady called Laura Taverner in 1870. That was also the year in which he was ordained priest, by the Bishop of London in St Paul's Cathedral.'

'London . . . I wonder if he's up there, sir? It's the best place to go, if a man wants to lose himself.'

130

'Yes, you may be right, Sergeant. In which case, we'll have to go up there and find him. But let's return to our friend Girdlestone's career. Very soon after his marriage, he embarked for India as a missionary, leaving Mrs Girdlestone behind him. She had to contain herself in patience until he returned, two years later, to become Vicar of Moor End, in Essex. What do you say to that?'

'That could have been the beginning of her consoling herself with alcohol, sir,' Bottomley replied. 'She might have started to drink in order to punish him for leaving her so soon after their marriage. I'd already wondered whether it wasn't something of that nature. Neglect.'

Jackson knocked out his pipe in the fireplace, and deposited it in a Benares brass bowl in the hearth. He gave a snort of disgust.

'Perhaps so, Sergeant. It was very good of Mr Mays to dig out these facts for us, but where is all this ancient history leading us? A fortune is missing from the cathedral funds, and we've the evidence of our own eyes that Dean Girdlestone is the man who's made off with that fortune—'

'Yes, sir, that's what the evidence shows. But Mr Girdlestone's an enigma. At first sight, he seems to be a man with his eye on preferment, a man who'll leave his new wife to fend for herself while he does his obligatory stint as a missionary. And yet, sir, he's the same man

131

who went on to lead a blameless life, respected wherever he went.'

'Yes, Sergeant, I take your point. He was six years at Moor End, and then he moved to Sedley Vale. We've both heard what heroic things he did there, during the cholera epidemic in '80.'

'And his wife wasn't with him, sir. Where was she? None of this may sound relevant to a fraud on Ancaster Cathedral, but you never know. First him, then her. He went out to India. Where did *she* go, and why? Did Mr Mays tell you when Mrs Girdlestone appeared on the scene again?'

'Well, she was certainly with him when he was appointed Archdeacon of Manningley, and was still with him when he moved from there to be Rector of St Philip's, Mayfair. She's been with him ever since, and he's found himself reunited with two old school chums, Canon Walter Parrish, and Prebendary Nicholas Arkwright, now Acting Dean of Ancaster.'

'Arkwright . . . Somebody told me that Prebendary Arkwright had been passed over, sir, for the post of Dean. That could have bred a dangerous resentment. I think I'll keep an eye on this Arkwright, if you're agreeable, sir.'

'What? Yes, of course. But the whole thing *feels* wrong, Sergeant! There's a lot more digging and delving to be done if we're to bring the truth to light.'

Sergeant Bottomley smiled, rather absently. His mind seemed to be elsewhere.

'Sir,' he said, 'the Ancaster Revel starts tonight. I'm minded to ride out there, and cast a general eye over things. I agree with you; the whole thing feels wrong. There's something that we haven't seen, or that we don't know about. I'd like to mingle with the crowds over at Ancaster tonight, and see if I can read a few minds.'

*   *   *

As soon as the light of day had dimmed to a mere glimmer in the east, the bells of Ancaster began to ring in the Revel. The single high tenor bell of St Mary in Campo was rung with special gusto. (Hadn't their Rector just been appointed Dean? About time, too! He should have got that post five years ago.) In the town centre the full peal of Ancaster's parish church, St Edmund at the Gate, vied for mastery with the stately monotone of the modern bell in the tower of the Town Hall.

The streets of Ancaster were lit by gas, and the tall lamp standards had been hung with festoons of summer flowers, and sheaves of what seemed to be dried wheat stalks. There were coloured lamps and lanterns everywhere, in the windows of the closed shops, in the upper storeys of countless houses, and in all the public gardens. It was a warm, dry night, and the whole town was thronged with revellers. Only the cathedral bells were silent, and the precinct gates locked. Dean Girdlestone had not approved of the idolatry associated with the Ancaster Revel.

Conrad Arkwright and Caroline Parrish wandered through the lively streets, listening to the continuing echo of footfall, and the laughing and chattering of the crowds. Lights seemed to be glowing everywhere they looked.

When it was fully dark, the music began. A number of licensed bands had come in from outlying country towns to play a seemingly endless repertoire of Tudor music. It lent a curiously disturbing enchantment to the town, as though, for one single night, it had turned its back upon the rational modernity of the nineteenth century.

They made their way slowly through the streets until they reached the end of Friary Street. They mounted the thirty steps into Cathedral Green. The noise of revelling receded, but was always there as a background to their conversation. They walked along Dean's Row, towards Canon Parrish's house.

'It was magical down there, Conrad,' said Caroline. 'I never imagined that Ancaster could have that atmosphere of—of a fiesta, or carnival. And yet they're not the right words to use, because it seems so English, with the old Tudor music.'

'It is English, Caroline, and it celebrates

something more than the Guardian Angels. I think it's a survival of some ancient pagan festival that was suppressed at the Reformation. Did you see those festoons of dried wheat stalks? They're saved from the last year's harvest, and brought out just for tonight. At the end of the harvest, they carry sheaves of wheat up to the top of the cathedral tower, and put them in a brazier, ready for the next year's Revel. They continued to do so even after Dean Girdlestone had forbidden it. Nobody really knows what those sheaves represent.'

'It was magical,' Caroline repeated, 'but eerie, too.'

'Yes, there's something rather spooky about it all! I remember my father saying to me, when I was a boy, that all our ancestors came out in the spirit to celebrate with us when the Revel began. I always looked forward to it, but I was relieved when it ended!'

There was a strong perfume of night-scented stock rising from the gardens of the houses in Dean's Row. It seemed to emphasize the warmth of the summer evening, and the odd feeling that Ancaster had become enclosed, cut off from the mundane world of Warwickshire lying around it. Magical . . . That was the word that Mr Bottomley had used, when they had spoken together on the train, nearly a fortnight ago. 'Ancaster's a magical town,' he'd said, 'but it's also a haunted town.'

He had been right.

She saw Conrad glance up at the dark bulk of the cathedral tower, and frown.

'Years ago—not all that many years ago, if the truth be told—there were hundreds of coloured oil lanterns hanging in the precinct trees on this night, and the gas chandeliers were left alight in the cathedral nave. All the windows glowed with light, as though the old girl was taking part in the festivities. That was before Dean Girdlestone came—in old Dean Cunningham's time.'

'Conrad, do you think—?'

'I don't permit myself the luxury of thinking about Dean Girdlestone's predicament,' said Conrad abruptly. 'I always got on well with him, despite my father's rooted dislike for the man. Beneath all that puritanical zeal there was a good heart, the heart of a decent man, Caroline. I never thought he was as ruthless as people made out, and I'll reserve judgement on him until he's found, and made to give an account of himself.'

There was a sudden stir in the air, and the sound of many voices came to their ears, together with the high-pitched tones of flutes, and the staccato beat of a kettledrum.

'They're going to light the great bonfire in St Michael's Square, Caroline. Don't go in to Number 7, yet. We can skirt the railings here to the right, which will bring us to the old south churchyard. You mustn't miss the lighting of the bonfire.'

It was as they rounded the end of the railings, and stepped off the path on to the rough turf, that the men in St Michael's Square kindled the bonfire. Within a minute the tinder had caught alight, and the whole carefully arranged heap of dry wood and tarred rags exploded in leaping orange flame. The impact of the fire was so startling that the crowd of onlookers simply stood for a while, absorbing the fierceness of their festal pyre. The burning wood crackled and hissed. Huge sparks, and shards of burning wood flew into the air, to be lost in the blackness.

Caroline stood in silence beside Conrad Parrish. As the fire burned more fiercely, the area behind the cathedral began to define itself in the light of the bonfire. She could see down the slope towards the square where she and Conrad had met Mr Solomon earlier in the day. It looked different, now, its houses suddenly endowed with flickering orange frontages, sinister and demonic. An amorphous crowd of men stood in the square, watching the flames, and seemingly impervious to the great heat.

Surely she knew that man—the one standing on the fringes of the crowd to the right? A burly, untidy sort of man, clutching some kind of parcel tied up with string? Was it Sergeant Bottomley, the detective? She peered across the grass and down through the smoke

137

and haze of the bonfire, but the man had gone.

And then she became aware that another figure was standing near the entrance to the south churchyard, a figure that was contriving to keep itself from the light by moving discreetly to the shade of the taller tombstones. She saw Conrad start in surprise.

'It's Father!' he said. 'He's come to see the beginning of the Revel. Let's join him.'

But at that moment, they heard a murmuring in the crowd and, looking down the grass slope towards the blazing bonfire, they saw the unmistakable figure of Mr Solomon. He was talking rapidly to a little knot of men who seemed to be grasping staves in their hands. He pointed up the slope towards the cathedral, to the spot where Nicholas Arkwright was standing.

Caroline caught her breath as the whole crowd of men suddenly surged forward out of the square towards the open grass below the cathedral precinct. They came on silently, with an air of surly hesitancy in their gait, as though expecting some kind of rebuff. They were led by the men with staves, dark, anonymous figures in the summer night.

Nicholas Arkwright suddenly emerged from the shade of the churchyard, and stepped forward. He looked very calm, and very elegant in his fur-collared black overcoat and tall silk hat. There was an indistinct murmur from the crowd, and the men with staves detached themselves from their companions. They spoke hurriedly together, evidently electing a spokesman. The chosen man stepped forward, and nervously cleared his throat.

'Asking your pardon, Mr Arkwright, sir,' he said, 'but we're wondering if you won't consent to light the Angel Fire this year?'

There was a pause, and it seemed that the whole crowd held its breath. Then, from the rear of the throng of men, Josiah Solomon stepped forward. He was holding a burning torch, which cast strange shadows across his face. To Caroline it seemed that the man was holding back some anticipation of a private triumph.

'As one old Ancastrian to another, sir,' he said, in a voice loud enough for the whole crowd to hear, 'I'd like to add my voice to that request. It's long years now since the Guardians were shown their due honour. We're all waiting upon your consent, Mr Dean.'

As he uttered Nicholas Arkwright's new title, an almost diabolical smile of triumph contorted rather than lit up Solomon's features. Nicholas Arkwright looked at his old friend, and then at the sea of eager but respectful faces turned to look at him. It was a heady moment. He experienced a sudden surge of pride, an awareness that at long last he had come into his rightful inheritance.

Dean Arkwright gave his answer.

'I shall be pleased and honoured to do so, Mr Solomon.'

While the whole crowd began to cheer and whistle their approbation, Solomon stepped forward with the blazing torch, and handed it to the Dean. Holding the flaming brand firmly in his right hand, Arkwright lit the tarred poles of the men at the front of the throng. He watched them as they ran across the grass towards the entrance to a flight of turret stairs leading up to the tower.

*   *   *

Nicholas Arkwright quickly left the men and their torches, and returned through the south postern into the dark cathedral church. He was soon back in the St Catherine Chapel, where he had been for the last hour. He had come there to give what the Prayer Book called 'humble and hearty thanks' for his deliverance from his persecuting nightmares, and for his appointment as Acting Dean of Ancaster. This night—the first night of the Revel—had provided him with the heady delight of sudden popular esteem, out there on the sward in the light of the bonfire, acceding to the ritual reverence that had once been paid to the Ancaster Guardians.

Arkwright sat down in his favourite pew, and by the light of the few candles he had lit about the chapel, let his eyes fall upon the image of old Bishop Parr, lying, marble eyes ever open, on his florid tomb.

The throng of onlookers outside the cathedral waited, necks strained to discern when their fellows emerged on to the parapet below the great clock face on the north side of the tower. They had drifted into the precinct, and arranged themselves in an orderly crowd on the north side of the great church.

Here they were! Four bright, flickering lights suddenly appeared high up towards the sky. In a moment, a huge flame rose with a roar from a hidden brazier, and the faces of the four Ancaster Guardians sprang into sight. Immediately a band of flutes and kettledrums began to play a haunting kind of anthem, and the crowd joined in some ancient ritual song.

And then, one of the men high up on the tower uttered a shriek so loud, that it rose like a judgment above the band. The instruments ceased abruptly, and the crowd fell silent. The man who had shrieked now began shouting down to the crowd, but no one could make out what he was saying. His companions had disappeared. The faces of Michael, Raphael, Gabriel, and the faceless image of Azrael gazed without involvement towards the dark north. The man uttered a cry of despair, and threw his flaming torch down from the tower, so that it looked to the men below like the burning Lucifer falling from heaven.

141

In the St Catherine Chapel, Dean Arkwright heard the cry, and wondered what it could portend. He stared at the rows of gleaming red garnets adorning Bishop Parr's carved marble vestments, and marvelled that there were so many of them. They seemed to be increasing as he watched them. They defined themselves as red spots, leaping up from the marble—more, and more again.

Arkwright glanced up to the ceiling, and knew then that the spots were not leaping up from the marble, but falling rapidly, thick and red, from the cathedral roof.

CHAPTER SIX

THE SCARLET WITNESS

Sergeant Bottomley stood on the perilous ledge above the clerestory, and looked up at the cathedral tower. Some ten feet above him, a strong flame, whipped to a frenzy by a roving wind, still burned in the brazier on the parapet below the great gilt clock face. Near the brazier, the four carved Guardians, inscrutable and indifferent to the silent sea of upturned faces in the cathedral gardens below, gazed out through the darkness towards the north.

On a roof twenty feet below him, the body of a man lay sprawled in what appeared to be a dark, stagnant pool of blood. The body was starkly visible in the light shed from the brazier fire, and the long shadows playing over it conveyed an unsettling suggestion of movement. The dead man was fully clothed, and there was a bedraggled, broken appearance to the body that reminded Bottomley forcibly of a dead blackbird that he had once found lying in the rain behind his farmhouse.

Bottomley spoke to someone who was standing behind him in the dark recesses of the cathedral roof, though he continued to look down at the sight that had sent the man with the tarred pole into shrieking hysterics half an hour earlier.

'Do you recognize that dead body, Mr Solomon? Can you give a name to it, I mean?'

'Yes, Mr Bottomley. That's our previous Dean, Mr Lawrence Girdlestone. Poor gentleman! He was always tripping over things,' volunteered the Clerk of the Works. 'Clumsy, he was. And he'd sprained his ankle last week, falling down some steps, which didn't help matters. He came up here quite a few times on his own this last week or so. I warned him how dangerous it was. "Stop fussing, Solomon", he'd say. And there's the result of it. A tragic accident.'

Bottomley said nothing. He came in off the ledge, and stood in the sloping space above the cathedral vaulting. He saw that there were

143

other men there, vague lurking shapes in the gloom. It was beginning to grow cold.

'Mr Solomon,' said Bottomley, 'I must get down there now, somehow or other, and examine the body. After that, it had better be left there until morning. There's nothing useful or decent that we can do in the dark. As soon as it's light, we'll have to devise some way of bringing the body down. It's going to be a tricky business.'

Josiah Solomon rose to the occasion. He gave some brief orders to the men standing in the darkness of the roof-space, and they moved somewhere out of sight.

'Mr Bottomley,' he said, 'those men will lash three ladders together, and sling them down like a kind of bridge to where poor Mr Girdlestone's body lies. It'll be quite safe for you to clamber down. I'll see that the brazier fire's kept alight.'

'Thank you very much, Mr Solomon. You're very accommodating, if I may say so. Do you have any suggestions about tomorrow's business?'

For answer, Mr Solomon stepped out on to the ledge, and looked down at the body. Bottomley glanced at the Clerk's face. It had a curious inscrutability, as though it had been carved out of teak, but there seemed a rather shocking gleam of triumph in the man's dark eyes.

'That roof below us, Mr Bottomley, adjoins

144

the roof of the St Catherine Chapel, which is due for restoration this month, as soon as the Revel's over. The tiles have already been raised, prior to being removed. Early tomorrow morning, soon after sunrise, my men and I will strip a section of the roof, and when that's done, and you judge the time is right, we'll carry the body over the leads, and lower it down in a timber-sling to the floor of the chapel below. So everything will be done decent and decorous.'

At that moment, three workmen appeared out of the gloom, hauling a contraption made from three ladders and stout rope, which they pushed carefully out of the access door. It settled itself with a number of creaks and bumps, and Sergeant Bottomley made his way gingerly down to the appalling human ruin spread-eagled across the leads of the roof below.

*   *   *

Josiah Solomon watched Bottomley as he scrambled down the rickety contraption of ladders by the light shed from the hissing brazier on the north parapet of the tower. He'd sent a man up with orders to replenish the Angel Fire, so that this policeman could see to do whatever he was going to do. The flame was now burning lustily, and as bright as a beacon.

Yes, it was Dean Girdlestone, right enough; but then, he'd known that before ever this Sergeant Bottomley had stepped forward from the crowd when Bert Rivers had uttered that shriek, and thrown his blazing torch from the tower. Miss Caroline had been there, too, with Mr Conrad. Curse Dean Girdlestone! He'd spoilt everybody's triumph that evening. This was yet another Ancaster Revel that he'd blighted with his presence . . .

What was Bottomley doing now? He was kneeling beside the body, trailing his fingers through the blood. Well, every man to his trade . . . Now he was looking at his hand. Poor Nicholas Arkwright! It had been his moment of triumph, the Dean of Ancaster standing among his own, and consenting to light the Angel Fire. And then, only minutes later, he'd come running into the cloister like a man pursued by demons, his hands flecked with gouts of blood as big as thunder spots . . . Canon Parrish, thank goodness, had appeared from somewhere, and taken poor Nicholas away.

Bottomley was leaning right over the body, now, lifting the head with both hands. Now he was slithering and sliding across the roof— he'd better be careful, or he'd go plummeting down on to the nave pavement!

The important thing was to make sure that Dean Arkwright remembered what he, Josiah Solomon, had said to him in the St Catherine

Chapel last Thursday. 'You came in here just after two o'clock, and you've been here, fast asleep, ever since.' He'd asked him the time, and he'd told him the truth: four o'clock. Let him believe what he'd been told, and all would be well.

Josiah Solomon saw that Bottomley was clawing his way back across the framework of ladders to the safety of the dark spaces in the cathedral roof. His face was bleak, almost expressionless, but even in the flickering torchlight Mr Solomon could see the smouldering anger in the man's grey eyes.

'I'm much obliged to you, Mr Solomon,' said Bottomley, 'you've been a great help to me tonight. I've finished down there, now—for the moment, at any rate. The body of Dean Girdlestone can be moved tomorrow morning. We'll take it down to the police mortuary in Canal Street. It's an unusual death, as you'll appreciate, Mr Solomon, and the police surgeon will need to conduct an examination. I think you told me that you're the Clerk of Works?'

'Clerk of *the* Works, Mr Bottomley, if you'll excuse me. That's the traditional name given to the post. Climb back here, into the roof space. It's getting cold out there on the leads.'

It was a relief to clamber back into the dim recesses of the vast cathedral roof. Mr Solomon had procured a hand lantern from somewhere, and by its faint light Bottomley saw that the seemingly empty spaces were, in fact, serving as stores for all kinds of building tackle and equipment. It was dusty, and gloomy, but the roof area, he realized, was a living place.

Bottomley followed Mr Solomon down a temporary wooden staircase to a dim platform, from which they gained access to a turret stair in the thickness of the wall. In a few minutes' time the two men had reached the safety of the cathedral pavement.

*   *   *

'Dead?'

Millie Parrish invested the word with the shock and disbelief that she felt at the news that her husband had brought her. She stood at the window of her little parlour on the first floor of Number 7, the fingertips of one hand resting on the panes.

'Yes,' said Walter Parrish. 'His body was lying on the roof of the nave, about five feet across from the St Catherine Chapel. Presumably, he'd lost his footing up there, and fallen to his death. Some time last week, by all accounts. Poor Lawrence! Sergeant Bottomley went up on to the roof last night. Whatever he found up there, he's keeping his own counsel, according to Mr Solomon.'

Millie was looking up at the cathedral tower. She could see men swarming along the parapets, and climbing down the stout wooden scaffold poles rising above the nave roof.

'There are men up there, Walter,' she said.

'They're preparing to bring Lawrence's body down through the roof of the St Catherine Chapel. Mr Solomon's arranging it.'

Millie turned angrily from the window, and sat down. It was very early, and the house was cold. She hugged herself in her quilted dressing-gown, and sat down near the empty fireplace.

'Mr Solomon! He never liked poor Lawrence. "Yes, Mr Dean, no, Mr Dean"—but if looks could kill, Lawrence Girdlestone would have died long ago—'

'Millie!' Walter's voice held mild reproach, but there was a warning edge in his tones that was not lost on his wife. What was he implying?

'You said that Lawrence had met with an accident—'

'I said "presumably", but there are other possibilities. I know perfectly well that Solomon never liked Lawrence Girdlestone, which is all the more reason not to talk about "if looks could kill". Solomon has been a faithful servant of Ancaster Cathedral for most of his lifetime. Be careful, Millie.'

Millie looked at her husband, and suddenly realized that he was still wearing clerical evening dress. He had not been to bed. He had roused her from sleep at just after seven, and she had been so shocked by his news that she never thought to ask him why he had not changed. He seemed to read her mind, and offered her some explanation.

'Late last night, Millie, after you'd retired, I decided to sit up late in the study. At about half past eleven, a knot of men called at the front door, and asked for me. Would I come and look after Dean Arkwright? There'd been an accident, they said, an accident to Dean Girdlestone. Poor Nicholas was in a terrible state, but he seemed to rally when he saw me. Fortunately, Conrad and Caroline arrived almost immediately—they'd been watching the bonfire, and all the rest of the fatuous mummery.'

'What did you do then?'

'I hurried the three of them back to the Prebendary's House. They're still there. Caroline insisted on staying, and I must say I was very pleased about that. You'll hear the rest of the story from her, when she finally returns to Number 7.'

'And what about you? Have you had no rest at all?'

'It was after two o'clock when I got home. I lay on the sofa in the study until Jessie came in at six to light the fire. Then I went across to the cathedral. Solomon was still there, and I got him to take me up to the roof. I—I saw poor Lawrence, lying where he'd fallen. I think he must have been there for days.'

150

Millie Parrish put an arm round her husband's shoulders and gave him a kiss on the cheek.

'I'll get dressed now, Walter, have a bite to eat, and then go next door. Whether she wants me or not, Laura mustn't be left alone.'

She paused at the door, and said, 'Thank you for looking after Nicholas. You always have, haven't you?'

Walter Parrish treated her to one of his rather sad, elfish smiles.

'Yes, my dear, I've always looked after Nicholas. I expect I always shall.'

*   *   *

'Dead?'

Mr Alfred Markland put down his pint of brown ale carefully on the little round marble-topped table, and looked at the man who had just told him about Dean Girdlestone. The man was a decent enough fellow, one of the market porters who were forever in and out of the Ancaster Arms in the cattle market.

'Dead as a door nail, is your Mr Girdlestone,' said the porter, wiping his lips on a ragged sleeve. 'I expect he slipped and fell. Gentlemen like that shouldn't go up them sort of places. I must go. There's a cart of vegetables due any moment.'

The man hurried out of the little public bar, and Mr Markland sipped his beer delicately and thoughtfully. Well, well! Who would have thought it? He addressed himself to the only other occupant of the bar, an aged, befuddled man in an old black suit, who was sitting at a table near the door.

'So Dean Girdlestone is dead, Maurice,' he said. 'I never liked him, as is well known, but I was never one to bear a grudge.'

' 'Course you weren't, Mr Markland. No one would ever say that about you. So he's dead? Slipped and fell, so that feller said—the one who's just gone out.'

'Well, as to that, Maurice, I'll reserve my judgement. You know he was being investigated by the police? It was largely my doing, that, you know. I'm sorry it's come to this, but I've always done what I consider to be my duty.'

' 'Course you 'ave, Mr Markland. You've always done your—what was it you said?— your duty. So he was being investigated, was he? The Dean?'

'He was, Maurice, and that's why I don't think it was an accident. Suicide, that's what it was.' Mr Markland treated old Maurice to a smug, self-congratulatory smile.

'Suicide? You mean he jumped deliberate?'

'Deliberate. Stands to reason, I think. It'll all come out when the police have looked into it. I saw the detective inspector myself, you know. *And* the superintendent. Very grateful they were, I must say.'

152

'Suicide? Well, that's not what I'd expect from a clergyman. Not from a Church of England man, at any rate. I can't answer for Baptists, and such.'

'It's a sad world in many ways, Maurice. Well, duty calls, as they say. Revel or no Revel, I must get down with pen and ruler to the cathedral books.'

Mr Alfred Markland rose from the table. This Tuesday was going to be one of those days where everything went right. He bade old Maurice a cheery farewell, and sauntered out of the Ancaster Arms. The bleary-eyed old man looked at the open door malevolently, and snorted in disgust.

'Bloomin' hypocrite!' he muttered. 'Him and his duty, and his grudges, and his ugly mug! The trouble with people like him,' old Maurice continued, addressing the empty bar, 'is that they're neither one thing nor the other. He's too educated to be a working man, and he's not educated enough to be a gentleman. That's why he hated that poor Dean of his, who, by all accounts, was a gentleman down to his boots, and with money behind him, too. One of these days Alfred Markland will hate one of his betters a bit too much, and then he'll come a cropper.'

*　　　*　　　*

When Millie called at the Deanery, she found

Laura Girdlestone sitting at her husband's desk in the library. She was writing away furiously, the quill pen scratching over the paper. She smiled when she saw Millie, rose from the desk, and kissed her on the cheek.

'I knew you'd come, Millie. I can't take it in, you know. They only told me at seven this morning. I feel frozen up inside—numbed, you know. I must write these letters as soon as possible. There are so many people to inform. All the London folk, of course, and the people from Kent. They can send wreaths, if they like. Have you breakfasted yet?'

'No, I thought I'd come straight away. Walter's only just told me. Dear Laura, I'm so sorry! I don't know what to say.'

Laura Girdlestone strode to the fireplace and gave a vigorous pull to the bell rope. The summons was answered almost immediately by the footman.

'Forrest,' said Laura, 'get them to lay breakfast for two in the dining-room. Mrs Parrish and I are in need of sustenance. And now,' she continued, seating herself once more at the desk, 'while we're waiting, I'll just dash off a letter to Dowbiggin & Holland. Or should I telegraph? There's not much time . . . No, I'd better write. They'd think it odd.'

The quill pen resumed its frenetic scratching. Millie looked at Laura's bright, feverish eyes, and noted the firm determination of her expression. It looked as though writing letters at this time was her means of coping with grief.

Dowbiggin & Holland? Surely they were the famous London funeral furnishers? Was Laura already planning her husband's funeral?

Laura suddenly threw down the quill, and picked up a sheet of blue notepaper. She thrust it imperiously into Millie's hand.

'Read that!' she cried. 'That came while I was still dressing. I read it out to that mewling cat Ballard, and she started her blubbering and snuffling all over again. Read it! It's from that man Jackson, who came here to root through Lawrence's desk last week.'

Millie read the letter. It asked Mrs Lawrence Girdlestone to present herself at Canal Street Police Mortuary, in order to confirm the identity of a man lying there dead as the body of her husband, Dean Lawrence Girdlestone.

'He says you are to come at five o'clock this afternoon, but that you may send a substitute, someone who knew Lawrence well. Why not let Walter go? You must be spared this ordeal, Laura—'

'No! I will see this man Jackson myself, and hear what he has to say. I'll go down there in the Dean's carriage. The coachman had better wear crape in his hat . . . I've a lot of things to do this morning, Millie. I must capture the house-keys from Ballard. I am the mistress here! I wonder, should I give her a month's severance? Perhaps not. She's a sly jade, but she knows my ways, and we're used to each other—the cat and the mouse, you know. There's the breakfast bell. Come on, Millie, let's fortify ourselves for the day's doings. And at five o'clock this afternoon, I'll go and see what they've done to the Dean.'

*   *   *

Despite the warmth of the summer afternoon, it was cold in the stone-floored chamber of Canal Street Police Mortuary. One or two gas jets burned dimly on their brackets. The only windows were mere slits beneath the ceiling, but the walls had been whitewashed, which helped to lighten the place.

The attendant drew back the white sheet from the face of the man who had been found dead on the roof of Ancaster Cathedral. Inspector Jackson looked not at the corpse, but at the impassive face of the woman standing beside him. She flinched slightly, and soon averted her eyes, but her reactions were utterly empty of emotion. Jackson thought: she's as cold as he is. She's as cold as this freezing chamber.

'Yes, Mr Jackson,' said Laura, 'that is my husband, Lawrence Girdlestone. I had a premonition that something like this would happen.'

'You feared that he would meet a violent

death?'

'I am not surprised that he did so. He was an incorrigibly clumsy man, prone to accidents. He was the only person I knew who could fall *up* as well as down stairs. On this occasion, he climbed where he was not welcome, and that juggernaut, Ancaster Cathedral, was the death of him. But this is not the place for me to expatiate on the matter.'

A handsome, well-set-up woman, thought Jackson, soured by something, presumably in her marriage to Lawrence Girdlestone. What age was she? In her mid-forties, but looking younger. She dressed well, and with meticulous care, but her eyes betrayed a kind of desperate recklessness. She seemed to be holding herself in check by a monumental effort of will. He watched her as she glanced with distaste around the room. She showed no fear or disquiet at the presence of the other sheeted figures lying on their narrow tables. In response to a brief nod from Jackson, the attendant covered the dead man's face.

'What is the custom here?' Laura Girdlestone's voice continued its even, haughty tone as she unclasped her handbag.

'One shilling to the attendant, ma'am.'

Mrs Girdlestone handed the man a shilling. He muttered a word of thanks, and left the room. Laura stirred impatiently.

'Are we to stay here freezing for ever, Mr Jackson? I fail to see what else you want me to do.'

Jackson made no reply. He preceded Mrs Girdlestone out of the silent, cold room and into a small panelled office, where a fire was burning dimly in a rusty grate. Sitting in an upright chair near the fire was a distinguished grey-haired man in his sixties, with a handsome, intelligent face, and long, delicate hands. He was wearing a pearl grey suit and matching frock coat. On a table beside him he had deposited a well-brushed silk hat, and a pair of fawn kid gloves.

'Mrs Girdlestone,' said Jackson, 'this gentleman is Dr James Venner, the police surgeon. Dr Venner, this lady is the widow of the unfortunate Dean Lawrence Girdlestone.'

Dr Venner inclined his head in greeting, but said nothing. He looked at Laura Girdlestone with what Jackson knew to be a deliberately contrived lack of interest. Venner, thought Jackson, would have seemed more at home in a box at the opera than in the office of a police mortuary. Evidently Mrs Girdlestone was thinking along the same lines, because Jackson saw her start in surprise. He motioned to another chair, and Laura sat down.

'You told me just now, Mrs Girdlestone,' said Jackson, 'that you had had a premonition of your husband's death. Did you also fear that he was going to be murdered?'

'Murdered?' Laura Girdlestone's voice held an infinity of scorn. 'I told you that my

158

husband was a clumsy man, prone to accidents. He had been advised not to go climbing up ladders and scaffolds—Solomon, the works foreman, warned him not to do so. Mr Girdlestone, as always, knew better than anyone else. And so this appalling accident— an accident of his own making—has taken him from this world. Murder? I think not.'

It's early days, thought Jackson. Whatever is motivating this woman to defy me will become clear in the fullness of time. Some things, though, could be done straight away. He turned to the elegant man sitting in the other chair.

'Dr Venner,' he said, 'is there any evidence to support Mrs Girdlestone's theory that Dean Girdlestone died as the result of an accident?'

'None at all, Inspector. Mrs Girdlestone, your husband did not die as the result of a fall, whether accidental or otherwise. He was killed—murdered. You must take my word for it. I have conducted a preliminary examination of your husband's body, and the cause of death was almost immediately apparent to me.'

Mrs Girdlestone glanced at Dr Venner with a kind of mutinous distaste. She drew the folds of her stylish coat around her, as though to shut him out of her world.

'They were saying that the Dean had committed suicide,' she said. 'I found that suggestion equally offensive. This ludicrous idea that he'd embezzled money from the

159

cathedral funds was the first outrage to common sense. My husband was a wealthy man, and I must admit that he was a generous man where money was concerned. And he was a principled man, too, according to his lights. He would never have stooped to anything so mean as theft.'

Mrs Girdlestone laughed. It was an unpleasant, joyless sound.

'And as for suicide—well, Mr Girdlestone had such a high opinion of his own importance to the world, the universe, and to society in general, that he would not for one moment have thought of depriving us all of his beneficent company. So "suicide" can be ruled out of court as a viable verdict. And "murder"—well, in the hands of a physician determined on such a verdict, I suppose it will be a self-fulfilling prophecy.'

A slight flush of vexation rose to Venner's cheeks, but he said nothing. Inspector Jackson strode to the door of the mortuary office, and threw it open.

'There's nothing else I need to ask you at present, ma'am,' he said. 'What I must do, though, is point out to you very forcibly that your husband was murdered, and that I am empowered as a Crown Officer of the Law to investigate that murder. You, and your household, must look to be visited by me, vested with warrants, as and when necessary, and accompanied by other officers. On such occasions, you will be entitled to have your friends present.'

Had those words had any effect? Had she sensed his anger at her slanderous suggestion about Venner's integrity? Yes. She was more subdued, now, and she'd had the grace to cast her eyes down in something approaching shame. She rose from her chair, and said diffidently, 'Very well, Inspector Jackson. I will consider what you have told me. I should be obliged if you would give me notice of your coming visits.'

Laura Girdlestone bowed stiffly to Dr Venner, and Jackson conducted her from the dreary building to her waiting carriage.

Venner briefly recalled what Sergeant Bottomley had told him earlier, as the two men had sat alone by the fire in the mortuary office, waiting for Jackson and Laura Girdlestone to arrive.

'There was a pool of congealed blood on the roof, sir,' Bottomley had said. 'I ran my fingers through it, and guessed that it was three or four days old.'

'You were always good with blood, Sergeant Bottomley. Particularly in that slaughtering business last year, at Burton Viscount. Go on.'

'I examined the head, sir, and saw that the back of the skull had been crushed in with a blow from some kind of hooked or pointed instrument. Although the body had fallen on its back, the face had not been marred.'

'What did you do then, Sergeant?' Venner had asked.

'I eased myself a few feet across the roof, sir, to a patch where the tiles had been raised from the roof of what they call the St Catherine Chapel. A trail of blood led to a kind of little boxy area beneath the tiles, a space between two joists, I suppose it was. The blood from the body had drained down the sloping roof into this little area, and it was still liquid. That's what dropped down through the rotten ceiling on to Dean Arkwright, who was sitting in the chapel underneath.'

'I'm inclined to think, Sergeant,' Venner had said, 'that the strong sunlight up there on the tower had kept that little reservoir of blood liquid. It wouldn't have been the brazier that they'd lit up there. It's odd, though . . . It reminds me of the old superstition that a corpse would bleed afresh if approached by its murderer. Still, that's nonsense.'

'Is it, sir?' Bottomley had said. 'Well, there were one or two folk around the cathedral that night who had no love for Dean Girdlestone, and a lot of liking for mumbo-jumbo. So maybe the poor Dean's blood was a sign.'

Venner started out of his reverie as Inspector Jackson came back into the office.

'Upon my word, Dr Venner,' Jackson began, 'I'm sorry to have subjected you to that unpleasantness from Mrs Girdlestone—' Venner held up a hand to silence him.

162

'That woman, Mr Jackson,' he said, 'is under the influence of ardent spirits. I suspect that she is on the verge of alcoholic addiction. I should keep an eye on Mrs Laura Girdlestone, if I were you.'

Dr Venner rose abruptly from his chair, and removed his pearl grey frock coat, folding it carefully, and placing it across the chair back. At the same time, a diffident young man in black appeared from the mortuary chamber. He handed Venner a rubber apron, and tied the strings behind the surgeon's back.

'Well, Inspector,' said Venner, turning back his shirt cuffs, 'Roberts and I will conduct the autopsy now. It may reveal some interesting extra bits of information, but my preliminary examination showed me at once that poor Girdlestone's skull had been crushed in with a heavy, hooked object of some kind, as Sergeant Bottomley maintained. Despite the frantic widow's theory to the contrary, Lawrence Girdlestone was murdered.'

CHAPTER SEVEN

FREED FROM EVERY SNARE

Dean's Row was basking in the sun when Jackson and Bottomley called upon Laura Girdlestone two days after her visit to the police mortuary. The mellow brick house fronts with their white sash windows conveyed their usual air of genteel prosperity. Several carriages were drawn up outside the Deanery. Two coachmen in livery, who had drifted away from their charges, were talking together on the lawn in the cathedral precinct. Evidently Mrs Girdlestone had company that Thursday morning.

'Perhaps she won't see us after all, sir,' ventured Sergeant Bottomley. 'I don't think she likes the police very much. Very hard on Dandy Jim she was, on Monday.'

'She was, Sergeant. I'd have thought her ill-bred if I'd not been making allowances for her situation. But Dr Venner's a tough nut to crack! As for Mrs Girdlestone, she'll see us, all right. We're here by appointment, remember. I've allowed her two whole days to recover her poise, if that's the right word. I'm in no mood for nonsense today.'

In response to Jackson's knock the front door was opened by a powdered footman, who

164

was wearing a black crepe arm band. He glanced briefly and rather doubtfully at the card that Jackson had given him.

'Beg pardon, sir,' he said, 'but do you want to see Mrs Girdlestone immediately? She's with Canon Parrish at the moment.'

'I'm here by appointment, young man,' Jackson retorted, 'and I'm on time. You have my calling-card there. Take it to Mrs Girdlestone at once.'

The footman inclined his head, and walked swiftly away down a dim passage leading from the hall. From where Jackson and Bottomley stood, they could hear the muffled sound of a wheezy harmonium being played rather too lustily for its own good. After a minute or two the footman returned, and conducted them to a door at the end of the passage. Bottomley glanced quickly at the little cubby-hole under the stairs, but Daft William was not there.

The man threw open the door to reveal a square, stuffy, over-furnished room, the contents of which had evidently been chosen to intimidate rather than reassure. There were high presses of dark oak, and a great deal of brassware. A narrow window looked out on to a corner of the rear garden.

Two people paused in the middle of a conversation to look at the police officers. One was Canon Parrish, who was sitting on a music stool in front of the harmonium. He smiled a greeting at both men, but there was something almost sheepish in the smile. Jackson wondered why.

The other person in the room was Mrs Girdlestone. She was dressed in black, though Jackson could see that she had not yet been measured for full mourning. She sat bolt upright in a black oak chair, holding a thick hymn book. Her dark eyes regarded them with a kind of restless insolence, but her voice was calm, and seemingly well controlled.

'Very well, Forrest,' she said, 'there's no need to announce these gentlemen. Please close the door.' Without altering her position on the uncomfortable chair, she said to Canon Parrish, 'Those two hymns, then, Canon, will suffice, I think. That thing by Thomas of Celano is particularly apt:

Day of wrath and doom impending,
David's word with Sibyl's blending!
Heaven and earth in ashes ending!

It sets the right tone, you know, and would echo in some way my late husband's great erudition. The other thing by Watts is a trifle sentimental, but then, Mr Girdlestone had a certain romantic side to his character, albeit rarely revealed. Perhaps you would just play that once again? Verse two, I think.'

'Laura—'

Mrs Girdlestone ignored the desperate pleading in Parrish's voice.

'Verse two!' she repeated.

Sergeant Bottomley thought to himself: She's playing to the gallery today, the gallery being *us*!

Inspector Jackson, looking into her eyes, thought: This woman is under the influence of strong liquors, but behind that poisoned miasma there lurks a determination to mock her dead husband's memory. No wonder Canon Parrish looks cowed.

The harmonium lurched into life, and after a few introductory bars, Parrish began to sing. He had a good tenor voice, which he tried to temper to fit the small, oppressive room.

'In heav'n they dwell, with spirits blest,
How kind their slumbers are,
From sufferings and from sin released,
And freed from every snare.'

Mrs Girdlestone had not removed her eyes from Jackson's face. She remained looking at him as she suddenly joined in the last two lines of the funeral hymn's second verse, her high soprano jarring eerily against Parrish's tenor. Her careless tone and attitude conveyed to Jackson a frightening mixture of secret glee and gloating triumph.

The music ceased, and Walter Parrish rose from the stool.

'Thank you, Canon, for agreeing to come this morning,' said Mrs Girdlestone. 'The funeral will be on Monday. It will be a private affair, for friends and family. That is what the Dean would have wanted. The furnishers have already arrived, and are working in the drawing-room. I must speak now to these police officers. Perhaps you will see yourself out? It will save time if I don't ring for Forrest.'

Canon Parrish glanced briefly at Jackson, and it was a glance that seemed to say: 'I must speak to you alone, when you have finished here.' Parrish smiled rather sadly at Laura, and left the room, closing the door quietly behind him. When Laura spoke, her voice was free of the hideous mocking tone that she had employed when Canon Parrish was present.

'I have kept you standing, Inspector Jackson,' she said, 'and you, Sergeant Bottomley. Please be seated. I have the funeral furnishers in the house, and there is much to be done. You have told me that my husband was murdered. At first, I expressed incredulity, but now, of course, I must accept what you have told me. If you will send me that doctor's address—Venner, was it?—I will pen him a note of apology.'

Come, now, thought Jackson, this is much better! Perhaps I can establish a few facts without wasting time bandying words.

'Murdered . . . It seems so strange, Inspector, so utterly out of character . . . Oh, dear! I know that sounds silly, as though to be murdered could be out of character, but that's how it seems to me. My husband would have been quite happy to die in the pursuit of duty, but he would not have approved of being the victim of murder.'

'Well, ma'am, murdered he was, brutally and cruelly, in an area of the cathedral roof above the nave. I wonder why he should have been there? He had seen Sir Charles Blount that afternoon, and your maid Ballard saw the Dean quit this house shortly after Sir Charles had left. Did he mention to you that he was going up into the cathedral roof?'

'He did not. In any case, I was upstairs in my boudoir, suffering from a bout of indisposition. On all such occasions, the Dean thought it prudent to lock me in my chambers. I was an inconvenience, you see—an embarrassment, if you like.'

As she spoke, Jackson saw the light of pent-up resentment rekindle in Laura Girdlestone's eyes. Evidently, the episode of sweet reasonableness had passed.

'My late husband, Inspector, had three great loves in his life—wine, clothes, and power. He was a rich man—which is why these charges of fraud against him are so foolish—and we live well, as you can see. We were married at St Paul's, Knightsbridge, and I thought that he would have settled for a living somewhere in Town. That, at least, would have made things a little more bearable. But my late husband immediately began his search for preferment, which took him first to India, and then to various provincial English backwaters. We had two very civilized years when he was Rector of St Philip's, Mayfair. Then, his wanderlust returned, and we came to bury ourselves here.

'Wine was his first love. At one time, I assumed that *I* was his first love. I was mistaken. He collected wine, and our cellar here is justly celebrated for its rare vintages. It will raise a small fortune when I sell it off. In his love of wine he was following his father, Mr Jethro Girdlestone. He started a wine account for him with one of the old London wine-houses—Molinari's, I think it was. When not preoccupied with clothes and power, my husband would be down there in the cellar, cherishing his vintages. That I could take no interest whatever in the matter did not further my own cause, I can tell you. Am I boring you, Inspector?'

'No, ma'am, not at all. It might be prudent if I were to talk to your husband's father, Mr Jethro Girdlestone—'

The sardonic widow laughed.

'By all means talk to Jethro. Much good may it do you!'

'Where can I find him?'

'In Highgate Cemetery. You can talk to him there as long as you like. For all eternity, if that takes your fancy. Jethro has been buried there for fifteen years.'

This bitter woman, thought Jackson, has been possessed by the demon of resentment, and speech is her form of self-exorcism. She can't stop.

'So, wine. Then clothes. For my husband, clothes made the man. He lavished money on his tailors, his boot-makers, his shirt-makers . . . He had his own dressing-room upstairs, with fitted wardrobes and full-length mirrors—'

Sergeant Bottomley, who had been sitting very uncomfortably on the harmonium stool, suddenly spoke, and the unexpected sound of his voice caused Laura Girdlestone to utter a shriek of alarm.

'Would you say, ma'am, that the late Mr Girdlestone was an elegant man? Him having all these fitted wardrobes, and fancy tailors, and so forth?'

'Elegant? What has that to do with the matter in hand? He was always well dressed— expensively dressed. But no, he wasn't elegant. He was a solid, heavy man, a stumbling, bumbling kind of man, you know. Elegant? If elegance has anything to do with this affair, then you'd better go and look at Prebendary Arkwright—Dean Arkwright, I should say. He wears anything with panache. An old gardening jacket would look elegant on Nicholas Arkwright.'

Sergeant Bottomley smiled, but said nothing. Evidently he was satisfied with Laura's answer. Jackson glanced at him, and wondered what lay behind his apparently irrelevant question. Mrs Girdlestone continued to talk.

'So, there was wine, and clothes, and finally, power. My late husband enjoyed the exercise of power, both in public and private life. He was satisfied—fulfilled—when he had rendered others subordinate to himself. We all writhed under that lust for power. It made me the woman whom you see now. It rendered his subordinates sly and obsequious, while seeking any opportunity to secure his downfall. Perhaps you should seek his murderer among those who had been diminished by his lust for power.'

A forbidding frown marred Mrs Girdlestone's brow. Her breast heaved with a sudden onset of indignation.

'And there may have been other lusts that were concealed from me. I've sometimes wondered about that creeping, mewling cat. She knows I can prove nothing, and that I'm bound to her, for my sins. Very prim and proper she is, but you can see the insolence behind her eyes.'

Jackson realized that Mrs Girdlestone was talking about her maid, Ballard. Evidently, she thought that the Dean had added women to his predilection for wine, clothes and power. Was any of this rigmarole of hers true? Time would tell.

The door opened, and Ballard came into the room. She was wearing black, with long mourning bands falling from her lace cap. She looked pale and exhausted, but she regarded her mistress with scarcely concealed pity. This young woman, thought Jackson, is the type of servant who remains stubbornly loyal, and her mistress knows that well enough.

'Madam,' said Ballard, 'the people from the mourning warehouse will be here in five minutes to measure you for your dress and veils. And the furnishers want to know if it's convenient for them to hang the funeral festoons in the hallway now.'

'Tell them to get on with it, Ballard. These gentlemen, I assume, will be leaving now.'

Inspector Jackson rose from his chair, and bowed to Mrs Girdlestone.

'Thank you, ma'am,' he said, 'for seeing us both today, and for giving us your frank appraisal of the late Mr Lawrence Girdlestone. As you know, the coroner will release the body today for burial. The inquest has been adjourned for a week, while I pursue my enquiries. You are now quite free, ma'am, to arrange the details of your late husband's obsequies.'

Rather to Jackson's surprise, both women smiled at his choice of word. Was there, in fact, a secret bond of friendship underlying the tearful obsequiousness of the one, and the reckless bullying of the other?

'*Obsequies*, indeed! How quaint! My late husband was scarcely a royal duke. A funeral will suffice. But I can promise you, Inspector, that it will be a funeral worthy of a Dean of Ancaster. Nothing obscure and mean. Lawrence Girdlestone will go to the grave in style!'

Ballard showed them out into the hall, and handed them their hats from the hall table. As they stepped out of the house into Dean's Row the harmonium recommenced its plaintive whining, and they could hear Laura Girdlestone's shrill soprano essaying yet another funeral hymn.

A black carriage had just stopped at the kerb, the sunlight gleaming off its brass lamps. Two men and a lady, all dressed in deepest black, alighted, and were shown into the house. The people from the mourning warehouse had arrived to measure the mistress of the Deanery for her widow's weeds.

*   *   *

At the far end of Dean's Row a narrow alley led to a shallow flight of steps which took the two detectives up to a sheltered public garden. There was a plot of grass, a few park benches, and a couple of rather tired flower beds. The two men chose a bench in front of an ivy-covered wall, and sat down.

'In a few minutes' time, Sergeant,' said Jackson, 'I'm going to call on Canon Parrish, and ask him about the Girdlestones. I like that man. Parrish, I mean.'

'I met his niece, sir, Miss Caroline Parrish, on the train from Latchford Halt. She was just coming here for the first time. I heard in the town that she's becoming sweet on Dean Arkwright's son, Mr Conrad Arkwright.'

'Is she, now? Well, I was going to suggest that you paid a surprise call on your Prebendary Arkwright—Dean, I should say—while I'm closeted with Canon Parrish. I see you've got your brown-paper parcel with you. Back there in the Deanery you were clutching it to your bosom as though you thought Mrs Girdlestone would take it off you. I suppose it's a present for your Prebendary—Dean, I should say.'

Bottomley rummaged round in one of the pockets of his overcoat, and produced the stub end of a cigar and a box of wax vestas. He placed the remains of the cigar delicately between his lips, and succeeded in lighting it. The match flared up between his fingers, and he dropped it with a little bleat of pain.

'You'll burn yourself to death one of these days, Sergeant,' said Jackson. 'Your horrible collection of butt-ends will reduce you to a cinder.'

Sergeant Bottomley smiled absently. He was mentally recording the fact that Arkwright was now 'your Prebendary'. The guvnor had evidently decided that Arkwright was Bottomley's affair. Mr Jackson had other fish to fry.

'Sir,' said Bottomley, puffing away at his cigar, 'it strikes me that this fraud business won't wash. Everybody's telling us that Mr Girdlestone was rich. Mr Mays got hold of his bank balances for you, and they showed us that he *was* rich—'

'Yes, Sergeant, and the answer to that problem lies in London. That's where he banked. That's where his late father conducted his business. I may have to visit his bankers— what were they called? Cooper & Partners, of Lothbury. And it's quite likely that Canon Parrish may know something about Girdlestone's affairs. They'd known each other for a lifetime, so I'm told.'

'And then, sir, there's the business of Mr Girdlestone's murder.'

Herbert Bottomley frowned, and his face was shadowed by a kind of bleak despairing expression that Jackson knew well. It meant that his sergeant had become personally involved in—and personally affronted by—the crime that they were investigating. Bottomley threw down the stub of his cigar, and ground it into the path.

'That poor man had been struck down, sir, with a vicious instrument of some kind— something picked up on the spur of the moment, perhaps, a mattock, some kind of clawed tool. He was left exposed on that cathedral roof for the crows to find, and for the rain to soak and stain. What had he done to deserve that? Was it hatred, sir? Or envy? Who stood to gain from his death?'

'Well, Sergeant, I suspect you already know the answer to that last question. Mrs Girdlestone, for one. She stands to come into a tidy fortune, doesn't she? And no one could accuse her, Sergeant, of being heartbroken over her husband's death.'

'She couldn't have struck him down like that, sir. She wouldn't have had the strength. And I can't see her climbing up ladders in an afternoon tea dress.'

'Neither can I, Sergeant. But what about an accomplice? That man Markland told me that Arkwright had been pipped to the post in the marriage stakes by Girdlestone. All you need is a disenchanted wife and an embittered former suitor, like your Prebendary, to hatch a very pretty little plot. The wife gains her liberty, together with a fortune and the disappointed suitor gains the position of Dean. So that's one line of enquiry. Then, of course, there's that dusty imp of a man in the works office—Solomon.'

'Yes, sir. I've not overlooked Mr Solomon. He's one of those true pagans you often find in old churches and cathedrals. They worship the place itself, its bricks and stones, and its old customs, and God help anybody, priest or layman, who tries to interfere with all those things. Yes, I've not forgotten Solomon. I've

177

asked around over the last few days, sir, dropping a question here, and a little hint there. Solomon was in the cathedral all Monday afternoon, and so was Dean Arkwright. It may mean nothing, sir, or it may mean everything. Perhaps I'll find out this afternoon.'

*　　*　　*

Saul Jackson sat back in the comfortable chair that Canon Parrish had drawn forward for him, and felt truly relaxed for the first time that day. When he had rung at the door of Number 7, it had been answered by a cheerful, homely woman who told him that her name was Jessie, and that he was expected. She had led him into Walter Parrish's little study, and closed the door.

'Your servant told me that I was expected, Canon,' said Jackson.

'So you were! I knew you'd want to hear some kind of explanation, or excuse, for that mocking charade just now at the Deanery. Laura is a well-educated woman from a very good background, and yet she's so far forgotten herself as to use me—*me*!—as an instrument of her celebration of her husband's death! I sat there, playing the harmonium, and singing those hymns, all the time realizing that she was exulting at having been released from bondage to a man who no longer loved her.'

Jackson looked at the slight, puckish clergyman sitting opposite him, and peering at him through round, gold-rimmed spectacles. He had met this type of man before—a man without guile, so open in his dealings that he found it difficult to cloak honest truths in euphemisms.

'Do you know why she behaved like that,' Parrish continued, 'even though two police officers were present?'

'She was not herself—'

'She was drunk!'

It was an ugly word for such a man to use of a woman. Jackson suddenly realized that Parrish had chosen that particular brutality as a form of protest against the dead man rather than the living woman.

'We were all young things together, you know, Inspector, which somehow makes it worse. Lawrence, and Nicholas Arkwright, Laura Taverner, Millie and I. We went to the same parties, stayed at the same houses—'

Parrish rummaged through a drawer in his desk and produced a large photograph, mounted on a gilt-edged card. He handed the photograph to Jackson.

'That picture was taken in 1868 at a place called Vaux Hall, in Essex, the home of a family called Morton. Over on the right, you'll see two dashing young men, the sons of the house, Gussie and Tom Morton. Gussie was my particular friend at Cambridge, and Tom

179

was a friend of Nicholas Arkwright at Oxford. That's why you can see all the members of our little crowd there, on the terrace. It was at Vaux Hall that our different worlds met.'

Jackson looked closely at the photograph. It had faded to a golden brown, but the detail was sharp and clear. Parrish leaned across from his chair, and pointed out the various figures.

'There's Nicholas Arkwright, standing on the left, looking terribly young and earnest. That's Lawrence Girdlestone standing beside him, again, looking too solemn for his age. It was the slow photography, you see. They were both only twenty-three when this picture was taken.'

'And there's you, sir! I'd have recognized you immediately! And this beautifully dressed girl with the parasol and white gloves—why, it's your good wife!'

'Yes, that's Millie. And next to the two brothers, Inspector, you'll see a beautiful young woman sitting in a basket chair. Very elegant, isn't she? Very much untouched by the world. She was only twenty. That's Laura Girdlestone.'

Jackson handed the photograph back. He could see how all these cathedral folk had been forging links among themselves by visiting country houses together, thirty years earlier.

'She was Laura Taverner, then, Inspector.

She was the only daughter of Mr Piers Taverner, a landed gentleman in Sussex. Mr Taverner was acquainted with the Morton family. And so we mixed and mingled, and then went our separate ways, until Providence brought us together again in this place. We met as people changed by time and circumstance, Millie and I long married, and the parents of three daughters. Nicholas Arkwright long widowed, and the father of one fine son. And the Girdlestones—'

Canon Parrish rose abruptly, and opened a cupboard. Jackson heard the clink of glasses.

'Inspector, I know there are various conventions in your profession about drinking on duty. Nevertheless, I am going to offer you a glass of old malt whisky, as I dislike drinking alone. There you are.'

How strange, thought Jackson, that he could feel thoroughly at home in this high-ranking clergyman's study, whereas the Deanery next door had seemed to him like an alien and rather frightening land. He thanked Parrish, and sipped the golden liquid appreciatively.

'Lawrence Girdlestone laid down a famous cellar, you know. His father's besetting sin was drink, and he encouraged his son to follow suit. It was Lawrence's subtle flaunting of his head for drink that ultimately lured poor Laura into the web of intoxication and dependence on strong liquors. We all connived in the fiction of Laura's bouts of "indisposition". Caroline—my niece—tells me that Laura was virtually imprisoned in that house.'

'Dean Girdlestone—'

'Dean Girdlestone did nothing to rescue her! Preaching, too, has been in vain. Neglected and undervalued, she has withdrawn into a world of cynicism and self-abasement.'

Jackson was silent for a moment. The clergyman's anguish for Laura Girdlestone's situation was palpable. It was not the time for soothing suggestions.

'The late Dean Girdlestone, Canon, has been accused of fraud against the cathedral. Although I am now engaged in a murder enquiry, the original charges remain to be confirmed or refuted. I'm going up to London very soon, to interview one of the directors of Dean Girdlestone's bank. Would you, sir, know of any useful contact I might consult about the late Dean's finances? You and he obviously moved in the same circles—'

Canon Parrish held up a hand to enjoin silence.

'Just one moment, Inspector—I'm recollecting something I once heard from a man who's now a bishop in the Scottish church. He told me that both the Girdlestones—the father and son, I mean— were intimately concerned in some kind of charitable enterprise. The Maple Trust. That was its name. I know nothing about it, but you might care to seek it out. My Scottish bishop mentioned that it was based in London somewhere. You might care to follow that lead. The Maple Trust.'

CHAPTER EIGHT

THE MAN WHO KNEW THE TRUTH

Nicholas Arkwright, alone in the front parlour of the Prebendary's House, permitted himself a luxurious sigh of contentment. In spite of Monday's grim experience in the St Catherine Chapel, the week had gone well. He had called at Number 7 on the Tuesday morning, and the Parrishes had received him warmly, brushing aside his apologies for the previous night's doings, and making him stay for lunch.

The Revel had limped along for a while after the horrors of the Bank Holiday night, and had then re-established its ancient hold over the townspeople. The Fools' Mayor had been elected and paraded around the streets on a decorated and docile horse. On Wednesday morning the Civic Service had taken place, his first official appearance in public as Acting Dean. He had missed the familiar huddle and gossip of the Canons' vestry, donning his robes in the lonely splendour of what had been poor Lawrence Girdlestone's private vesting room. He had rather enjoyed being led in by the beadles with their staves, and had been conscious of the many necks craning to see him as he took his place for the first time in the Dean's stall. Canon Hall, as Rector of St Edmund at the Gate, Ancaster's parish church, had preached. His sermon had been about the need for sobriety and vigilance. Very apt, really, at the end of the Revel.

Nicholas glanced around the room. It was some years since he had ventured into the parlour, preferring to live in cramped comfort in the rear portion of the old Tudor house. There was Joanna's flat-topped Broadwood piano, the empty wing armchair facing his beside the fireplace, and the old Queen Anne sofa, which Mr Worden, the optician next door, had pronounced to be a genuine antique.

All the things in that room belonged to his earlier, vanished life with Joanna, when Conrad was a little boy. Waiting for him now, socially staid and architecturally chaste, was Ancaster Deanery, Number 5, Dean's Row. When Laura was ready to vacate the coveted house, he would move in . . .

Where did he stand now, in life's pilgrimage? He was on the threshold of irrevocable change. The resentments and frustrations of the last five years could be set aside, and poor Girdlestone left to rest in peace. He recalled how thankful he had always been for the friendship of Walter Parrish. He had known him from school-days, and had been delighted when Walter had been appointed by Bishop Grandison as Vicar of the Cathedral Parish. Walter was a man with a truly pastoral heart. Then he thought for a while of Caroline and Conrad, and wondered whether the three of them would evolve into a new family, with himself at the centre of things . . .

He'd already received a good number of letters, containing congratulations, or invitations to dine, among them a letter from Sir Charles Blount. He searched for it in the pile of letters on the desk, and admired its pale-blue envelope, the vigorous handwriting on the front, and the aristocratic crest embossed on the back flap. He extracted the single sheet of paper from the envelope and read it for the second time.

My dear Arkwright
Heartiest congratulations on your appointment as Acting Dean. You'll understand, now, why I urged you to stay your hand! I knew that poor Girdlestone was to be offered a bishopric, and I had already suggested to the Foundation that the office of Dean should go to you as soon as it fell vacant. The circumstances are very

different now—tragically different, but we had no hesitation in appointing you, albeit temporarily, in Girdlestone's place. I intend to throw a dinner here at Ladymead in your honour, at which I very much hope that your friends the Parrishes, and Miss Caroline Parrish, will be present.
Once again, my congratulations!
Charles Blount

It was time to pen a suitable reply. Arkwright drew the writing desk nearer to his chair, and selected a fresh sheet of writing paper. For a minute or so his pen moved rapidly over the paper. He would show appreciation of Sir Charles's kindness, but there was no need to be unduly profuse. Charles Blount loathed obsequiousness, and in any case he and Nicholas were old Ancastrians—like Josiah Solomon, and the bibulous gatekeeper, Obadiah Syme.

Nicholas's right index finger had become stained with ink. He picked up the pen-cloth, and wiped his hand. But what was this? *It wasn't ink, it was blood, and he was frantically wiping it off his hands.* He threw the bloodstained handkerchief away from him in horror—and saw that it was only the innocent ink-stained pen-cloth lying demurely on the table. His eyes were playing him tricks.

His heart beating with shock, Nicholas Arkwright looked across the room to the piano. There, on its flat top, beside a pile of books, was the handkerchief, washed and ironed, that Mr Solomon had posted to him without comment on the day following Lawrence Girdlestone's death. What did it mean? There had been a dream of sorts, something to do with a handkerchief—

There came a heavy knock at the front door. Looking out from the parlour window into Friary Street, Dean Arkwright saw the solid, rather ungainly figure of Sergeant Bottomley standing on his front doorstep. A few minutes later, Bottomley was sitting opposite him in the study.

Arkwright looked with growing apprehension at the red-faced, gently smiling detective sergeant. He glanced once again at the man's card, as though to reassure himself that someone who looked rather like a cattle-dealer was, in very truth, Detective Sergeant H. Bottomley, of the Warwickshire Constabulary.

'I expect you know why I've called on you today, sir,' said Bottomley, and then stopped. He fixed Dean Arkwright with an almost demonic smile of encouragement.

'Well, Sergeant, I suppose your visit's to do with poor Lawrence Girdlestone's murder—'

'You see, sir,' said Bottomley, depositing his brown paper parcel on the floor beside him, 'Dean Girdlestone was murdered in the cathedral at around three o'clock on

Thursday, the third of August. Now, a cathedral's not like a house, where you can make a quick search of a number of rooms, in order to find your culprit. A cathedral's full of hidey-holes—old chapels, and vaults, and secret spaces.'

Sergeant Bottomley stopped talking, and seemed to fix his gaze on the garden, which glowed in the afternoon sun beyond the French window. There was an unexpectedness about this man that Arkwright found unnerving. He was forcibly reminded of Bishop Grandison, sitting behind his desk in the palace, playing cat and mouse.

'Among those secret spaces, sir,' Bottomley continued, 'was the St Catherine's Chapel, where, according to Mr Solomon, whom I spoke to yesterday, you spent the fatal afternoon fast asleep in a pew.'

'I did, Sergeant. I'd never done so before, and I don't suppose I'll ever do so again! And while I was sleeping, and dreaming, poor Dean Girdlestone was being done to death! It doesn't bear thinking of.'

'Asking your pardon, Mr Dean,' said Bottomley, 'but it does bear thinking of. You see, when Mr Solomon kindly told me about your gigantic nap in the chapel, he also fixed for me the fact that two people, at least, were present in the cathedral at the time of the Dean's death. Himself, and you, sir. I asked him what he'd been doing all that afternoon if

188

he could swear positively that you had been in the chapel without moving out of it. He said he'd been "here and there", and I couldn't say him nay.'

'No, I don't suppose you could deny the truth of what Solomon told you. He must have been present all afternoon. That was why he could speak so positively about my long sleep in the chapel.'

Bottomley sighed, and shook his head. It was a kindly gesture, tinged with a certain impatience.

'You've provided each other with an alibi, sir, an alibi which can't at the moment be shaken. Don't you see how certain uncharitable folk could put a sinister interpretation on that alibi? You cover for him. Or he covers for you—'

'But that is outrageous, Sergeant! Are you daring to suggest—?'

'I'm suggesting nothing, sir. I'm pointing out to you the way some minds will work. There are other possible combinations of the folk in Dean's Row that could point to a conspiracy to murder. Murder, Mr Dean, is a terrible business, which is why people like my guvnor and me can never allow themselves to be involved too closely with the family and friends of the victims. Truth is what we're after. Truth, and justice. You were Mr Girdlestone's friend, weren't you, sir?'

'I—yes, I had known him ever since my

189

school-days. My mind is reeling from the veiled accusations that you have made, Sergeant—'

'Not accusations, sir. They're just possibilities. Mr Girdlestone was cruelly murdered by a blow from some kind of hooked instrument. While I was talking to Mr Solomon yesterday, I saw an old empty stone coffin full of adzes, and crowbars, and other tools of the mason's trade. Very convenient, and very handy for all concerned, if I may say so. I've heard that you and Mr Solomon were fast friends, too, sir, from childhood.'

Sergeant Bottomley stooped down, and picked up his parcel. Arkwright watched him, fascinated, as he slowly undid the string, and then removed the brown paper wrapping. He produced a leather-bound quarto book, fastened with brass clips.

'And here's a journal that was kept by another very old friend of yours, Mr Arkwright. It's a kind of diary kept by the late Dean Girdlestone, and I've put a marker here beside a passage that I think you should read. It may give you food for thought, sir.'

Bottomley stood up, and handed the journal to Arkwright.

'I'll be on my way now, sir. When you've finished reading that book, perhaps you'd be good enough to return it to the folk at the Deanery? I'll just leave you with a little thought, if I may, sir: beware the power of friendship. If wrongly handled, it can lead a man to destruction.'

When Bottomley had left the house, Nicholas Arkwright returned to the study, opened Lawrence Girdlestone's journal at the marker, and began to read.

No one seeing my present success, and, perhaps envying my high social position as Dean of Ancaster, would believe that I was afflicted with the burden of feeling at all times inferior to a man who has been a friend and companion throughout a lifetime, a man who, as a mere boy of 14, saved my life by an act of instinctive bravery. Prebendary Arkwright is that man . . .

Nicholas sat quite still, as though transfixed and, as the meaning of the words sank further into his consciousness, he felt the whole tenor of his life shift, reform, and settle down in a new place, and with a new perspective. The time of seeking help from Bishop Grandison had passed. He must struggle now with his conscience courageously, and alone.

* * *

Saul Jackson steadied his feet on either side of the roof ridge, and looked about him. According to Sergeant Bottomley, he was standing near the spot where Dean Girdlestone's body had been found, but there was nothing to be seen now, apart from some discolouring of the leads at the spot. A warm wind was blowing from the south, disturbing the rather eerie silence of the place.

Jackson's alert eyes scanned the rooftops of the ancient houses bordering the cathedral precinct. The upper storeys of the many residences in Dean's Row and Abbey Yard were hidden by the soaring roofs and turrets of the cathedral, but at one spot the afternoon sun glinted off a single arched window set in a high, triangular sandstone gable. The lower sash of the window had been flung up, and for a moment Jackson fancied he saw the sudden gleam of a telescope. Someone was evidently watching them—someone who had a clear view of this particular section of the cathedral roof.

Jackson turned round, and glanced up at the doorway leading from the cathedral roof. Bottomley had retreated into the roof space, and his place at the open doorway had been taken by a middle-aged man dressed very smartly in the regulation uniform of a police inspector. He had a good-humoured, slightly incurious face, and the air of someone waiting patiently to be given a set of straightforward orders. He had welcomed the presence of Jackson and Bottomley with a mixture of formal courtesy and genial relief.

'Inspector Traynor,' said Jackson, 'can you identify that bit of sandstone roof over there? It's about three hundred yards south-east. There's someone there who might be able to tell us something. Somebody with a telescope.'

'That? It's the top storey of what they call the Abbey Gatehouse, Mr Jackson. That's the gate that you passed under when you came here this afternoon. It's the way in to the cathedral precinct.'

Jackson clambered cautiously back to the door, and allowed Traynor to give him a hand. Traynor hauled him over the threshold, and into the roof space.

'And there's someone living there, is there? In the Abbey Gatehouse.'

'Yes, Mr Jackson. There's a sort of tenement up there over the arch, and it's occupied by a man called Syme. Obadiah Syme. He's the general porter, and gatekeeper. Syme's a devious, sly kind of man, and I've had my eye on him for years. A shifty individual altogether.'

'Has he got a criminal record?'

'No, he hasn't, but that's probably more through luck than judgement. He spends more time than he should in the alehouse, and he's got some shady friends. But he's not a villain, Mr Jackson, not what you and I would call a villain, leastways. Do you want to ask him a few questions? He's at home now, by the look of things.'

                    *   *   *

Obadiah Syme greeted his visitors with a kind
of writhing, placatory unctuousness. He all but
bowed the three men into the large room
above the gatehouse, when they had climbed
the steep stone stairs set in the massive wall,
and knocked on his stout oak door.

'Why, Inspector Traynor! This is an honour,
sir! And these gentlemen are your friends?
Any friend of yours, sir, is a friend of mine. Sit
down, gentlemen. You've caught me at a slack
moment, before the calls of duty take me down
to the lodge again.'

It was not an easy thing, thought Jackson, to
find a place to sit down in that squalid place.
There seemed to be no distinction between
living and sleeping quarters, just an
amorphous continuity of broken furniture,
rags, old mattresses and grimy blankets, and
packing-cases used as tables for the reception
of stale and decaying scraps of food. The room
was full of liquor bottles, some half empty, and
the close atmosphere reeked of stale beer. The
three men stood at the door, and observed
their unshaven, loose-mouthed host.

'This gentleman is Detective Inspector
Jackson,' said Traynor curtly. 'That other man
is Detective Sergeant Bottomley. We're all
here to investigate the murder of Dean
Girdlestone.'

'Oh, to think of that good man done to death! Picked up like a rag doll, and thrown down on to the roof! Even our clergy aren't safe! Perhaps we'll all be murdered in our beds—'

'Like a rag doll? What do you mean by that?'

Inspector Traynor's voice echoed sharply from the stone walls of the room. Jackson watched his uniformed colleague, and realized that it would be better not to interfere. Traynor knew the wiles and ways of his own customers. Best let him be.

Traynor stood in front of the cowering porter, who was sitting on a broken wooden chair near the fireplace. He stooped, placed his hands on his knees, and looked Syme straight in the eyes.

'Like a rag doll, was he? And thrown down on to the roof? Who told you that? Or if you saw it that day through that telescope of yours, why didn't you tell anybody about it? Or were you in with the man who did it, and kept mum until today, when the drink loosened your lips? Accessory to murder—that means, Syme, that when we hang the man who did it, we'll hang you, as well—'

'I was afraid to speak, Mr Traynor!' The porter's voice rose to a shriek. 'I'm a poor man, and there's many who are prejudiced against me. Besides, my sight's not good, and my hand's not always steady. But I had nothing

195

to do with the murder. Dean Girdlestone was very good to me. There's some who wanted to dismiss me, but he wouldn't hear of it.'

'What did you see, Obadiah?' asked Traynor, softly. 'Just tell these gentlemen and me. That was my little joke, you know. Nobody's going to hang you. Not yet, leastways.'

'It was that Thursday afternoon, sir. I set my old clock on the mantelpiece there right by the cathedral clock most afternoons. I use that old brass telescope on the window sill there to see the time. Well, it was just on three when I turned my telescope on to the tower, and at that moment I saw—I saw a figure, sir, a man, bent forward, and carrying what seemed to be a body in his arms. He came out of that door above the clerestory, and threw the body down on to the roof. I thought he glanced this way for a moment, and I dropped the telescope with fright, and when I looked again, he'd gone.'

Jackson had walked over to the window, and trained the telescope on the gap between the roofs. He could see the door quite clearly, but the nave roof below was hidden by the stone gables and turrets above the great cathedral windows.

'And you didn't see who it was?' asked Traynor. 'That would be too much to hope for.'

'No, sir.' For a moment the porter's shifty

eyes failed to meet the inspector's steady, rather contemptuous gaze. 'No, sir. All I can say was, that it was a man. It's been a heavy burden on my conscience, gentlemen, and I'm relieved now that I've told you. I hope you won't hold my secrecy against me? A poor man feels powerless, unless he had good friends in high places. Dean Girdlestone was a good man, and so is Dean Arkwright. Very generous and understanding—'

'You're to keep this to yourself, do you hear?' said Traynor, curtly. 'Not a word to anyone, or I'll be back to ask more questions.'

The three policemen left the unctuous porter to his own devices, and made their way across Abbey Yard.

'So he was killed in the roof space, most likely,' said Jackson, 'and then hauled out of that door, and dumped out of sight on the roof. That was a very good piece of work, Inspector, if I may say so. That man Syme probably knows more than he cares to admit. Killed in the roof space . . .'

'There was a lot of blood up there in that stone chamber above the cathedral ceiling,' said Sergeant Bottomley. 'There was blood on the floor, and splashed on to the doorposts. I've been thinking about adzes and mattocks, and other handy things hanging around the cathedral. But I'm wondering now, sir, whether there wasn't a bit more premeditation about this murder than we think.'

From his window high above the abbey gateway, Obadiah Syme watched the police officers as they made their way into Dean's Row. They'd have found out, anyway, he thought. That's why they'd come, because they could see that this was the only spot visible from the cathedral roof. Maybe they'd seen the gleam of his telescope today, as he'd watched them at work. It had been a slip on his part, but no great harm had been done. He'd been cute enough to plead bad eyesight as his excuse for not seeing who the killer was, and they'd believed him! Just as well, all things considered: it wouldn't do to betray the goose that laid the golden eggs.

CHAPTER NINE

HOLLOW PAGEANT

At just before ten o'clock on the morning of Monday, 14 August, there came a stir and bustle from the knot of onlookers flanking the Abbey Yard side of the gatehouse, as the funeral cortège of Dean Lawrence Girdlestone began its progress through the arch. It was a dry, misty morning, with the smell of chimney smoke about the streets, and a pale disc of sun behind the clouds. Six black horses, their dusky funeral plumes nodding in the breeze, loomed out of the mist, straining to pull the massive glass-sided hearse that gradually defined itself as it approached over the cobbles. The toiling horses were preceded by a squat, bearded man in top hat and morning coat. He carried a slender wand, which he used to measure his steps as he ordered the pace of the procession. Six younger, clean-shaven men in full black walked beside the horses.

Caroline Parrish turned to Millie, who was standing beside her on the pavement outside Number 7. They were clad in mourning, and wearing half-veils, ready for their journey, which would take them first to the cathedral, and then out to the municipal cemetery. All the cathedral clergy were already in choir, ready vested for the funeral service.

'Who is that man?' Caroline whispered. 'I've never seen the like of him before. It was a simple, homely affair when poor Uncle Alexander was buried.'

'That's the funeral furnisher, my dear. He's paging the hearse. Going in front of it from the house to the graveyard. It's a bit old-fashioned to do that, these days. I can't think what possessed Laura to go to this extreme. Poor Lawrence wasn't an ostentatious man. He'd have hated this . . . And look! Here are the chief mutes.'

Two figures emerged from the mist as the procession rumbled nearer, two men who seemed to Caroline to be the stuff of nightmares. Both were slightly built, and not very tall, but their stature was heightened by top hats swathed entirely in clinging crape. They were both clad in black from head to foot, with thick, wide sashes of marbled black silk slung across their bodies. Each man carried a kind of implement attached to a pole, but the poles, too, and whatever they carried, were hidden under palls of crape, which the men clasped firmly to the poles with black-gloved hands.

The true horror of these beings lay in their expressionless faces. Each man was bearded, but beneath the beard you could see the sternly set mouth, looking as though it had never smiled. Their eyes were fixed, dead, and staring into nothing. They looked like two guardians of the gateway to hell. Caroline closed her eyes for a moment, and when she opened them again, she found that the mutes had taken their places in the procession behind the furnisher.

Millie made some remark, but her words were lost in the noise of stout iron tyres grinding on the cobbles as the massive hearse was brought to a halt in front of Number 7. The first mourning carriage stopped behind it, precisely in front of the Deanery. Both Caroline and Millie stepped back on the pavement, as though to distance themselves from the grim vehicle.

The hearse, and its surmounting set of trembling plumes, rose nearly ten feet above the pavement. The driver, sitting high up on his seat above the horses, was enveloped in black capes, and clutched the reins in black-gloved hands. He looked as though he had been carved out of wood, as one more luxurious and useless extravagance. There was a good deal of gilt and ornamental ironwork, tasselled coach-lamps, false pillars and velvet canopies, and there, behind the polished glass, discreetly shaded by golden curtains, and embraced by fronds of the morning mist, lay the ponderous ebony coffin of Lawrence Girdlestone.

The door of the Deanery opened, and Laura Girdlestone, followed by the faithful Ballard, stepped out into the road. Laura was completely hidden from sight by the most extravagant mourning dress that Caroline had ever seen. It had a train, which slithered over the flags as Laura approached the first coach, and her all-enveloping veil fell to her waist. She did not even deign to glance at the monstrous hearse, but as she was handed up into the coach by one of the men in black, her veil was blown aside by the breeze, and Caroline saw the wicked smile of triumph that fleetingly crossed the widow's face. Then the veil fell down again, and Laura was gone.

The great hearse seemed to grow bigger by the minute, filling the narrow carriageway of Dean's Row with its threatening bulk, and shutting out the light. Caroline turned her eyes

201

away, and looked down the Row towards Abbey Yard. She gasped in surprise, and clutched Millie's arm.

'Look!' she whispered.

Stretching in an unbroken line far back into the mist was a string of plumed mourning carriages, each drawn by a single horse, with a man on the box, and flanked by two attendants in black. Others were still coming through the gatehouse, and the noise of their gradual approach resembled the rumble of distant thunder. How many were there? Twelve? Who could they be for? A few distant relatives on both sides had come to Ancaster on the previous day, lodging in various hotels. They were assembled near the entrance drive to the Bishop's Palace, and would step into one carriage when the moment came. But there was no one else. Neither Lawrence nor Laura had any close living relatives. The carriages would progress to the graveyard empty.

Millie and Caroline were helped into the second carriage, and the door was closed. Then, for a matter of ten minutes or more, the great hearse was slowly turned round in the narrow road, to the accompaniment of a discreet tattoo of wand-taps on the cobbles, delivered by the furnisher. It was a skilled and well-executed manoeuvre, but chilling in its disregard for the dignity of the man in the fine ebony coffin. The hearse proceeded on its way back to the gatehouse, and each mourning carriage turned skilfully to follow it, the furnisher's taps from his wand accompanying the whole bizarre ritual.

Millie Parrish, speaking almost between clenched teeth, said to Caroline, 'She must have known that it would be like this. She must have known; but she doesn't care.'

*   *   *

The cortège, preceded by the furnisher, made its ponderous way along St Michael Street, where a crowd of curious onlookers had already gathered, until it arrived at the great west door of Ancaster Cathedral. The vehicles came to a halt, and the massive ebony coffin was borne into the nave by six bearers, and placed on a velvet catafalque.

It was with a feeling akin to shock that Caroline saw that the cathedral nave was virtually empty. Laura, she remembered, had insisted on a private funeral. The canons and other senior clergy were vested in the choir, but the long pews were deserted apart from the handful of distant relatives who had arrived on the previous day, and the serried ranks of hired mutes, including the two guardians of the gates of hell.

The brief ritual, however, banished some of the crushing gloom and unease of the occasion. The service was sung by Canon Parrish, the choir gave beautiful renditions of

Laura's chosen hymns, and a brief, moving address was given by the Acting Dean, the Very Reverend Nicholas Arkwright.

Once outside, the actors in the great theatre of death reassembled, and orchestrated the progress of the monstrous hearse through the town centre of Ancaster, in the direction of the old town bridge across the river, further upstream. The cathedral clergy, their white surplices billowing in the breeze, had occupied three of the carriages, but the procession seemed overblown and vulgar, so that a considerable crowd of people gathered to watch the show. Caroline, sitting mutely beside Millie, looked out of the window of their carriage, and saw a few men pull their hats off as they passed, but once or twice she saw people point, and shake their heads. One or two even laughed.

'It's my opinion,' said Mr Markland, Chief Clerk of the Cathedral Treasury, who was standing on the crowded pavement in Foregate, 'that Mrs Girdlestone's gone too far, this time. All those empty carriages—when all's said and done, she's the only real mourner! She's gone too far. It's not as though Girdlestone was a bishop, or a nobleman, or anything like that.'

Mr Solomon, standing beside Markland in the crowd, gave vent to a low laugh, and nudged the clerk in the ribs.

'All it lacks, Mr Markland,' he chuckled, 'is a

nice brass band. That'd cheer things up a bit.'

Sergeant Bottomley had taken up a position at the lower end of Foregate, where the town centre began to merge subtly with the modern residential suburb of Miller's Ford. Many people stood at the upper windows of the liver-bricked villas, watching the grand progress of the late Dean Girdlestone to his final resting-place.

Bottomley could see Daft William in the crowd, smiling uncomprehendingly, and looking up at a woman in the smock of a market-woman, who was presumably William's mother. What was it that the boy had said to him, that day in the Deanery? Something about 'a week's grace' . . . He must remember. Whatever it was, something told him that he'd missed an important pointer to the truth.

Bottomley removed his hat as the plumed hearse rumbled past over the setts. The first mourning coach followed, and he caught sight of Laura Girdlestone. She had thrown back her veil, and her pallid face stood out in stark contrast to the Stygian veils.

Unless I'm very much mistaken, Bottomley thought to himself, that lady is very near to a nervous crisis. Very near indeed.

*   *   *

Once out of Miller's Ford, the procession found itself passing into open country. The

205

early mists had dissipated, and a hot orange sun hung over the summer fields. They crossed the River Best by means of the old town bridge, and almost immediately saw the modern Gothic chapels and towering monuments of Ancaster Municipal Cemetery, lying serenely in its enclosure of sandstone walls and fledgling willows.

The cortège made its way along a wide, straight avenue between the monuments until it reached the spot where Lawrence Girdlestone was to be interred. The six bearers, preceded by the furnisher and the terrifying chief mutes, carried the ebony coffin over the grass, followed by the black-veiled widow. It took only a few minutes for Walter Parrish, officiating as vicar of the cathedral benefice, to pronounce the committal, and then the coffin was lowered into the grave.

It was then that the most bizarre feature of the funeral took place. The long phalanx of empty mourning coaches had lined up along the avenue. Now, their drivers opened the doors, and each removed a heavy, ornate wreath. They walked in silence to the area of grass beside the open grave, and solemnly piled up the wreaths in vulgar profusion against the adjacent stones.

Saul Jackson stood in the shade of a drooping willow near the gates, watching the spectacle. The clergy in their robes had all obscured their personalities in the duties of their calling, so it was not possible to imagine what Canon Parrish or Dean Arkwright were thinking. The widow moved awkwardly and automatically, occasionally guided by a touch from her maid, but she gave no sign of any true engagement with the rites.

He watched the mourners disperse. They were a pathetically small crowd for so pompous a display of funeral splendour. He could see the gravediggers approaching through the headstones and crosses, their wide spades at the ready. But what was this?

A line of people was approaching the graveyard along a narrow country lane beyond the boundary wall. They were country folk, some of the men wearing peasants' smocks, and the women still in their daily working dress. They opened a small gate in the rear wall of the cemetery, and filed in, heads bowed, and arms full of freshly cut flowers. Without acknowledging the official mourners and their attendants, the country folk made their way to the grave, and reverently laid down their tribute on the grass.

Jackson suddenly realized who they were. The village of Sedley Vale was less than a mile from this spot. These were the survivors of the cholera outbreak, the men and women whom Lawrence Girdlestone had helped so selflessly in the terrible year of 1880. One of the women in the group turned, and saw him. She smiled a greeting, and then turned away with the others towards the rear gate. It was Sarah Brown.

*   *   *

'Wicked, wicked woman!'

Millie Parrish, divested of her mourning, seemed heedless of the fact that Jessie was helping her into her usual day dress of fawn silk. Millie's eyes flashed with an anger that was very rarely kindled. On such occasions, she tended to throw convention to the winds. Jessie tiptoed out of the room, and closed the door.

'But Millie—'

'There's no "but" about it, Caroline. I felt ashamed to be part of that charade. That hideous funeral car! It was like something out of a nightmare . . . And all those empty carriages—at least, not empty, because she'd had them filled with overblown wreaths, to mock him in death.'

A tear rolled down Millie's cheek.

'We were all young together, Caroline, which makes her action all the worse. Poor, clumsy Lawrence, with his awkward ways and blunt manner of speaking . . . How she must have hated him, to do that to his mortal remains today! I've never felt so angry in my life—'

Jessie suddenly appeared in the dressing-room where Millie and Caroline were sitting, her good-natured face moved with alarm.

'Oh, ma'am,' she whispered, 'Mrs Girdlestone's here! She wants to see you. Shall I show her up, now?'

'Wants to see me, does she?' asked Millie tearfully. 'Very well. Show her up, by all means.'

In a few moments Jessie ushered Laura Girdlestone into the room. Caroline looked at her. She was still in her dress of full mourning, but had discarded her long veil. She looked ghastly, but her hair was perfectly arranged, as though Ballard had hastily taken her in hand before she called at Number 7. She moved with a curious stiffness, as though she was not fully in control of her own limbs.

She opened her mouth to speak, but the enraged Millie forestalled her.

'You wicked, wicked woman!' she cried. 'How dare you show your face here after what you've just done to poor Lawrence! You knew how modest he was, and how he hated pomp, and so you deliberately debased his poor dead body with that heathen fantasy of a funeral—'

Laura Girdlestone began to scream. She staggered, and would have fallen if Caroline had not caught hold of her. Her eyes stared unblinkingly at some undefined point in space. The screaming continued, sustained by great gulps of air. It reminded Caroline of a little girl's tantrum, but it was not that.

The door opened, and Nicholas Arkwright stepped into the room. He had changed back into his usual immaculate clerical dress, and looked from his placid expression as though he had just called by invitation to partake of afternoon tea. Laura's screaming stopped abruptly. Something approaching intelligence came flooding into her staring eyes. Nicholas, almost apologetically, held out his hand.

'Come on, Laura,' he said, ignoring the others, 'I'll look after you.'

Nicholas Arkwright and Laura Girdlestone left the room together.

*   *   *

It had not been an easy task for Jackson to locate the offices of The Maple Trust. He had called on various well-known charitable institutions in London, but had received very imprecise answers. The Maple Trust? Yes, it was a very discreet affair, funded by income from investments, and donations from a prominent industrial concern. A public affair? No, it was a family trust. Very discreet, and shy of all publicity. You could try asking at Truscott & Smith's, the solicitors in Fetter Lane. They had some connection with it.

Mr Smith, of Truscott & Smith, had been cautious at first, but had gradually warmed to Jackson as the inspector unfolded the tale of Lawrence Girdlestone's cruel death. Yes, he would certainly point Jackson in the right direction. He would need to speak to a man

210

called Pendlebury. He'd find him in Holy Cross Almshouses, just off Theobald's Road, and behind Red Lion Square.

Holy Cross Almshouses had proved to be a gem of Elizabethan black-and-white timbered architecture hidden beyond the high brick buildings of the surrounding streets and squares. It was built around a central garden, brilliant with summer flowers, and boasted a minute chapel, a matching hall, and twenty-four small dwellings for aged and indigent couples. In a dim room at the back of the chapel, Inspector Jackson found Mr Edwin Pendlebury, solicitor and commissioner for oaths.

'This story that you've told me, Mr Jackson,' said Mr Pendlebury, 'is the kind of thing that arises from ignorance and misapprehension. A sum of money goes missing—in this case, fifteen thousand pounds, from the treasury of Ancaster Cathedral. Who has been dealing in large sums of money recently? The Dean. *Ergo*, the Dean is a fraud.'

Pendlebury was an alert, bright-eyed man approaching fifty. He wore pince-nez, which he now pulled off the bridge of his nose and angrily threw down on the table at which he sat. Jackson was content to wait. He sat opposite the lawyer, in a chair that faced the open door of the little office which housed the ledgers of The Maple Trust. He could see a couple of aged almsmen walking across the

211

grass, puffing away at clay pipes. Pendlebury spoke again.

'Part of the trouble, of course, is that the Canon Treasurer at Ancaster, a man called Hugh Nicholson, is out of the country. He's gone to visit his son at Taormina, in Sicily. I don't suppose anyone thought to write to him? Or to telegraph the British Legation there?'

Jackson shifted uncomfortably. This man Pendlebury was right. Ancaster had exerted its insidious parochialism, and no one had thought to look beyond its narrow confines for the answers to some urgent questions.

'You've brought me this written epitome of the case, which is very good of you, Inspector. It tells me that this information was lodged against Dean Girdlestone by the chief clerk, a man called Alfred Markland. Why did he not make contact with Nicholson? These are not rhetorical questions, Inspector; they're questions that need to be answered.'

'I'm aware that this Markland may have been over-zealous, sir,' said Jackson. 'That's why I have been as discreet as possible over this fraud business. But you'll realize, sir, that it's now peripheral to a case of murder—'

'Yes, yes, indeed. A most foul and wicked crime! Even the London papers have deigned to notice it. Did you ever meet Lawrence Girdlestone, Inspector?'

'No, sir. I know him only by report.'

'Exactly, and no doubt the reports came

212

from his various clerical rivals and cronies up there in Ancaster. Well, The Maple Trust has nothing to do with that place, and our view of Girdlestone is based upon the man's deeds. He was fond of quoting that text, you know, about faith without works being dead. And another text he liked was the one that says, "Do good by stealth". The Maple Trust, Mr Jackson, exists to throw a lifeline to the poorest people in our country. These almshouses were rescued from dereliction by the trust, and restored to be the thriving sanctuary that you see now. There are dozens of such places financed by us. We are the people behind a number of cottage hospitals. We run refuges for poor children . . .'

Pendlebury paused in his account, and seemed to be lost in thought. He suddenly tapped his pince-nez sharply on the table, and frowned.

'And all the money to pay for this great charity came from Lawrence Girdlestone and his late father, Jethro! Lawrence entered the church, but his fund of charity was well established before ever he did that. Lawrence played an active role in the dispensing of charity, but he was not a trustee. I'm a trustee—a lawyer turned accountant. Among other trustees we number Mr Gladstone, and the Bishop of London. I will not allow Lawrence Girdlestone's name to be sullied by this slander. He was a man with an unboundedly generous heart.'

'And the fifteen thousand?'

'The fifteen thousand may well have been spirited away from Ancaster, as this man Markland avers. I don't know. It's none of my business. But if it's true, then you'll have to find out who took it, because it wasn't Lawrence Girdlestone.'

Pendlebury picked up the epitome that Jackson had given him, and adjusted his pince-nez. He glanced down the sheet of paper, and then tapped it with a fingernail.

'You see here? It says that this man Markland saw Girdlestone withdraw a hundred and fifty pounds in sovereigns from Mason's Savings Bank at Sedley Vale. Quite right! He loved to deposit sums from the trust into these little country banks, and use them to pay for charitable deeds in the area. He had five accounts of that sort with country banks in Warwickshire, one at Sedley Vale, another at a place called Fort Hill—I can't recall the others at the moment, but I'll show you them in the ledger, presently. He had several similar accounts with savings banks here in London. The man liked to go about doing good by stealth. I'll show you the relevant ledgers now, recording all those transactions. Dash it all, Jackson, the man was spending his own money!'

*   *   *

Saul Jackson looked up from his desk in the back room of Warwick Police-Office, and watched Herbert Bottomley, who was drawing thoughtfully on a new cigar. He had withdrawn himself into his capacious overcoat rather like a tortoise who had thought better of emerging from his shell. His eyes were narrowed in thought.

'Were you listening to me, Sergeant?' asked Jackson. 'He was entirely innocent of any plundering of the cathedral accounts. That man Pendlebury proved his innocence to me beyond any shadow of doubt. So where does that leave us?'

'It leaves us, sir,' said Bottomley, balancing his cigar on the edge of the window sill, 'it leaves us with some very interesting documents which require some explaining. I'm thinking of a small black notebook, bound with faded tape, formerly the property of that poor man whose body was paraded by his grieving widow through Ancaster like a freak show in a travelling circus.'

'This book, in fact,' said Jackson, holding up the book that he had found in Dean Girdlestone's desk. '"A List of the Sums Removed from the Cathedral Accounts, Compiled by me, Lawrence Girdlestone, Dean, 24 July, 1893." I'm getting too old for this business, Sergeant. Why did I think this was a confession? The Dean was quite clearly making notes of a fraud that he himself had discovered. That man Markland discovered it. The Dean discovered it. Neither had any consultation with the other—'

'No, sir, because the Dean moved in different circles from the clerk, and the clerk was envious of the Dean. That notebook gives a list of bank accounts in twelve different towns dotted around England, all opened under aliases, and providing a loving home for fifteen thousand pounds. So if Dean Girdlestone didn't open them, sir, who did? Or need I ask?'

'You'll burn the window sill if you don't do something with that cigar, Sergeant. No, I don't suppose you need to ask.'

Jackson picked up a single sheet of paper from the desk, and held it up.

'Maybe *this* provides the answer. You've read it before, but it'll do no harm if I were to read it aloud.

' "Dear Girdlestone
You have asked for time to make these depredations good. I cannot jeopardize my own standing as Hereditary Steward by conceding to your request. I will call upon you, as planned, next Thursday, when I expect you to offer me your resignation. Charles Blount." '

'How is Sir Charles Blount going to explain
216

that away? He told me that Girdlestone had asked him verbally for a week's grace when he called at the Deanery that Thursday afternoon. *But the Dean was innocent.* He could not have written the letter that Blount's note was meant to answer. Dean Girdlestone had committed no crime.'

'That boy Daft William said something to me that I've forgotten,' said Bottomley. 'I'll have to speak to him again . . . So what do you propose we should do, sir?'

'I think we need to move carefully and quietly, Sergeant. I'm going to make enquiries about our good baronet. I'm also going to get in touch with this Canon Nicholson, who's out in Italy. Meanwhile, you'd better carry on with probing your Dean Arkwright's conscience, together with that of his trusty old friend Josiah Solomon. Somebody tried to sully Lawrence Girdlestone's reputation, and then killed him, so that he couldn't answer back. I want that person safe and sound in my hands, so that I can deliver him to Justice.'

CHAPTER TEN

DINNER AT LADYMEAD

Caroline Parrish sat at the massive carved and gilded desk in Sir Charles Blount's picture gallery, and made a determined effort to give her mind to business. Sir Charles did not pay her to daydream, but it was difficult to prevent her mind from wandering back to the hideous funeral, culminating in Laura's nervous collapse, and Nicholas Arkwright's dramatic intervention.

Millie had been like an avenging fury, but when Laura had finally collapsed into a state of semi-trance, the mistress of Number 7 had been immediately overwhelmed with remorseful concern. But it was Nicholas Arkwright who had taken control of the situation. He had been preternaturally calm, almost apologetic, as he led Laura away.

The mass of ancient documents that she had been engaged to catalogue had revealed no priceless lost works by Dante or Petrarch, and there wouldn't be much sale for the kitchen accounts of a sixteenth-century Milanese advocate, or for the endless transcriptions of Latin sermons into Italian.

Caroline looked up from the desk as Mr Hayden came soft-footedly into the room from the extension. He looked very suave in his formal clothes, which he wore well. He smiled, and gave her his usual half-mocking bow.

'Miss Parrish,' he said, 'I've been contriving excuses to ask you a question, but the excuses were all either too subtle, or too silly, so I'm going to ask you plainly to satisfy my curiosity. What has happened to Mrs Girdlestone? I've heard that she was totally overcome after her husband's funeral.'

'Let me tell you what happened, Mr Hayden. After the funeral, Mrs Girdlestone became ill. That, I think, is not surprising, considering the great strain that she'd been under. She was immediately taken into the charge of Dean Arkwright, who has been a friend of hers, and of her husband, for many years. Dean Arkwright made arrangements for her to be removed from the Deanery, and from Ancaster, to a place where she can begin the long process of convalescence that will be necessary to ensure her recovery.'

Mr Hayden gave Caroline an amused smile, and sat down on a gilded rococo chair near the desk. He folded his hands delicately around his knees, and subjected her to a kind of impish scrutiny.

'You said all that, Miss Parrish, as though you'd written it down first, and then learned it by rote—good heavens! That blush of vexation tells me that I was right!'

'I *did* write it down, Mr Hayden, because Dean Arkwright and I thought it would be advisable to give a judiciously prepared answer to anyone crass enough to ask us outright about Mrs Girdlestone's condition.'

Mr Hayden laughed, but there was a slightly dangerous glint in his eye as he replied.

'"Crass", hey? I suppose I deserved that, though it's not a word most people would associate with me. Well, let it pass. And what happened then? Where is she? Or am I not supposed to know?'

'There, now, Mr Hayden, you've taken offence, when it was only my intention to tease you! Of course you may know. Mrs Girdlestone is staying in the empty parsonage house at Arden Leigh. She is accompanied by her maid, Ballard, and a resident nurse.'

'And Arkwright arranged all that? Good man. Will she be seeing a doctor?'

'Oh, yes. Doctor MacLeod will visit regularly, and they're bringing down an alienist from London.' Caroline smiled, and added, 'That bit wasn't learnt by rote!'

This time, Mr Hayden gave vent to a hearty laugh. He sprang up from the chair, and started to make his way back to the extension.

'Thank you for telling me all that, Miss Parrish. Sir Charles will be interested to hear about it. How splendid of Dean Arkwright!'

Caroline worked steadily for the next half-hour, preparing index cards for another batch of musty, dog-eared manuscripts. The bewildering array of shallow drawers was crammed with all kinds of discarded papers, including restaurant bills, yellowing theatre programmes, and invitation cards. Evidently, Sir Charles used the extravagant piece of furniture as a general repository for unwanted trifles.

At half past three, Caroline put her work

aside, and wandered out into the spacious hall of the house. The airy lightness of the place, provided by the large skylight in the roof, had attracted her from the time of her first visit, and it had become something of a habit for her to climb the wide stairs, and pause on each of the landings. On the first floor, she stopped to admire the fairy-tale clock that told the time of a hundred years back. Hadn't Sir Charles told her that it had been created for an Egyptian pasha? That would account for the five ponderous basalt figures of Anubis standing guard, as ever, around the clock.

From where she stood she could see up to the second floor, where the huge oil-painting of Sir Charles's Italian villa hung at the head of the staircase. The whole wall seemed to be occupied by the depiction of the long, stuccoed villa, with its classical portico, and frame of cypresses.

Five statues? Surely, last time she'd been up here, there had only been four? There had been five, when she'd first come to the house, but one had not been there on the last occasion that she'd noticed them. It had been on the day that Dean Girdlestone was killed. They were sinister figures, those jackal-headed monstrosities, but not as sinister as the black-robed guardians of the gates of hell who had preceded Lawrence Girdlestone to the grave.

The first statue seemed to be discoloured, as though there had been a vein of some intrusive mineral running through the basalt. Caroline stretched out her hand to pick it up.

'What are you doing?'

Caroline's heart gave a great leap of alarm, and the blood pulsed at her temples. She drew her hand back in fright, as though the image itself had rapped out those sharp, urgent words. She looked up, and saw that Sir Charles Blount was observing her from the second-floor landing. For a moment, she experienced a feeling of wild panic, but then the baronet smiled, and came lightly down the stairs to her side.

'You were admiring the painting of my Italian villa, I think?' he said. She nodded, not yet trusting herself to speech. She contrived not to look at the jackal-headed statues standing guard over the pasha's clock. Sir Charles glanced upward towards the painting.

'It deserves a better setting than that, Miss Parrish,' he said, 'but it's so confoundedly big, that it would dwarf far better works of art if I had it brought downstairs. You really must come out with us to Taormina one day, and experience the place. It's haunted by the spirits of the ancient Roman poets and philosophers; and surrounded by acres of enchanted woods. Some little way off, you will find the deep blue waters of the Mediterranean, and the magic of the little coastal ports.'

As Sir Charles spoke, the picture on the landing seemed to fade, to be replaced by something more vivid and real. Sir Charles was describing not a dead palace of antiquity but a living house, a place large enough to contain his overpowering personality. She had lost all fear of him, and felt instead the mesmerizing attraction that such men always held for her sex.

'However,' said Sir Charles, seeming to wake from his own romantic reverie, 'the villa can wait until later this year. My next concern will be a celebratory dinner for Dean Arkwright, here, at Ladymead. I'd value your opinion about that, Miss Parrish. In view of poor Girdlestone's death, and the recent funeral, do you think I should postpone it? I'd pencilled in next Monday, the 21st. What do you think?'

'I should go ahead with it, Sir Charles. Dean Arkwright is in sore need of some kind of respite from his many cares and troubles. By all means, make it next Monday.'

'It will be a small, intimate affair—not one of the great banquets that I give here from time to time. I want to thank him for all that he's done for Ancaster, but also for what he is doing for that poor, lost woman, Lawrence Girdlestone's widow. I expect you know that Laura Girdlestone was confined for six years to an asylum in the seventies? She seems to have made a complete recovery, but one can never be sure in these cases. So Arkwright deserves some public thanks for his care and concern.'

Still talking about Nicholas Arkwright, Sir Charles Blount accompanied Caroline downstairs. He seemed quite unaware that he had mentioned a dark episode in Laura's personal history that had been entirely unknown to her. And all the time that he was talking, Caroline was thinking about the jackal-headed statues. Had there been four? Or five?

*   *   *

Monday's celebratory dinner for Nicholas Arkwright at Ladymead saw Sir Charles Blount presiding from a ponderous carving-chair at one end of his long dining-table, which glowed with silver and crystal. Dean Arkwright had been placed at the far end of the table, facing his host. To Blount's right sat Millie and Walter Parrish, and Canon Hall, the Rector of Ancaster. Caroline sat to Blount's left, and next to her the Mayor of Ancaster, Alderman Thomas Hargreaves, an industrialist who owned the lead works in Pitt Lane. A widower, he was a solid man of sixty or so, with a florid face and close-cropped white hair. Beside the mayor was Mrs Hall, a small, taciturn lady, much given to smiling agreement with everything that the others said.

Oyster soup was served, and one of the waiters hired for the night poured chilled hock delicately into tall green fluted glasses. Arkwright savoured the embrace of extreme luxury, and sipped his hock.

'You're right, Sir Charles,' he said, looking down the long table at the baronet, 'we all misjudged him. I was the chief sinner in that respect. I had no idea of the regard in which he held me, or of the great good that he did by stealth. He and I disagreed occasionally, but I always respected him.'

'Did you?' The baronet's tone held a subtle hint of mockery.

'Yes, I did,' replied Nicholas stoutly. 'Respected him, I mean. But I should have given him more than mere respect.'

Yes, poor Lawrence had deserved more than mere respect. The Dean's anguished confession to feelings of inferiority in his private journal had liberated Nicholas from the toils of jealousy, leaving him curiously calm, no longer in thrall to festering resentments. The 'deformed and savage slave' that old Bishop Grandison had detected lurking in his body had departed.

It was as the empty soup plates were removed that Alderman Hargreaves began to talk about Lawrence Girdlestone. He was gifted with the ability to eat and talk at the same time, without doing injustice to either activity. He spoke with robust appreciation of the late Dean, whom he had known well, as they were both Commissioners of the Poor

Law.

'Dean Girdlestone gave a lot of money to Missions, you know,' he said. 'Not many people knew about that. Girdlestone was almost desperately modest, and didn't like people talking about his generosity. He established a splendid school in Mashonaland, and later funded a clinic there. All out of his own funds, you know. Wonderful, really.'

A savoury of anchovies was brought in. Arkwright covertly watched the Mayor of Ancaster, and saw how his eyes sparkled with affectionate recall. He began to recount what Girdlestone had told him about the mission school, at the same time making short work of the savoury.

Nicholas thought to himself: this is a memorial meal for Lawrence as much as a celebration of my good fortune. Quite right, too. He was already beginning to miss the Dean physically, expecting him to appear in the pulpit, or at the lectern, or to come striding along Dean's Row, hell bent on some new scheme or other . . .

Thank God he'd taken Laura away, before the wretched tongues began to wag! She was safe out at Arden Leigh. He'd already secured Bishop Grandison's consent to make use of the house until a new rector was appointed. Meanwhile, one of his own curates from St Mary in Campo would take the Sunday services at Arden Leigh.

226

Millie Parrish had shocked poor Laura out of her carapace of resentment by a kind of moral frontal attack. It had been at the expense of Laura's nervous stability, but it had been the best thing that could have happened to her. Another few weeks of that mad hatred of her dead husband, and she would have been back in St Clare's Asylum. No one, thank God! knew about that dark period of her early life. No one, in Ancaster, at any rate, apart from Sir Charles Blount. He knew, because one of his cousins had been a doctor at St Clare's when Laura was confined there. But Sir Charles was a born diplomat, and the soul of discretion.

Despite the many crosses that she had had to bear, Laura hadn't changed much over the years. Her hair was still raven-black, her dark eyes bright and restless. He and Ballard between them would cleanse the Deanery of poor Laura's dependent liquors later that week.

The suite of servants hired for the evening brought in roast saddle of lamb and its accompaniments. An impressive man in the livery of a butler poured out the vintage St Julien, 1880, with the necessary religious awe. The conversation drifted towards the subject of idolatry. Arkwright wondered whether it was Sir Charles Blount or Canon Hall, who had broached the topic.

'I must confess,' said Sir Charles, 'that

227

Girdlestone's fixation about idolatry vexed me considerably. He couldn't seriously believe that people actually worshipped "stocks and stones"—I wonder where that phrase comes from? Somewhere in the Old Testament?'

Walter Parrish paused with his fork halfway to his mouth. 'Milton,' he said, and consumed another tender portion of roast lamb.

'Wasn't there some talk of taking the Ancaster Guardians down altogether? Somebody mentioned it to me the other day. I wonder whether poor Girdlestone would have risked the wrath of the townsfolk by doing that?'

'Oh, but Sir Charles,' said Caroline, 'Dean Girdlestone had actually told Mr Solomon to begin taking them down. Mr Conrad Arkwright told me about it. You heard Dean Girdlestone say so, didn't you, Mr Arkwright?'

'Is that true, Arkwright?' asked Sir Charles. 'Had Girdlestone actually told Solomon to commit iconoclasm?'

'Yes, he had. Very insistent he was, too—'

Nicholas Arkwright felt himself turn pale. He was conscious of seven faces turned towards him where he sat in solemn state at the end of the table. Why had he said that? He'd never heard Girdlestone say any such thing! It had all been part of a bad dream. Solomon had reassured him that he had been sound asleep all that afternoon. Solomon . . .

'At least, that was the impression I got—a

228

general impression, you know. I can't actually recall any such conversation. In any case, the matter's purely academic, now. Nothing is going to happen to the Guardians.'

A welcome interruption came with the serving of a confection of water-ice, which was followed by cheese. Coffee was served at the table, and instead of the ritual port, a choice of liqueurs was offered. After half an hour the company rose and, as they left the dining-room, Sir Charles drew Arkwright aside. His manner was conspiratorial.

'Arkwright,' he said, 'can you give me coffee tomorrow morning, at about eleven? At your house, I mean. I'm going to pay a call on that fellow Syme, in the Abbey Gatehouse. I've seen you giving him money from time to time—I don't know whether that's wise, you know: it'll all go on drink. But that's by the way. I'm convinced that Syme knows something about Girdlestone's murder. I think he actually saw who did it, and I'm going to beard him in his den tomorrow, and task him with it.'

'You think he did the murder?'

'No, no, you're not listening to me, man! I think he knows who did do it. I'm going to get the truth out of him tomorrow, and when I've done so, I want to tell you, quite confidentially, at your house. May I call upon you?'

'Of course, Sir Charles. I shall look forward to seeing you. But really, Syme is just a devious would-be rogue. There's no harm in him. Walter Parrish is working on him, I believe, as a sort of pastoral project.'

'Well, we'll see. But come, the others will be wondering what's detained us. It's been a splendid evening, Arkwright! I hope that you'll regard this little celebration as the true beginning of your work here as Dean of Ancaster.'

'Acting Dean, Sir Charles! Though I must thank you most sincerely for this evening's hospitality. I feel very much at peace with everyone and everything tonight.'

'I'm glad. As for "Acting Dean"—well, leave things to the fullness of time, and the machinations of your friends. You may well find that the ultimate prize is virtually within your grasp.'

*   *   *

It was after eleven o'clock when Sir Charles Blount's carriage stopped in front of the Abbey Gatehouse. Syme hurried through the archway to open the doors, bowing and smirking, his hand held out, as always, for a tip. Canon Parrish smiled, but shook his head. Canon Hall seemed not to notice the man at all. Dean Arkwright, almost without thinking, pressed two half-crowns into his eager hand.

'Why do you indulge that horrible man, Mr Arkwright?' asked Caroline. 'The more

230

you give him, the more he'll expect.'

'Miss Parrish is right, you know, Mr Dean,' said Canon Hall. 'That type of man, given the opportunity, will begin to take liberties.'

'I suppose you're right, George,' said Nicholas to Canon Hall. 'And you, Caroline. But I'm sorry for the man. Everybody's hand seems to be against him, merely because he lacks some of the social graces. I'll think over what you've said, though. Good night. I'll see you all in the morning.'

Arkwright walked through the pleasant night air down towards the town wall. The line of gas lamps in Dean's Row threw pools of yellow light upon the pavement, and there were still lamps glowing in the windows of the gracious old houses. He descended the thirty steps into Friary Street, and let himself into his house. He paused in the hall to strike a match, and light one of the wall-mounted oil lamps. He removed his top coat, and groped his way along the passage to his study. He lit the candles on the mantelpiece, and sat down in his favourite chair.

What was it that disturbed the pleasant memories of the dinner at Ladymead? It was that remark of Caroline's about Solomon and the Ancaster Guardians. Girdlestone, she said, had ordered Josiah Solomon to take down the images. She said that he, Nicholas, had told Conrad about it. But that had been a dream, part of his long sleep on that fatal Thursday afternoon, when Girdlestone was murdered. They were words that he had imagined. Had he unconsciously let them slip out in some chance remark to his son?

Nicholas sat up in his chair. Somebody was standing in the garden—standing apparently motionless against the wall separating the Prebendary's House from Pitt Lane, and the ever-busy lead works beyond. It was that man Bottomley. What was he doing there? He must have come in through the garden gate. How dare he! What did it mean?

Nicholas Arkwright strode across the room, threw open the French window, and stepped out into the cool night air.

'What do you want? It's Sergeant Bottomley, isn't it? What are you doing here?'

Sergeant Bottomley moved out of the shadows into the light. He was dressed in a rather loud check suit, over which he wore his yellow overcoat open. He removed his hat, and gave Nicholas a clumsy half bow.

'I want to have a quiet word with you, sir, if I may. I came in the back way so as not to set the neighbours' tongues wagging. Most of the folk in this street know who I am by now, and what it is I do for a living.'

'You'd better come in, Sergeant. I must say, you choose the most unconscionable hours to pay your calls. Sit down there, and state your business.'

Sergeant Bottomley lowered himself

232

carefully into one of the two chairs flanking the fireplace. He removed his hat, and put it down carefully on the floor beside him.

'While you were dining with Sir Charles Blount at Ladymead, sir,' he said, 'I rode over from Warwick to Ancaster along the country lanes. When I got to that flat stretch of country above Ancaster Old Bridge, I saw the town cemetery spread out among the trees in the moonlight. I tethered the horse in the lane, and walked through the graves until I came to the spot where Dean Girdlestone lies.'

Nicholas Arkwright stirred uneasily. It was dim in the study, with only the candles flickering on the mantelpiece. He should have lit the two oil lamps. There was something eerie and disturbing about this big, clumsy man, sitting there motionless, and talking about his nocturnal visit to the cemetery.

'I stood beside that mound of flowers and wreaths, sir, all grey and pale in the moonlight, and I told him that I would seek out his murderer, and bring him to the gallows. Then I walked back to the lane, unhitched the horse, and rode here to Ancaster.'

Bottomley's voice was that of a Warwickshire countryman, quiet, and rather slow, but bearing a weight of earnestness that suggested a hidden menace. From somewhere in the obscure depths of his memory, Arkwright heard Lawrence Girdlestone's voice. He was telling Solomon to start work on

233

detaching the Ancaster Guardians from the tower. Could a man have heard such purposeful, coherent instructions being given by one dream figure to another?

'You know how he died, don't you, sir? Dean Girdlestone, I mean?'

'He was struck down—'

'Yes, sir, he was. He was murdered in the roof space, attacked with a heavy hooked instrument, and then his dead or dying body was hurled out on to the cathedral roof. There was blood everywhere, sir, on the doorposts, the threshold, the walls. That was the way of things: slaughtered, and thrown down like a carcass at the butchers. The Very Reverend Lawrence Girdlestone, MA, departed this life August the third, 1893, aged forty-eight years.'

The candles on the mantelpiece began to splutter, and go out. Nicholas rose unsteadily, and with trembling hands lit the two shaded oil lamps standing in the room.

'Why are you telling *me* these dreadful things?'

'I'm telling you these things, reverend sir, because while that murder was being carried out, you were sleeping like a little child in the St Catherine Chapel—sleeping for two hours, if Mr Solomon's to be believed. In all that time, Mr Arkwright, didn't you have any dreams?'

'Dreams? Yes, I did. I'll tell you what they were, Sergeant Bottomley, because I suspect that you don't trust me. I dreamt first that I was walking in the north transept of the cathedral. I fancied that I heard the Dean's voice. He was ordering Mr Solomon, the Clerk of the Works, to prepare the statues on the tower for removal to the south churchyard.'

Sergeant Bottomley had produced a very small notebook from his overcoat pocket, together with a stub of pencil. He began to write.

'Can you recall the Dean's exact words, sir? Or is it all just a jumble?'

'No, Sergeant, it was not a jumble. He said, "When your men have finished on the chapel roof Solomon, they can go up on to the leads and make some preliminary experiments in detaching those idols from the tower. If all goes well, they can be taken down, and lowered by winch into the old burial ground below the south wall."'

'And what did Mr Solomon say to that?'

'He said that the angels were very dear to Ancaster folk, and that they'd been there from before the Reformation. The Dean said, "I've decided that they must go, and go they shall! They are rags and remnants of superstition, and misleaders of simple faith."'

Arkwright heard Sergeant Bottomley sigh. The sigh was followed by at least a minute of silence. Then Bottomley spoke.

'Would I be correct, sir, in thinking that you were much the same age as the late unfortunate Dean Girdlestone?'

'What? Yes, he and I were the same age, give or take a few weeks.'

'So you are forty-eight, sir, which means that you've reached the years of discretion. Only little children confuse fact with fantasy. You must know, and therefore must admit, that what you've just described to me was reality, not dreaming. Why not admit, sir, that you walked out of that chapel and into the north transept, and that you did indeed hear the Dean and Solomon holding that conversation? You know that what I'm saying is true.'

'Solomon assured me that I was sound asleep for two hours—'

'Solomon may have been mistaken, sir. He could hardly have sat beside you for those two hours. Or perhaps he wanted to spare you any unpleasantness. I gather you and he have always been fast friends, despite the difference in class.'

'Perhaps. But how could I have walked in the north transept and not known that I was doing it? And of what importance is all this business of recollection?'

'Sir, on Monday, the thirty-first of July, you went to see Dr Arthur Savage MD, at Copton Vale, and he prescribed you some special medicine—'

'How did you know that? Good heavens, Sergeant, what possible business can that be of yours? What are you implying?'

'I'm implying nothing, sir, but it's an open secret here in Ancaster that you have been afflicted all your life with the falling-sickness. That becomes my business, sir, when I'm investigating a case of murder. Dr Savage and I know each other well. We were both involved in that Burton Viscount affair last year. So when I told him that I needed to know what he'd prescribed for you, he told me. I think that when you went "sleep-walking" out of the St Catherine Chapel on that fatal day, sir, you were suffering from an overdose of bromide.'

Herbert Bottomley retrieved his hat from the floor, and stood up.

'I'll leave you now, sir,' he said. 'I'm sure we'll meet again, some time very soon, when we can have a further talk. Perhaps there's more that you could remember about those dreams of yours.'

Nicholas Arkwright watched Sergeant Bottomley move lightly through the darkened garden. Presently, he heard the latch click on the rear gate. He was alone at last.

What if Bottomley was right? Those other dreams—he must face up to them and defeat their menace once and for all. He had dreamed of going up the ladders after Girdlestone. What if that had been true? And after that, what had he done? Yes! He remembered seeing a figure, its back turned, a figure in black broadcloth standing motionless

237

in the open doorway above the clerestory. He'd rushed forward, arms outstretched, to send his enemy falling to his death. But had his hands actually reached the figure? Surely, he could remember now, feeling the touch of the broadcloth on his open palms?

Nicholas Arkwright broke out into a sweat. This was something entirely new, something conjured up by that cunning sergeant's suggestions, and talk about bromides. Yes, the figure had stood in the opening, and he had pushed . . . Later, he had raised himself up from the floor, resting for a while on all fours, before staggering towards the open door. He had looked down, and seen Girdlestone's body spread-eagled on the leads far below. He had pushed the sight far away into the depths of his mind, and forgotten it.

And then? More darkness, followed by the horrible realization that he was sitting hunched up against one of the rough stone walls in the roof space above the clerestory. He had thought it was a dream. What if it had been the dreadful truth? He had looked at his hands, and they had been covered in blood. He had wiped it off with his handkerchief, and flung it away in horror. What if that had been true?

It *had* been true. Faithful Josiah Solomon had found that handkerchief, washed it, and posted it back to him. Josiah had known that he had killed Girdlestone, and had decided to protect him. That fact must remain a fast secret between the two men. Solomon must not be allowed to suffer the supreme penalty as an accessory to murder, if the truth ever came to light.

The blood was a problem. When, and by what means, had he struck the fatal blow? His recollections were still confused. He would bide his time, and see how things fell out.

CHAPTER ELEVEN

DEAN ARKWRIGHT'S FOLLY

'I was right about Syme,' said Sir Charles Blount. 'Apparently, he'd already admitted to the police that he'd seen Girdlestone's murderer throwing the body down on to the cathedral roof.'

Nicholas Arkwright had seen the baronet descending the thirty steps, and had opened the front door of the Prebendary's House before Sir Charles had crossed Friary Street. He looked pale, as though he had faced a difficult encounter with Syme. He had followed Nicholas into the study, and had flung himself down in a chair facing the window. The coffee was already brewed, and Nicholas had poured out cups for them both. It was just after eleven o'clock.

'He'd seen the murder committed?'

'Apparently. He told Inspector Traynor that he couldn't identify the killer, but his demeanour this morning suggests that he knows who it was well enough. Oh, yes, he knows, all right!'

Nicholas watched the baronet sipping his strong black coffee, and felt an unaccountable leap of fear. What had the wretched fellow seen? He felt once more the yielding warmth of broadcloth beneath his outstretched hands, and saw in his mind's eye the figure of Lawrence Girdlestone sprawled out dead on the nave roof. What had that appalling man Bottomley really thought, when he had encouraged him to see his dreams as fatal realities? And was that a gleam of knowing speculation in Blount's eye? Had Syme—?

'I wish you'd go up there now, Arkwright, and talk to him,' said Blount, putting his coffee cup down on the table. 'Talk to Syme, I mean. He's on the verge of making a clean breast of it, I'm sure, and a word from you will tip the scales. I know he has a high regard for you, and I've seen you giving him small sums of money, which I'm sure will have made him well disposed towards you. If anyone can prise the truth from him, it will be you.'

Why did Blount mention those sums of money? Perhaps he thought that he was paying Syme to keep silence? That look in Blount's dark eyes—fathomless, enigmatic . . . Did

240

Blount think that he, Nicholas, had murdered Girdlestone? And did he think that Syme had seen him do it?

Suddenly, Blount sprang to his feet, and stood looking out on to Arkwright's untidy garden.

'Do you know, Arkwright, I'm almost sure that Syme is lurking in your garden at this very moment, somewhere beyond that clump of laurel bushes! Just go out and see, won't you? If it's really he, we can clear up the whole business here and now.'

Nicholas Arkwright did not reply for a moment. He found himself staring at Blount's broad back as he stood, motionless, at the French window. For some reason, the baronet's presence suddenly unnerved him. He felt a curious tingling in his hands, and wondered in horror whether he was about to experience an attack of grand mal. Muttering a brief reply, he tore his eyes from the baronet's back, and left the room.

Arkwright was relieved to go out into the garden, away from those dark, speculative eyes. It was difficult not to feel that some unspecified disaster was approaching. Something dreadful was about to happen, but it was something amorphous, indefinable ...

There was no sign of Obadiah Syme in the garden, and the door leading out into Pitt Lane was locked. Arkwright returned to the study through the French window.

'There's no one there, Sir Charles,' he said.

The baronet had resumed his chair near the fireplace, and was finishing his coffee. He looked slightly guilty, and for the moment rather foolish.

'I'm so sorry, Arkwright,' he said. 'I felt sure that someone was lurking out there. Well, there's no harm done. Finish your coffee, and then oblige me by going up to Abbey Yard. A frontal attack from the two of us will surely persuade Syme to tell what he knows.'

*   *   *

As Nicholas Arkwright walked over the cobbles of Abbey Yard, the uneven surface seemed to shift and buck beneath his feet. Why did he stagger so? Perhaps he'd taken too big a dose of Savage's foul concoction that morning. Thank goodness the square was deserted! He felt desperately tired, and his mind was beginning to fill with unwelcome images. Part of his brain still conjured up the figure in broadcloth standing motionless in the exit to the cathedral roof. Why had his hands been soaked in blood? The cobbles heaved and shifted, and by the time he reached the gatehouse he had to steady himself by clinging to the rough masonry of the arch.

Syme looked surprised to see him when he opened the door of his squalid tenement above the gatehouse. The dim room seemed shapeless, and it wasn't possible to see Syme clearly among the mass of old packing crates and mattresses. He could hear his voice, though, at times slimy and devious, at other times rising to a kind of craven truculence, giving evasive replies to the few questions that Nicholas managed to ask him.

'Sir Charles had better keep his own counsel, Mr Dean, if he knows what's good for him . . . No, I didn't recognize anyone, I tell you. It'd be better for all concerned, sir, if you didn't ask any more questions. It mightn't be wise. What? No. But maybe one day I'll remember who the man was, and that would set the cat among the pigeons. You've always been decent to me, Mr Dean, so I'm advising you to take no more interest in the matter. Leave it to the police, to Inspector Traynor. You don't look well, sir, fearful pale, you are, and swaying on your feet. Go home, Mr Dean, and lie down. It's your sickness coming on . . .'

Syme's face glowed like a dim sun in a hazy sky, and his voice began to echo around the room. Nicholas staggered, and his hands slid across the top of one of the packing cases. He heard a plate fall to the floor, and found himself grasping a knife. Did Syme think that he was the man who had killed Girdlestone?

For a few moments all went black, and when Nicholas recovered his senses, he found himself all but falling down the narrow staircase in the thickness of the gatehouse wall. He felt as though he was in a trance. Why should he think of broadcloth? Why did he feel that his empty hand was still grasping a knife?

He was able to comport himself reasonably well as he made his way back along Dean's Row, and down the thirty steps. When he finally got into his house, he staggered into the study. The coffee pot was still warm, and he refilled his empty cup. Even the coffee tasted foul! He collapsed on to the sofa, and fell immediately into a fitful, haunted sleep.

*　　　*　　　*

Caroline Parrish had reached the end of her cataloguing work. The vast accumulation of old Italian letters and documents, and the tedious Latin treatises, had yielded to her methodical approach, and a decent card index of all the relevant items now existed.

There were, however, numerous more amorphous masses of paper in the many drawers of the antique bureau that seemed to be crying out for the attention of a dedicated tidier. It was nearly twelve, so she could spend half an hour putting all the mess into some kind of shape. She opened the top row of drawers, extracted the contents, and spread it across the writing-desk.

What a collection of useless detritus! Here was one side of a correspondence about new drains beneath the cathedral vestries, with many yellowed letters from someone called Canon Ellison, across which Sir Charles had scrawled brief comments in black ink. The letters dated from 1889. They had been screwed up, and should have been destined for Sir Charles Blount's wickerwork waste-paper basket in his study. Mr Hayden usually emptied the contents of the basket into the basement stove. Perhaps, on some occasions, he simply stuffed the unwanted paper into the drawers of the capacious writing-desk, to save himself a journey. Caroline smoothed the letters out, and put them aside to await a cardboard folder.

Here was a series of letters from Dean Girdlestone to Sir Charles, all on the stultifying subject of the composition of quorums for irregular meetings of the Foundation. These had been tied loosely together with faded pink twine, and thrust to the back of their particular drawer. It seemed hardly worth the trouble of preserving them, but they had better be given a folder of their own.

Here was another screwed-up letter from Dean Girdlestone to Sir Charles . . .

Caroline almost cried out with shock. The great white gallery seemed to spin round, and for a moment she thought that she was going to faint. It was imperative for her to get out of Ladymead and back to Ancaster as soon as possible. Neither Sir Charles nor Mr Hayden was in the house, so she could leave unnoticed. Her friend Nicholas Arkwright would have to see this letter. He would know what to do.

She thrust the letter into one of the large patch-pockets of her costume jacket, and all but ran from the house, her heart beating madly against her ribs. What if she met them, as they were coming back to Ladymead over the bridge? Would she be able to mask her fear and shock? To her relief, the elegant suspension bridge was deserted, but as she stepped on to it, she saw a sinister plume of black smoke arising from somewhere in the area of the cathedral. At the same time, she heard the distant clanging of a fire engine's bell.

*　　　*　　　*

In St Michael Street a considerable crowd had gathered to gaze mutely at the smoking ruins of the burnt-out upper storey of the gatehouse. The fire engine stood on the streaming cobbles, a tangle of hoses lying around its wheels. Its brightly-polished steam engine was gently hissing. Two strong shire horses stood patiently between the shafts. Caroline looked up at the empty windows, now mere gashes in the brickwork, each outlined with an irregular bursting star of soot. The exposed roof beams of the gatehouse still smouldered, but the fire had been extinguished.

The fire master, in his navy-blue uniform and shining brass helmet, appeared in the arch, and there was a murmur from the crowd. He was joined by a smart man in police uniform, and the crowd watched as they whispered to each other. The policeman turned to the waiting crowd.

'Friends,' he said, 'I've bad news for you. Obadiah Syme, the gateman, is dead. I'll ask you all to stand well back while the firemen bring the body down. Stand back! Leave the carriageway free.'

The people obeyed, but they did not disperse. Caroline heard someone say to his neighbour, 'What's happening in Ancaster? First the old Dean, and now Obadiah Syme. There's demons broke free in Cathedral Green.'

The crowd fell quiet again as four firemen appeared in the archway, carrying an unscrewed door, on which lay a sheeted figure. At the same time, a heavy, olive-green police van rumbled into sight at the end of St Michael Street. It drew to a halt in front of the arch, and the remains of the gatekeeper were lifted into it.

At that moment, Caroline saw Nicholas Arkwright appear at the gate. He seemed agitated, and he had begun to talk excitedly to the police officer. It was vital that Dean Arkwright saw the letter that she had discovered. She tried to force her way through the crowd, but by the time she had gained the opposite pavement, the police officer and the Dean had climbed into the van, the doors had been slammed, and the vehicle had rumbled off towards the town. One of the firemen had begun to reel in the hose. Caroline asked him a question.

'Where are they taking that poor man's body? Was he burnt to death?'

The fireman, a young fellow with a soot-smeared face, looked at her with an expression of scarcely concealed distaste. He'd no time for morbid busybodies.

'Inspector Traynor's taking him to the police mortuary in Canal Street, miss. Dean Arkwright's gone with him.'

He turned his attention to his work in a gesture of curt dismissal which made Caroline feel awkward and gauche. She noticed that he had not answered her second question. She was sorry about poor Syme, but she must not let his death interfere with her need to see Nicholas Arkwright. She turned her back on the ruined gatehouse, and walked rapidly down St Michael Street towards the cab rank.

*　　　*　　　*

Dr James Venner MD, still fastening the five 'doctor's buttons' on the right sleeve of his frock coat, came into the bleak mortuary office, where Inspector Traynor was waiting for him. Really, he thought, this uniformed policeman improved on acquaintance. He must have deliberately practised looking so stolid and unimaginative, because beneath the wooden exterior there lurked a very capable investigator who was nobody's fool.

'Well, Inspector, I've done an immediate post-mortem, as you requested. It's not something I like to do in the normal way of things, but you were right to suggest it. Obadiah Syme did not die as the result of the fire in the gatehouse. There was no soot or other products of combustion in the lungs, so he did not die of smoke inhalation. There were no significant burns on the body. There were tubercular lesions in both lungs. The liver was much decayed by cirrhosis.'

'And how did he meet his death, sir? The fire master—'

'The fire master was right, Inspector Traynor. Syme had been stabbed in the back, and the weapon removed from the wound. He was murdered, and the murder must have taken place within the last hour.'

Venner flicked away a particle of dust from his coat sleeve. Inspector Traynor seemed to be lost in thought. He looked not only puzzled, but slightly embarrassed. Perhaps, thought Venner, he missed the presence of Detective Inspector Jackson.

'Did you hear what I said, Traynor?'

'Yes, sir. Murdered, and the weapon removed. What kind of weapon do you think it was?'

'I'd say it was an ordinary kitchen knife—a small serrated knife, something of that sort. I've removed certain organs which I'd like to study at more leisure. I'll give you a receipt for them, and let you know later what I find.'

'Thank you, sir.'

Traynor shifted uneasily, and glanced towards the door that led into the general waiting-room of the police mortuary.

'Dr Venner,' he said, at last, 'I've got Dean Arkwright out there. He insisted on coming here with the body, and in the van he seemed to be behaving most peculiarly. Chatting, you know, and telling me how marvellous poor Dean Girdlestone was. A man doesn't usually behave like that when in the presence of death.'

'Dean Arkwright? Why should he want to accompany you?'

Traynor did not seem to hear the question.

'And he was asking me how Syme had died. "Was he burnt to death?" "Was he choked?" And then he said, "Was he attacked with a knife?" I don't mind telling you, Doctor, that I felt very queasy when he started to talk like that.'

'Do you want me to see him? I'm not a detective, of course, but I could probably give you some idea of his state of mind.'

Traynor uttered a sigh of relief.

'Would you, sir? I'd be no end grateful. I know Mr Arkwright quite well, and I can see that he's not himself today. He bore up well over the murder of poor Dean Girdlestone, but this business of Syme seems to have shaken him to the core.'

Traynor opened the door of the office, and the two men passed into the front room. Nicholas Arkwright sprang up from the bench where he had been sitting. Venner was shocked to see how pale the man was, and how his eyes darted rapidly from side to side, as though he found it impossible to focus properly on any particular object.

'Mr Dean,' said Traynor, clearing his throat nervously, 'this gentleman is Dr Venner, the police surgeon—'

'Doctor!' Nicholas clutched Venner's sleeve. 'He was murdered, wasn't he? Stabbed! You've examined him, haven't you? You must tell me what happened to him. You see—'

Venner glanced briefly at Inspector Traynor, who nodded his head.

'Yes, Dean Arkwright,' said Venner. 'Obadiah Syme was murdered. Stabbed in the back.'

'And then, sir,' Traynor added, 'the murderer set fire to the gatehouse, thinking to burn the evidence to ashes. The fire master told me how the fire was started, but I'm not at liberty to tell you that.'

Nicholas Arkwright suddenly smiled, and the anguish vanished from his face. He sat down again on the bench, and began to speak. The policeman and the doctor listened appalled to what he had to say.

'I had always envied Girdlestone his success, you see, even though I've since discovered that he felt inferior to me! I can't think why . . . He took all the prizes, while I limped into second place behind him. He took the girl I wished to marry, and married her. He took the Deanery of Ancaster, which everybody thought would be mine. And then, he began to plot the destruction of Ancaster Cathedral under the guise of a crusade against idolatry. I couldn't bear it. And so, on Thursday, the third of this month, I followed him up to the cathedral roof, and pushed him to his death—'

'Sir!' cried Traynor. 'Stop! I have to advise you that you are not obliged to say anything at this juncture, and you are entitled to have a solicitor present—'

'I must speak! I must confess, and rid myself once and for all of this burden of guilt. I pushed him to his death, and Syme saw me do it. I went there today, and spoke to him, and then . . . And then I seized a knife . . . a table knife. I don't remember what happened then. He saw me murder Girdlestone, and so I silenced him.'

Inspector Traynor had gone very pale. He looked pleadingly at Venner, but the doctor

252

had nothing to say. His thoughts were elsewhere.

'Dean Arkwright,' said Traynor in a low, shocked voice, 'you have confessed to the murders of two men to a police officer in the presence of a witness. Nothing as at this time substantiates your confession, but I am obliged to hold you in custody until proof of your assertions is forthcoming. You will understand that you have not been formally charged with any offence, but that your unsolicited confession obliges me to apply for a warrant to remand you in custody. You must come with me now to Primrose Street Police Station.'

Nicholas Arkwright rose to his feet. Traynor touched him briefly on the arm, but made no further move to show the Acting Dean of Ancaster that he had been formally taken into custody.

Dr Venner said nothing. He was thinking to himself: this man's confession has prevented him from succumbing to an epileptic seizure. He'd been able to see all the signs there as soon as he'd set eyes on him. But there was something else wrong with him, and he'd better go with him in the van to Primrose Street.

The three men left the cold mortuary, and crossed Canal Street to where the big olive-green police van was waiting. The constable on the box got down, and hauled open the heavy iron rear door. Traynor helped Arkwright up the two steps, and Venner followed. The constable slammed the doors, and shot the outside bolt. In a moment, the heavy equipage was lumbering out of Canal Street on its way to Ancaster Police Station.

*   *   *

'It's true, miss. I'm very sorry, but there it is.'

The mortuary attendant, a balding man in his forties, looked kindly at Caroline Parrish, and read the anguish on her face. Poor lass! She'll not want to believe that our Mr Arkwright was a double murderer, but it had been impossible not to hear his confession as he'd blurted it out in the vestibule. This wasn't the right kind of place for a young woman to visit.

'And he's been taken into custody? But it's not possible! I must see him, because he's got it all wrong—'

'He confessed, miss! I heard him myself. There's nothing anyone can do. You're Canon Parrish's niece, aren't you? Go and tell the Canon what's happened, if you like—but keep away from Primrose Street. It's early days yet, Miss Parrish, and in my opinion, the fewer people who know about this business the better.'

Caroline walked out of Canal Street and into the main Ancaster road, where she caught a cab to Cathedral Green. Once in Dean's

Row, she told the cabbie to wait, and rang the bell at Number 7. Jessie admitted her to the house, and informed her that both Canon Parrish and Millie were out visiting. Should she tell Jessie what had happened? No. That would only cause a diversion. She knew quite well what she had to do. She slipped into the deserted dining-room, and opened her handbag. She rummaged through its contents for a moment, and then with a little cry of satisfaction she extracted the card that Sergeant Bottomley had given her on the train from Latchford Halt to Ancaster.

Detective Sergeant H. Bottomley,
Warwickshire Constabulary.

What had he said to her? 'If ever you're in need of help, you can come and see me at the address written on the back of that card.' She turned it over, and saw that he had written his home address on the other side in a bold cursive hand: 'Dekker's Field Farm, Thornton Heath, Warks.' Pausing only to check that the letter she had found at Ladymead was still in the pocket of her costume jacket, Caroline left the house, and told the waiting cabbie to drive her to Ancaster Railway Station.

CHAPTER TWELVE

WHAT MR SOLOMON SAW

Caroline toiled upward through an empty meadow carpeted with daisies and dandelions which rose from the railway line at Thornton Heath. She had bought a third-class ticket at Ancaster, and had been told to change at Latchford Halt.

Mr Bottomley's friend the Latchford station master had talked to the driver of the little train that had clanked in from a siding, and the man had obligingly stopped at Thornton Heath's timber platform for her to alight. He had walked up from the engine to tell her that Dekker's Field was the third field beyond the meadow, and that she couldn't miss it. She'd thanked him, and he'd touched his cap, assuring her that it was no trouble at all.

It was a warm day, and the sky was a deep blue, darker than the open skies of Lincolnshire, but the silence of the meadow, and the tilled fields beyond, was familiar enough to her. She was used to the deep countryside, and if her journey hadn't been so urgent, she would have enjoyed her walk through the field paths towards the man who could help Nicholas Arkwright.

After a quarter of an hour, Caroline saw

ahead of her a long, low farmhouse nestling among the trees of a small dell. Smoke rose from a chimney towards the deep blue sky. She stepped off the path on to a stony yard, where a number of pigs and hens apparently dwelt together in uneasy amity. She wondered idly whether they were the hens that Mr Bottomley had been carrying home in a crate when she had first met him.

The yard was muddy and rutted, but Caroline was in no mood to be fastidious about clothing. She hitched up her skirts, and hurried through the mud and stones to the front door.

Her knock was answered immediately by a fair-haired girl of fourteen or so, who was carrying a cheerful baby girl on her hip. Caroline could hear the shrill cries of other children at play inside the house. The opening of the door had released the smells of stew and cabbage to mingle with what old Uncle Alexander had called 'farmyard perfumes'.

'Yes?' asked the girl, while the baby smiled a welcome at the visitor.

'Is it possible for me to see Mr Bottomley for a moment?' asked Caroline.

The girl turned away into the house. Presently, a door slammed, and Caroline realized that the girl had emerged into the rear yard of the farmhouse. She heard her call out lustily, 'Dad, there's a lady here to see you. You're to come at once!'

At that moment, a fair-haired woman wearing a black dress and a coarse linen apron stepped out into the yard. Caroline recognized her as the woman who had been waiting for Bottomley and his crate of hens at Thornton Heath platform on 25 July. Mrs Bottomley smiled a greeting, and her general demeanour reminded Caroline forcibly of Millie, contented with her lot in life, and good humoured in consequence.

'I hope you'll excuse my Poppy, miss,' she said. 'She's a bit boisterous, and hasn't quite learnt what's what when it comes to speaking to gentlefolk. Did you want to see my husband? He's out in the field at the moment, miss, so I'll take you round the house and across the lane. If it's police business you're on, you'll be better off speaking to him there.'

Behind the farmhouse, and across a narrow lane, there stretched a smallholding of about an acre, well tilled, and planted with a range of vegetables. Caroline was no stranger to fields of this type. She knew at once that this rural police sergeant also grew vegetables for market, and perhaps supplied eggs, fowl and the occasional cut of pork to neighbouring households.

Sergeant Bottomley was busy digging a trench, his coat lying in one of the furrows, but when he saw Caroline approaching, he stuck his wide spade into the earth, rubbed his hands on his moleskin trousers to free them of soil, and slipped into his coat. Mrs Bottomley waved to her husband, then turned away, and walked back to the house.

'Miss Parrish! So you've found a use for that card of mine, at last!'

'Oh, Mr Bottomley—Dean Arkwright's confessed to the murder of Mr Girdlestone! He's been arrested by that police inspector at Ancaster—'

'Confessed, has he?' said Bottomley. 'Well, I'm not surprised. I thought he'd do something like that, in the end. It's the strain, you see, miss—'

'But he's innocent! I *know* he didn't do it— look! This is a letter that I found this morning in the picture gallery at Ladymead. Read it, and then you'll see the truth.'

Bottomley took the letter from her, and motioned towards a small barn at the end of the field.

'You and I had better go and sit in there, Miss Parrish,' he said. 'No one will overhear us in there.'

Caroline followed him across the large field. She felt half stunned by anxiety, but at the same time relieved that she was about to confide her secret to this big, homely man with the grave manner, and the fine, grey eyes. As they walked, she unconsciously recorded what she saw, the long rows of potatoes (he'd lift those before the autumn frosts), the beds of fine Savoy cabbages waiting for the autumn harvest, the onions, the Brussels sprouts, and the untidy beds of carrots, constantly plundered early in the season before they had time to develop their mature toughness.

They reached the barn, and sat down side by side on a stout wooden bench. Only then did Bottomley open the letter. He read it aloud, holding the paper at a distance, as though in need of spectacles. Perhaps he had a pair, across the lane in the farmhouse.

'"Dear Blount, You will surely realize that I cannot under any circumstances cover up your frauds against the church. You must call upon me here, at the Deanery, on Thursday next, the third, so that I can do you the justice of listening to your plea of mitigation. I am minded to grant you a week's grace, during which time the money that you have taken must be repaid in full. Failing that, the police will immediately be informed.— L. Girdlestone, Dean."'

Caroline watched Sergeant Bottomley as he carefully folded up the single sheet of paper, and put it into one of the pockets of his jacket. He said nothing for so very long that Caroline thought he had lapsed into some kind of trance. Finally, he seemed aware once more of her presence in the barn.

'Where did you find that letter, Miss

Parrish?' he asked.

'It had been crumpled up, and thrust into a drawer of the desk where I work, with a lot of other unwanted scraps of paper. I thought it would do no harm to tidy them up. And so I found it.'

'But it shouldn't have been there, should it, miss? Would you have put a letter that showed you were guilty of fraud into a drawer where anyone could find it?'

'No. I would have destroyed it. I can't think what it was doing there.'

'That letter from poor Dean Girdlestone would have been delivered in an envelope, either by hand or in the post. It was probably marked "private and confidential". Sir Charles Blount would have read it, and—well, miss, what would he have done next?'

Caroline was intrigued by Bottomley's approach. Instead of making a dramatic statement about Sir Charles's guilt, he had brought his skills to bear on a humdrum detail of the baronet's daily round. And now he was inviting her to join in the investigation!

'Sir Charles always receives the mail in his study. He keeps some of his letters, but most of them are screwed up, and thrown into his waste-paper basket. The basket's always emptied by his secretary, Mr Hayden. He takes it down to the stove in the basement.'

Even as she spoke, she conjured up an image of the suave secretary carefully sifting through the contents of the basket, extracting anything that caught his fancy, and hiding it away in the wilderness of drawers in the great Louis XIV writing-desk. She put her mental picture into words, and Bottomley nodded his head in agreement.

'Well done, Miss Parrish!' he said. 'Now, let's just take that matter a bit further. If Sir Charles Blount throws away incriminating letters, and lets his secretary carry them off, it suggests to me that he and the secretary are accomplices—'

'You mean—'

'Please, miss, wait! Things are suddenly falling into place. That boy—Daft William— he tried to describe to me the words Dean Girdlestone and Sir Charles Blount had in the hallway of the Deanery on that Thursday afternoon. Poor lad, he wasn't so very good at describing things. " 'I'll give you a week, he said, and then they went away'." They were the words Daft William heard. I assumed at the time that they'd been said by Sir Charles Blount. But it was the other way round! The whole business of the fraud was the other way round! Those words had been spoken by Dean Girdlestone. It was he who was warning Blount that the game was up. And this crumpled up note—well, I suspect that our friend Hayden salvaged it in case he could make use of it later. He hadn't reckoned with your instinct for tidiness, miss.'

Bottomley's eyes narrowed, as though he was recalling a half-vanished memory.

'Hayden . . . You've met Miss Ballard, haven't you, Miss Parrish? Well, she told me about Sir Charles's visit to the Dean. I can remember everything that she told me. This is what she said: "The Dean and Sir Charles came out of the library into the hall. They were talking quietly. Sir Charles looked very grave. I thought the Dean looked cross, as though something had upset him."'

Caroline was quick to furnish Bottomley with an explanation.

'Sir Charles looked grave because he'd been detected in fraud. The Dean was upset because . . . because he knew that he shouldn't be giving Blount any chance at all to wriggle out of his predicament!'

'Precisely, miss. And then Miss Ballard said, "Mr Hayden came out of the study, and he and Sir Charles left the house." Mr Hayden had remained in the study alone, while Blount and the Dean were talking in the hall. Why? Because it was Hayden's job to thrust a false letter, supposedly from Blount to the Dean, in one of the pigeon-holes of the Dean's desk. I thought there was something odd about that desk. It was very tidy in the main, but the pigeon-hole in the centre was disturbed. Hayden had had to work quickly, I suppose.'

'Sir Charles Blount and Mr Hayden were accomplices in the fraud.'

'They were, miss. And I'm convinced that they were accomplices in something far worse than that. Blount went to the Deanery that day to finish the business. He was a fraudster, and the Dean had detected him in fraud. So, for that matter, had the Chief Clerk, but that's another story. Blount went there to finish the business. He went there to silence the Dean for good.'

Caroline gave vent to a little sigh of relief. She had been waiting for Bottomley to hint at the possibility of murder, because it meant that she could tell him something else that she knew without prejudicing him against her employer.

'Sir Charles had five statues of an ancient Egyptian god,' she said in low tones. 'They were kept in an alcove on the first-floor landing. Some days there were five of them, other days four, and then five again. They're made of basalt, and have sharp stone muzzles or beaks. One of them seemed to be stained red . . . Sir Charles forbade me to touch it.'

Herbert Bottomley sighed. He felt angry that a young woman much the same age as his daughter Nan should have to think in this way about the grim weapons of murder.

'You said that you weren't surprised that Dean Arkwright confessed to the murders,' said Caroline. 'Did you think he was guilty before I came to you with that letter?'

'Well, miss, I never said I thought Mr

264

Arkwright was guilty. I said I wasn't surprised that he'd confessed. It's a different thing altogether, you know. Dean Arkwright wants to atone for his hatred of a man who did nothing but admire and revere him all his life, a man whose cruel death opened the gates of promotion to him. Penitent folk do very funny things, Miss Parrish, as you'd soon find out if you were in my line of work. The police, I mean.'

Bottomley rose and buttoned his jacket.

'Miss Parrish,' he said, 'my guvnor, Inspector Jackson, isn't here at the moment. He's down in Dover. So I hope you'll let yourself be guided by me. This is a murder case, you see, and you can't act positively until you've got all the proof that you need. I now have one part of the Girdlestone mystery clear in my mind. The other half's at present in Mr Solomon's mind, and I'm going to get it out of him. Meanwhile, let Dean Arkwright go on believing he's guilty, so that Blount will be off his guard.'

They walked together in silence until they reached the lane behind the house. Then Bottomley turned, and spoke to her again.

'There's something else that I want you to do, Miss Parrish. If Blount is to be lulled into a false sense of security, you will have to go back to work with him at Ladymead. You'll have to act as though he and that secretary of his are as innocent as the babe newborn. Will you do that for me?'

Caroline thought of the dead Dean, and of Laura, on the verge of being saved from a life of drunkenness by the man who had nourished a quiet devotion to her for a lifetime. The first was waiting to be avenged, the second to be redeemed, and the third to be saved from the folly of his own remorse. She gave Sergeant Bottomley her answer.

*   *   *

Sergeant Bottomley leaned over the ancient stone coffin, and extracted from it a wicked-looking steel adze. He held it up for critical examination, turning it round so that it caught the light from the tall Gothic windows in the cathedral works office. Mr Solomon sat very still at his roll-top desk, where he had been checking the monthly bills tendered by the stone quarries.

'What do you use this lethal weapon for, Mr Solomon?'

Bottomley, who had been swinging the adze through the air, stopped, and began a minute examination of its sharpened edge.

'It's got many uses, Mr Bottomley, but mainly we use it to prise up grave-slabs.'

Bottomley threw the adze back into the coffin, where it fell among the other mason's tools with a clatter that made Solomon jump. The sergeant treated him to a friendly smile, and sat down on a bench.

'I'm trying to recall, Mr Solomon,' he said, 'the name of the last clergyman to be hanged for murder.'

'What do you mean?' Solomon's voice held the suggestion of truculence, but he had turned very pale.

'I mean that Dean Arkwright has confessed to the murder of Dean Girdlestone, and also to the murder of Obadiah Syme. He's in custody at this very moment, Mr Solomon, and he's made up his mind to face up to the truth—the truth that all his dreams and visions were actually realities. He wasn't sleeping like a little infant for two hours in that chapel, was he? He came out into the north transept, and it was there that he heard you talking to the Dean. He heard *you*, Mr Solomon! The Dean was telling you to take those idols down from the tower, and you were objecting. But the Dean won the argument, didn't he? Because that's what would always happen where the Dean's wishes were concerned.'

Bottomley selected a stout sledge hammer from the coffin, tested it for balance, and then threw it back among the tools.

'You know how Dean Girdlestone was killed, don't you?' he asked. 'He was murdered in the roof-space, attacked with a heavy hooked instrument and thrown down on to the cathedral roof like a carcass at the butchers. Plenty of lethal weapons here, Mr Solomon, for a man who hated the Dean enough to kill him—plenty of weapons here for a determined killer—or his accomplice.'

Mr Solomon had begun to sweat. He mopped his brow with a handkerchief, and Bottomley saw how his hand trembled.

'When Dean Arkwright hangs,' said Bottomley sternly, 'any accomplices will hang with him. Anyone who aided and abetted him in his wicked murders. Accessories before and after the fact of murder—'

'I never—'

'You saw him, didn't you, Mr Solomon? After you and the Dean had finished talking about the idols. The Dean parted from you, and then you saw Nicholas Arkwright follow him. You wondered what your old friend was going to do. Perhaps you feared the worse, and followed him to see that he did nothing foolish—'

Josiah Solomon saw that he had been offered a way of escape. He sprang up from the desk in his agitation, and the colour rushed back into his ashen face.

'Yes! That was it! Mr Arkwright could never look after himself. Even as a little boy he needed a strong lad like me to watch over him. If you don't believe me, ask Canon Parrish. He's another man who's had to look after Nicholas Arkwright. Nicholas is a clever man, Mr Bottomley, and a distinguished clergyman. But he's also a great baby, asking his pardon for being so familiar.'

Bottomley looked gravely at the black-suited Clerk of the Works, with his trademark patina of stone dust. Here was a man of tenacious loyalty, a skilled craftsman, and an effective manager of men. How odd it was that such a decent sort could be so dim!

'Tell me what happened, Mr Solomon,' he said. 'All of it, mind! And don't try to stray away from the sober truth—I've a very good idea what must have happened up there in the roof-space.'

Solomon said nothing for a while. His normal air of confidence seemed to have deserted him. When he spoke, it was in a low voice, as though he was afraid that unseen witnesses were hearing what amounted to a confession of complicity.

'I was curious, you see, Sergeant, curious, and also concerned. I honestly didn't know at that moment where Dean Girdlestone was going. He just walked away from me in that impatient way that he had. I saw Mr Arkwright following him, and I kept out of sight behind the pillars, watching where they both went.

'Well, Dean Girdlestone went into the baptistery, and I saw him open the little door behind the font that leads to the winding stair up to the roof. I knew then that he was going to look at what he called the "idols", because that particular stair would take him out on to the walkways just below the north face of the tower. A few minutes after Dean Girdlestone had mounted the stair, Mr Arkwright came into the baptistery from the crossing, and followed him.'

'He went through the little door, and up the stairs? How did he look?'

'He didn't look very well. He was staggering a bit, and I thought to myself that he was going to have one of his fits. He'd suffered from fits all his life. He opened the door to the winding stair, went in to the stairwell, and closed the door behind him.'

'And what did *you* do?'

'I entered the walls through another door further down the south aisle, and mounted to the roof-space above the clerestory. It was a weird experience, Mr Bottomley. I couldn't see anybody from where I came out, but I could hear footsteps crossing and re-crossing, and I fancied I heard the murmur of voices. I walked along to that space where you and I talked on the day after the Dean's body was found. You remember that part of the roof-space, don't you? It's where the temporary wooden staircase is.'

'Yes, I remember it. What happened then?'

'At first, it was as though no one had been up there at all. It was suddenly very quiet. I couldn't see the door to the roof from where I stood. I'd have had to mount the ladders to do that. I walked out of the chamber, and along the narrow passage that would take me back to the stair. Then, suddenly, the footsteps started again, and I heard the sound of someone stumbling. Then I heard a voice cry, "Arkwright!" There was a scuffling, scrambling sound, and then silence.'

Solomon dabbed his brow with the handkerchief. He looked pale and haunted.

'What happened next?' asked Bottomley.

'I ran back the way I'd come, and I found Mr Arkwright sitting on the floor, leaning against the wall of the chamber. He was wiping blood from his hands.'

'So you must have suspected then, Mr Solomon, that he'd murdered the Dean. But you didn't know for certain, did you? Perhaps you thought that Mr Arkwright had had an accident.'

'No! I thought nothing of the kind. I thought that he must have done away with Girdlestone, though, of course, I had no proof of that. So I kept out of sight until Mr Arkwright got to his feet, and staggered away. He wasn't well. It was either the falling sickness, or the potions he had to swallow to drive it away.'

'You saw Dean Girdlestone's body, didn't you?'

'Yes. When Mr Arkwright had gone, I went up the ladders, and looked out from the door in the roof. I saw the Dean's body lying below. I knew he was dead. And I determined there and then to protect my old friend from the consequences of his own folly. I went down to the St Catherine Chapel with some tea, and persuaded him that he'd been there asleep for the previous two hours. So there you are, Sergeant Bottomley. It was a nightmare—a nightmare that we're never going to wake up from, apparently.'

The two men sat in silence for a while. Then Bottomley stirred, and looked round the airy chamber, with its tall Gothic windows, its massive blocks of stone awaiting the attention of the masons, and at the Clerk of the Works, sifting, shrunken and compromised, at his roll-top desk.

'Is this particular little bit of the cathedral consecrated?' asked Bottomley.

'Hey? I suppose so. I've never thought about it. It's always been the works office.'

'Well,' said Bottomley, 'let's give it the benefit of the doubt, and say it's just an ordinary place. You and I will smoke a cigar.'

Bottomley produced a battered cigar-case from his pocket, opened it, and offered it to Josiah Solomon. The Clerk of the Works looked at him thoughtfully for a moment, and then selected a slim cheroot.

'I think it would be agreeable to all parties,' said Bottomley, after his cigar was well lighted, 'if we forgot this conversation entirely. That'll simplify matters no end. Thanks to you, I know exactly what must have happened up there on that Thursday afternoon. I know a decent man when I see one, Mr Solomon, and I'm as sure as I can be that whatever harm you may have wished on Dean Girdlestone in theory, in fact, you wouldn't hurt a fly. You haven't got the gift of wickedness.'

Solomon drew on his glowing cigar. He said nothing, but his eyes were moist.

'There's a curious little incident,' said Bottomley, 'that I'm minded to share with you. On the afternoon of the Dean's death, I was examining his papers in the library of the Deanery. Suddenly, I felt that there was a presence there, someone or something that wanted to tell me that all the evidence we were collecting was false and untrue. Whatever that presence was, I heeded its warning, and sure enough, the charges of fraud against the Dean turned out to be totally unfounded.'

'Perhaps it was Dean Girdlestone's spirit,' said Solomon in awe.

'Perhaps it was,' Bottomley replied. 'Whatever the truth of it may be, I'm still heeding its warning. You said that you heard a voice cry "Arkwright" when you were up in the roof-space. Was it Dean Girdlestone's voice?'

'Well, I suppose it must have been, Sergeant. It stands to reason, doesn't it?'

'As a matter of fact, Mr Solomon, it doesn't stand to reason at all. It could have been someone else's voice, couldn't it?'

'Yes, I suppose so. But I can't imagine whose!'

'*I* can,' Bottomley replied. 'But that's another story altogether.'

He stood up, took a last look around the room, and offered Solomon his hand.

'Goodbye, Mr Solomon,' he said. 'Everything's square now between you and me, but I can see that you're depressed about Dean Arkwright. If I were you—and this again is just between you and me—I wouldn't give up hope.'

CHAPTER THIRTEEN

THE MAN AT THE CLERESTORY DOOR

Inspector Jackson took a yellow telegraph form from the inner pocket of his coat, and spread it out on the little round table at which he was sitting in the Albatross Tea Rooms in Dover. He'd read it several times before, but it would do no harm to look at it again while he was waiting for his visitor. The message was in police code, but Jackson was able to translate it without resort to a code-book.

Dean Arkwright held in custody. Has confessed to murder of Girdlestone and Syme. Await instructions. Bottomley.

274

So that was that. All the pieces in the secret chess game had obediently made their moves at the behest of the Grand Master. Unfortunately for him, not everyone on the board was content to be a pawn in his game. The whole grand strategy had all the hallmarks of the amateur. Did that man think that the police were stupid?

Jackson put the telegraph form away, and glanced out of the window and along the Esplanade. Police business had brought him to Dover on a number of occasions in the past, and he had always found it a pleasurable experience. The ancient town had many quiet attractions, and from where he sat he could see the White Cliffs away to the east, shining in the sun.

Ah! Here he was, walking purposefully along the Esplanade, a young man—or youngish—wearing a rather rakish suit, and a beribboned straw hat. It was only as he neared the front steps of the Albatross that Jackson could see his clerical collar.

The Reverend Paul Nicholson had met Jackson on the previous day. The inspector had been waiting for him on the quay as the mail packet from Calais had docked. The two men shook hands, and Nicholson sat down at Jackson's table.

'It was good of you to give me a night to recover from my journey, Mr Jackson,' he said, placing his straw hat on the floor beside his chair, and mopping his brow. He had a head of curly black hair, and a sun-bronzed face. 'I usually come back by sea when I'm on furlough, but this was by way of being an emergency. So I crossed Europe by train. But never mind me. My father was horrified to receive your report. Horrified, but angry, too. As Canon Treasurer of Ancaster, he knew all about Dean Girdlestone's charities, but he's a discreet man, and was aware that the Dean liked to do good by stealth. If that silly ass Markland had only waited for my father to return—'

'You can't blame Mr Markland, sir,' said Jackson. 'It certainly looked to him as though Dean Girdlestone had perpetrated the fraud, and there's no doubt at all that fifteen thousand pounds is missing from the cathedral funds. But I'll admit that he jumped to the wrong conclusion.'

'This missing money—does anyone know where it's gone?'

'Oh, yes, sir. We know where it's gone, and who's got it, but that's confidential, as I'm sure you'll realize.'

To Jackson's surprise, the young clergyman said, 'It's Blount, isn't it?'

'Well, sir, I'm really not at liberty to say—'

'We saw a report of Girdlestone's death in a continental newspaper. Father was very upset. You probably know that I'm chaplain to the English colony at Taormina? I suggested to

Father that he stay another week or so at my house in Sicily, while I came back here to see you. I can tell you some very interesting things about Sir Charles Blount.'

Jackson beckoned to a waiter, and ordered coffee for two. When they had been served, the Reverend Paul Nicholson began his story.

'I live in the town of Taormina,' he began, 'where there is a sizeable English colony. On the hillside above the town is Sir Charles Blount's residence, the Villa San Paolo.'

Mr Nicholson sipped his coffee, and glanced out of the window at the busy port. He was evidently arranging his thoughts.

'About six months ago, Mr Jackson,' he continued, 'the Villa San Paolo was suddenly put up for sale. At the same time, a good number of its priceless works of art were sold in the Italian art markets. It created quite a stir out there. People wondered, you know, whether Sir Charles Blount had gone bankrupt.'

'So the villa was shut up?'

'Yes, but then, earlier this year—in June, I think it was—the notices of sale were withdrawn. Apparently, Sir Charles had changed his mind. So there it is, Inspector: either Blount had suddenly come into money, or he was able to borrow on the strength of some kind of guarantee. I thought you should know.'

Jackson said nothing for a while. He was

thinking of how convenient £15,000 would have been to a man in desperate circumstances. Blount was the head of an old, established family, which had forged strong links with Church and State. He was also a dynamic, reckless kind of man, with a passion for art. He was, no doubt, kind and concerned in his own fashion, but he was one of those predators who would strike without remorse once his personal security was threatened.

'Was Sir Charles Blount popular with the locals? With the Italian folk, I mean.'

'Oh, yes. He speaks Italian fluently, and had many friends in Sicily and southern Italy. He loves the Mediterranean, and its ancient cultures. He has another house, you know, in Tangier, a place which appeals to him, I suppose, because of its romantic history, and the fact that it manages to maintain a kind of independence from French and Spanish protection. Sir Charles is a good friend of the sultan, so I'm told.'

Inspector Jackson finished his coffee, and stood up.

'You've been of tremendous help, Mr Nicholson,' he said. 'I'll bid you farewell, if I may, as I have much to do. Perhaps we'll meet again, some time, in Ancaster.'

'Prebendary Arkwright, is he—'

'*Dean* Arkwright, sir, is at present helping the police with their enquiries. And if anybody asks you what that means, the answer is, that it means just what it says, "helping". Good day, sir.'

*　　　*　　　*

The village of Arden Leigh was essentially a cluster of ancient cottages set in a grove of chestnuts some nine miles out of Warwick, on the road to Henley-in-Arden. There was a village green of sorts, little more than a patch of rough grass, across which you walked to gain entry to the tiny Saxon church. Beyond the graveyard, where a few somnolent sheep nibbled the turf, lay the seventeenth-century parsonage. It was a very quiet place, and Canon Parrish, looking out of its parlour window, thought what an ideal retreat it would have offered his friend Nicholas Arkwright from the tensions of cathedral life.

Arkwright! Really, whatever could have possessed him to confess to Girdlestone's murder? The police were denying that they were holding him, but everybody knew that they were. He must have convinced himself— and them—that he was guilty. Or perhaps he secretly relished playing the martyr? He'd always been a self-dramatizer.

Parrish had consulted old Bishop Grandison at the palace. 'Let Nicholas stew in his own juice,' he'd said. 'I've done all I can. The rest's up to him. He's probably acting out yet another of his silly fancies.' It wasn't very elegant language from a Cambridge DD, but it was true enough. Meanwhile . . .

Meanwhile, Conrad Arkwright had come blazing up from Southampton on the night express, bent on rescuing his father from the clutches of the law. Caroline, bless her, had gone back without fuss to her work at Ladymead, and Sir Charles Blount, hearing of Laura's illness, had sent a very beautiful gift of flowers and fruit.

Walter Parrish delved into his waistcoat pocket and produced his watch. Two o'clock. What date was it? Thursday, the twenty-fourth. Arkwright had been taken to Primrose Street two days ago, and no one had seen him since. What was the silly man up to? What about the Deanery? What about Caroline and Conrad?

The rectory parlour was long and low, with many-paned Jacobean windows at either end. Low beamed, and with old tapestries hanging on the panelled walls, it exuded a feeling of peace and contentment. Old Bill Davenant had been rector of Arden Leigh for fifty-four years, and had lived happily in this old place, first as a husband, then as a widower, until his death earlier in the year at the age of 94. The peaceful atmosphere of the old parsonage had been his legacy to his successor.

A door opened, and Millie Parrish came into the room.

'How is she?' asked her husband. Millie sat

down in a carved oak chair near the open fireplace. How poised and elegant she looked! In all the years of their marriage she had never failed to delight him with her cheerful pleasure in his company.

'Laura is more herself, now, Walter, though she bitterly reproaches herself for her conduct. She's lost all her mad resentment against poor Lawrence, and I think she's as horrified now as we were about that terrible funeral.'

'Well, Millie, she must strive to forget all that. She'd been possessed by her own frustrations, and turned into a parody of herself. And whose fault was that? It was Lawrence Girdlestone's neglect that turned Laura aside from her true self.'

'But Walter, poor Lawrence is dead—'

'Well, what difference does that make, my dear? The evil that men do lives after them. Lawrence's neglect turned Laura to drink.'

They were silent for a while. Walter crossed the room, and looked out at the quiet rectory garden at the rear of the house. There was a dovecote, and a row of beehives, but the lawn was overgrown, and cried out for the attentions of a lawnmower or a couple of hungry sheep.

'Doctor MacLeod says that Laura's mind will regain its equilibrium within the month,' said Millie. 'And as for being a drunk—what a horrible word!—well, he told me that Laura was simply drinking as an act of defiance, and as an attempt to draw attention to her sense of isolation. She's not in the toils of alcohol, as we thought, though he'll remain resident here with Nurse Stone until he's absolutely sure. He says that she'll stop drinking, now that . . .'

'Now that poor Lawrence is dead. That's what you were going to say, isn't it? What a tragic business! What a clotpole the fellow is! Nicholas Arkwright, I mean. Why didn't he do the thing properly that evening, a lifetime ago, at Vaux Hall? Then Laura wouldn't have married the wrong man—'

'No,' Millie interrupted, 'and that poor, blundering, hero-worshipper Lawrence Girdlestone wouldn't have married the wrong woman!'

Ballard opened the door, and beckoned to Millie, who joined her. The two women left the room, and Walter Parrish resumed his stance at the front window of the parlour, looking out at the quiet churchyard, and the line of chestnuts that formed its border with the lane beyond.

Poor Nicholas! The Very Reverend Nicholas Arkwright MA, Dean of Ancaster— and prize idiot! He'd always been a mite too concerned about winning prizes—and prizes, for him, had included both Laura Taverner and the Deanery of Ancaster. He'd been a prize-winner at school, and still kept his little array of athletics trophies in his study at the Prebendary's House. But the small silver cups were forlorn and tarnished, as though reflecting the settled hopelessness of their owner's later life.

Walter Parrish recalled himself to the present. There was a lot of work to be done. He'd always looked after Nicholas Arkwright, and it looked now as though he'd have to pick up some of the pieces that the idiot had left lying about. Arkwright had brought Laura out to Arden Leigh to recuperate, and that had been a brilliant move. But then, he had chosen to confess to Girdlestone's murder, leaving Laura to get better without his tender ministrations! Well, he'd just have to take over where Nicholas had left off.

Walter sat down at the late rector's desk, found himself pen, ink, and paper, and began to compose a letter. When he had finished writing it, he took an envelope, and addressed it to Augustus Morton, Esquire, Vaux Hall, near Maldon, Essex. It was time to make creative use of the past.

*   *   *

As Sergeant Bottomley entered the room in Primrose Street Police Station where Nicholas Arkwright was lodged, the Dean looked up from the large Bible that he had been reading, and greeted him with a mournful smile.

'My Nemesis,' he said. 'Wherever I go, and whatever I do, I can't escape from you.'

Bottomley said nothing for a moment. He glanced round the room, noting the plain wooden table, the two chairs, and the truckle bed, made up with sheets, pillows and blankets. A noticeboard on the wall was plastered with police notices. An unlit gas fire stood on the hearth of the little fireplace, and there was a round mirror hanging above it.

'How are you, Mr Arkwright?' he asked at length.

'I'm as well as a prisoner can be, Sergeant. This cell is comfortable enough, and the food is passable. Inspector Traynor has listened carefully to my story, and I am awaiting my fate with as much equanimity as I can muster.'

Sergeant Bottomley sat down at the table, facing Dean Arkwright. He thinks this is a cell, he mused, but in fact, it's the cosy little billet provided for the night constable, with bed, board, and all found. Inspector Traynor had been too kind-hearted to lodge the Dean of Ancaster in a real cell.

Bottomley produced a tiny notebook from one pocket of his yellow overcoat, and fished around in the other until he had found a stub of pencil. He began to question Arkwright, from time to time jotting down brief comments in the notebook.

'When you were brought in here on Tuesday, sir,' said Bottomley, 'you were examined by the police surgeon, Dr Venner. Can you recall what he did?'

'He submitted me to a cursory medical examination, Sergeant. A very presentable gentleman I thought he was, though economical with words. He looked into my eyes, and then made me open my mouth. I asked him what he was doing, but he made no reply. Elegant, but a little churlish. Then he left the cell, and the door was closed.'

Well, well, Bottomley thought, for a man who's determined to put a noose round his neck, our friend the Dean is decidedly perky. And not at all economical with words. Perhaps I've called at the right time.

'Dr Venner didn't say much, sir, because he's not allowed to talk to prisoners. But it may interest you to know, sir, that when he first saw you, in the waiting-room at the mortuary, he realized that there was something wrong with you.'

'Well, I myself feared that I was about to have an epileptic seizure—'

'Yes, sir, but I don't mean the falling sickness, which Dr Venner told me was very much to the fore on that occasion. It was something else. He suspected, sir, that you had been given a dangerous substance called chloral hydrate. He could smell it on your breath, and when he examined you here at Primrose Street, he was quite sure.'

'Chloral hydrate? I've never heard of it. And I've never taken it, to my knowledge.'

'Chloral hydrate, sir, forms chloroform in

285

the brain, and chloroform, sir, is what they give you before an operation, if you're lucky. Well, somebody gave you a dose of that stuff, sir, on the day that you sauntered out to visit the late Obadiah Syme at the Abbey gatehouse—'

'Good God!'

'Exactly, sir. Now do you see why no one here wants to accept your story at its face value? You were seen staggering along Dean's Row by Canon Hall's housemaid, among others. She thought you were under the influence, sir, asking your pardon for the coarse expression. And you were seen staggering back by one of the cathedral gardeners whom I dug out, saving your reverence, from a little shed he had near the railings on the north side of the precinct.'

'A gardener?'

'Yes, sir. Very willing, he was, to lean on his spade and have a chat. That gardener said you'd reached the steps down into Friary Street well before the fire broke out in the gatehouse. What did you do, sir, light a slow-match?'

'The fire? Surely, that was a terrible accident? I never—'

'Oh, and where did you hide the knife? The knife you used to stab poor Mr Syme in the back? I searched your house, sir, and it wasn't there. We sifted through the ruins of the gatehouse, and it wasn't there, either. We found some table knives, but they didn't look as though they'd been used to stab anybody.'

Sergeant Bottomley leaned forward, and began to speak with a quiet and controlled urgency. Arkwright listened to him with total attention.

'Sir Charles Blount called to see you on Tuesday morning. While he was there, did you have anything to drink?'

'Yes, we had coffee.'

'Had you invited him to have coffee with you, sir?'

'Yes. Well, actually, he invited himself on the previous evening, after the dinner that he gave for me at Ladymead. He proposed calling on Syme, and then on me, at the Prebendary's House.'

'And could Sir Charles Blount have put any of this substance, this chloral hydrate, into your coffee without you seeing, sir?'

'Sir Charles Blount? What a preposterous idea! Of course not. At least . . .'

'What is it, sir?'

'Well, he did ask me to search the rear garden of my house, claiming that he'd seen Syme lurking among the bushes there. I must say that at the time I thought it a silly idea, and when I returned to the study, Blount looked rather shamefaced—guilty, you know. Guilty . . .'

'That's when he slipped the chloral hydrate into your coffee. He put some more in your coffee pot, you know. Dr Venner analysed the

287

dregs. I must say, sir, that it was very convenient having you here under lock and key, and unable to raise an objection to our search warrant—you being a prisoner, Mr Dean, and accusing yourself of murder.'

Bottomley watched Arkwright as he digested the significance of what he had just told him. The man looked dumbfounded. Was it time to prompt him a bit more? Yes.

'I've seen Mr Traynor's notes on your confession, sir. Very full and frank, if I may say so. We both noticed that you had difficulty about the blood. You couldn't tell the inspector how you got blood all over yourself. Why was that?'

'It was on my hands. I thought I was dreaming when I wiped it off, but you showed me that it wasn't a dream. It was real blood. Somebody found my bloodstained handkerchief, and sent it back to me.'

'I suppose that "somebody" was Solomon, wasn't it, sir? That would be like him. But never mind Solomon for the moment. That blood on your hands came from the lintels of the door, and from the walls. You say you pushed Dean Girdlestone to his death. Dean Girdlestone was *not* pushed to his death. He was bludgeoned to death, sir, in the roof-space, before ever he reached that door out on to the roof. And he was carried out on to the ledge, and thrown down—thrown, sir, not pushed.'

'But—'

Sergeant Bottomley held up a large hand to stem a possible torrent of words.

'One moment, sir, if you please. You never struck him down, which is why you can't account for the blood. And you never pushed him, because he wasn't pushed. So why did you say that you did?'

'I did, Sergeant! Ever since that terrible day I've felt the sensation of my hands meeting the broadcloth of his coat as he stood on the threshold of the roof door—'

'But he *didn't,* sir! He *didn't* stand on the threshold of the roof door. So perhaps it was someone else you pushed, and maybe it wasn't much of a push, and maybe you collapsed, or fainted, before you could see who it was?'

'But it must have been Girdlestone! I felt the broadcloth on the palms of my hand—'

'Maybe you did, sir, but it was the man's *back* that you were pushing, so you couldn't have known it was the Dean. Not for certain. The man you pushed was someone else, and he was standing there on the threshold, looking down at his handiwork. He'd just murdered the Dean, you see.'

'But I heard him call my name. "Arkwright!"'

'No doubt you did, sir. When the man felt the pressure of your hands on his back, he naturally turned round, and when he saw who it was, he uttered your name in surprise. He

289

knew you, you see. But before you could recognize him in return, you had fainted. And when you recovered, smeared with blood in your struggles to right yourself, the man had gone. That was when Mr Solomon came across you, sir, and proceeded to cover up what he thought were your tracks.'

Nicholas Arkwright had listened fascinated to Sergeant Bottomley's reconstruction. Part of his mind marvelled at the cleverness of this basically humble man's thought processes. Another part, the more visual part, began to see once more the back, clothed in broadcloth, of the man who had stood on the ledge. As he conjured up the picture, the background faded, to be replaced by the French window in his study, and the image of Sir Charles Blount standing motionless, looking out into the garden. It was the same back.

'Sergeant—'

'You've seen it all now, sir, haven't you?' said Bottomley. 'Best not to mention any names for the moment, but you'll see well enough that the man who murdered Mr Girdlestone almost certainly murdered Mr Syme; and knowing that your presence in the roof-space on that day was too frightening for comfort, the same man had begun the preliminaries of murdering you as well.'

'Murdering *me*? Surely he wouldn't take such a terrible risk?'

'There'd be no risk involved, sir! He'd

simply manoeuvred you, with a little help from the chloral hydrate, into presenting yourself as a candidate for the gallows. It would have been the Law, sir, who removed the threat to his security for good and all.'

CHAPTER FOURTEEN

THE EAVESDROPPER

Superintendent Mays picked up the letter that Caroline Parrish had found in the Louis XIV desk, glanced through it, and then addressed his audience of two.

'Inspector Jackson,' he said, 'and you, Sergeant Bottomley, this letter from Dean Girdlestone to Sir Charles Blount is proof positive that Blount is an embezzler. The Dean writes of "your frauds against the church". He says the money must be paid in full, or the police will be informed. Have I drawn the right conclusion, or is there something I've missed?'

Jackson looked with quiet appreciation at his superior officer. He was a man who pined for the kind of action denied him by his rank, which placed him in an office for most of each day. He compensated for his enforced inactivity by giving his total attention to the particular case in hand.

'No, sir,' said Jackson. 'You've missed nothing. That letter gives us a prima-facie case against Blount. It won't be difficult now to ferret out the details of his scheme to extract fifteen thousand pounds from Ancaster Cathedral. It would arise from him being an authorized signer of cheques and other instruments. That man Hayden was his delivery boy, travelling round the country from bank to bank.'

'Precisely. So we'll set the fraud aside for the moment, and give our whole attention to murder. You've both shown me how Blount turned the whole situation round, posing as the discoverer of the fraud, and presenting poor Girdlestone as the villain. Then, in order to silence Girdlestone, he killed him. Sergeant Bottomley, remind me of the details, will you?'

The three men were consulting together in Superintendent Mays' office at Peel House, the police headquarters in Copton Vale. Bottomley stirred in his chair, gave vent to a rather moist cough, and launched into speech.

'Sir, Sir Charles Blount and his secretary arrived at the Deanery on the afternoon of Thursday, third of August, when they were granted an interview. When the interview was over, Blount came out into the hall with the Dean. We've established that the Dean said to him: "I'll give you a week's grace", or words to that effect. Soon afterwards, the secretary Hayden came out of the Dean's library. I think that his job had been to plant Blount's fake letter to Mr Girdlestone in the Dean's desk—'

'So it was a premeditated conspiracy?'

'Yes, sir. And once Hayden had put that letter there, Dean Girdlestone's fate was sealed. If ever he found it, he'd immediately expose Blount to the authorities. So it's obvious, sir, that the Dean would have to be silenced immediately.'

'So what happened next? That's a good point about the Dean's fate being sealed. Well done, Sergeant.'

'Thank you, sir. Now, I questioned an old codger I found leaning on his spade in the cathedral grounds, and one of the things he told me was that this Hayden was carrying a kind of satchel with him. Heavy, he said it was. I reckon, sir, that the satchel contained one of a set of heathen gods that Sir Charles Blount kept in that museum of a house of his in Ladymead. I heard about those gods from my informant, Miss Parrish. A very handy murder weapon, sir. A kind of half human dog, with a sharp stone muzzle. That's what I think, anyway. It's all very amateur, sir, but premeditated for all that.'

'What happened next?'

'Well, sir, the Dean went climbing up the ladders into the cathedral roof, on what you might call his legitimate business—his lawful occasions, as they say. And Sir Charles Blount followed him, and murdered him. Then he threw his body down on to the roof. At that point, Prebendary Arkwright came staggering up—'

'Arkwright! Yes, Sergeant, I'm glad you've mentioned him. Jackson, I've had a visit from Inspector Traynor. He brought this man Arkwright's son with him, a kind of firebrand, an ex-soldier, who's working for the Ordnance Survey. You were in Dover that day. The son demanded everybody's scalp—except for yours, Sergeant Bottomley. In your case, he wanted your head on a plate. Traynor can't get rid of this Arkwright out of his police station, and wondered whether I could do anything. See to it, will you, Jackson?'

Sergeant Bottomley shuffled uncomfortably on his chair. He looked positively abashed.

'Sir,' he said, 'it might be better if I were to get Mr Arkwright out of the choky. In a way, it's me who put him there in the first place. I had a feeling about him, you see. He was one of those men who want to be guilty, so as to make up for shady things they've done in the past. You could see by looking at him that he was a poser, one of those men that like to draw attention to themselves.'

'I know what you mean.' Mays nodded his agreement. 'And you, Jackson, hey? We've all met those peculiar people who rush to confess to crimes that they've never committed. We hanged one of those once, when I was still in London. Very sad. For his relations, you know.'

'Yes, sir,' Bottomley continued. 'Poor Mr Arkwright's got a lot to contend with. As well as wanting to be guilty, he's filled to the brim like an overflowing horse-trough with witches' brews and chloral hydrate. Blount slipped him the chloral in his coffee. The brews are supplied by Dr Savage. So poor Mr Arkwright doesn't know whether he's coming or going at the moment. I don't think a spell in choky will do him much harm, asking your pardon, sir, for speaking so boldly.'

'Not at all, Sergeant, though "choky" is not a very professional word, is it? And the old man—the witness whom you found in the cathedral grounds—surely "old codger" isn't very precise? What is an old codger, anyway?'

'Well, sir, it's just a manner of speaking. An old codger's one of those ancient fellows with just a couple of teeth left in his mouth, the type of old chap who's got one foot in the grave, sir. This one actually had a spade—very convenient, with the graveyard just a few yards away. A codger, sir.'

'Very interesting, Sergeant. Take care not to use such expressions in written reports. Oh, and while I remember: this informant of yours, Miss Caroline Parrish, is she going to be safe in that house—what's it called?—Ladymead? She's a very brave young woman to agree to your request, and go back there as though nothing has happened. I think—I think you'd better get her away from there now, before we appear on the scene. Make her go home, or send her somewhere safe.'

Superintendent Mays rearranged the papers on his desk, and then leaned forward earnestly. He joined his hands together, and glanced at both men before speaking.

'This is a clear case of murder, perpetrated by Sir Charles Blount to mask his fraud. We need to base our actions on that one charge, the murder of Dean Girdlestone. The original fraud, and the subsequent murder of the man Syme, will be investigated, but it is the capital charge relating to the death of Lawrence Girdlestone that needs to engage our attention.

'It's Monday today, the twenty-eighth. A new week, Officers, in which we should see this business brought to a conclusion. I'll apply for the necessary warrants today—warrants of search and arrest. All the preliminary work should be done by Wednesday. I want you both to go to Ladymead on Thursday, and take Blount into custody.'

Mays gathered his papers together, and rose from his desk.

'I'll give you my usual advice,' he said, as they moved towards the door. 'Read the charges carefully and fully. If the accused interrupts, you must read them in full for a second time. Don't be intimidated by rank or title. Don't feel that you mustn't use physical restraint against a gentleman if it seems necessary. Good luck to you both. And well done! Meanwhile, there's no need for us to startle our quarry prematurely. Keep the whole matter close to your chests.'

*   *   *

As Caroline crossed the suspension bridge to Ladymead, she was conscious of the sunlit waters of the River Best moving idly beneath her. It was a quiet day, and the atmosphere on Riverside was calm and tranquil. It was vital to create the impression at Ladymead that nobody knew anything about the murders, and that Sir Charles Blount could go on his desperately wicked way with total impunity.

Nevertheless, she was very apprehensive. She had loved working at Ladymead, but had very soon realized what a strange, Bohemian kind of house it was. There were no resident servants, only day maids, and a few skilled people paid by the hour. For banquets and dinners, like that given for Nicholas Arkwright, Sir Charles employed professional caterers. Otherwise, the house was curiously empty, a series of galleries for the exhibition of sculpture and paintings rather than a genuine home.

She entered the cool hallway of the house, automatically glancing up the staircases to the great skylight in the roof. It was very quiet, and she walked through the deserted drawing room and into the gallery without encountering a single soul. Her chief purpose was simply to be there, as her work was now finished. She selected an old book from one of the shelves between the windows, and sat down at the Louis XIV desk to read. Part of her mind followed the text, but another part sought flight from Ladymead to Arden Leigh, and Laura Girdlestone. She longed to have some part in poor Laura's recovery. Doctors and nurses were all very well, but the intimate companionship of a woman friend could work wonders on someone afflicted with depression.

Caroline was so absorbed in her thoughts that she failed to realize that voices were coming from the adjacent drawing-room. She sat quite still, straining her ears to hear what was being said. Evidently, Sir Charles and Mr Hayden had returned to the house—if, indeed, they'd ever left it. It was a vast place, and you could be swallowed up in parts of it without the other residents even knowing that you were there.

'But they *must* know, Sir Charles,' Hayden was saying, 'what you and I did that day.'

'They may suspect, Hayden, but they have no proof. No concrete proof, that is. The valise in which you carried the statuette is lying safely at the bottom of the river. Likewise, the little kitchen knife which I'd reserved for Syme. He saw too much, and wanted too much. Very early this morning, I removed the offending figure of Anubis, and buried it in the shrubbery behind the kitchen garden. Miss Caroline Parrish was beginning to show a dangerous interest in it.'

'Is she here today? I haven't seen her in the house.'

'She may be here, but I'm not sure. I never held her to specific times. But now, Hayden, let me tell you once again what we must do.'

Sir Charles Blount's voice dropped to a whisper. Caroline froze in terror at the great Louis XIV desk. It was chillingly clear that neither man knew that she was in the gallery.

After a while, Blount and Hayden began to talk in more normal tones, and Caroline was forced to listen. It was now out of the question for her to move, or to make her presence known.

'Dean Arkwright will be released any day now,' Hayden said. 'It's an open secret in the town that the police don't accept his confession of guilt.'

Caroline heard a scraping of chair legs on the marble floor, and knew that Sir Charles had shifted his position. Most chairs, modern or antique, seemed too small to contain his vast frame.

'Quite frankly, Hayden, I'm glad to hear it, though the chance of using him as a scapegoat was too good to miss! I felt a lot of remorse about that, and I'm pleased and relieved that nothing came of it. I'd better tell you how the business of incriminating Arkwright came about.

'After I'd sent that self-righteous busybody Girdlestone to his Maker, I stood looking down at the spot where I'd thrown him, in order to reassure myself that the fellow was well and truly dead—'

Caroline heard Hayden make a little sound of disgust. Sir Charles's voice came louder and more emphatic.

'I detested him, I tell you, and his power to change and destroy the old order here in Ancaster! Your genteel fastidiousness, Hayden, is out of place. I hated him for driving his young wife into an insane asylum while he carefully laid the foundations of his career. It was no thanks to him that she ultimately recovered. But I wanted no unnecessary suffering for him, you understand. I'd dreaded that possibility all along. In the event, I needn't have worried. He was dead before his body hit the roof.'

Caroline shuddered. She thought: I must not be sick. If I begin to retch, they'll hear me. She suddenly recalled the dinner at Number 7, and Dean Girdlestone's reaction when Uncle Walter had mentioned the possibility of her working for Sir Charles Blount. He had paused in the act of lifting his wineglass to his lips, and a strange, disturbed look had come into his eyes. That was because he'd known, then, that

Sir Charles was an embezzler.

'And then Arkwright turned up?' Hayden prompted.

'He did. I don't mind telling you, Hayden, I nearly died of fright! I was so startled that I called out his name, but almost immediately I saw that the poor fellow was virtually in a coma. He'd no idea who I was. But it was a nasty moment, I can tell you. That's when I conceived the idea of letting him take the blame. I wonder whether you can understand why?'

'Oh, yes, sir, I can. Arkwright tried to push you off the ledge, didn't he? He obviously thought you were Girdlestone, and tried to murder you. So there was murder in his heart; and there's no great difference morally between conceiving an evil deed, and carrying out such a deed. So he was entitled to a share of the consequences.'

Sir Charles chuckled. Again, Caroline heard the creaking of a chair. She wondered whether she'd ever be able to creep away from the desk, and seek refuge in the hidden extension.

'A nice distinction, Hayden,' said Sir Charles. 'You should have been a theologian. But enough of these things. Arkwright, as you say, will be released, and Inspector Jackson will then turn his attention to me. Well, poor man, he'll find that the bird has flown. Birds, I should say. Bellini's *Madonna and Child with Lilies*, alas! has been eagerly acquired by

Stevenson, the art dealer in Old Bond Street. He gave me a thousand guineas for it, and that will be more than ample to spirit us both away before the good Jackson has even noticed.'

'What about the—er, the proceeds, you know?'

'The fifteen thousand pounds? It's safe and sound, my dear Hayden, in the Bank of Naples. At the end of this year I'll part with the Villa San Paolo, and move all my assets to Tangier.'

Caroline could hear both men stand up. If they came into the gallery, she would have to pretend that she'd heard nothing. They, in their turn, would pretend to believe her . . .

'Well, Hayden, you've turned up trumps over this affair, and you'll not find me ungrateful. You know the plan. All you have to do is to carry out your side of it, and all will be well.'

Sir Charles laughed again. He seemed to Caroline to be totally without conscience. She suddenly recalled her Uncle Walter's humorous description of him as a vampire. He had not been far wrong. Hayden made some suitable reply, but Caroline did not hear what he said. Both men had evidently decided to leave the drawing-room the way they had come into it. The blood began to flow once again through Caroline's stiffened limbs. She got up very slowly from her chair at the desk, picked up the book she had been reading, and tiptoed along the gallery into the extension.

Murderers! That cultured man with the energy of a tiger, prowling around his magnificent sunlit mansion, and his elegant, handsome secretary, had conspired together to cover a common fraud by committing murder! The house suddenly took on the atmosphere of a trap, a light glass box from which there was no exit. The paintings, the sculptures, the collection of ancient books—how many of these things had been acquired through treachery and fraud? That very day she would leave the blighted place for good.

Gathering her courage, Caroline hurried out of the extension and back into the main gallery. Hayden, his face convulsed with rage, was waiting for her at the Louis XIV desk.

'What have you done with it?' he cried.

One of the drawers was open, and her cardboard files were strewn over the desk.

'What do you mean, Mr Hayden?'

She knew quite well what he meant. He was looking for Dean Girdlestone's letter to Blount, which he had thrust to the back of that particular drawer. He would have used it to establish a hold over Sir Charles if the baronet ever tired of his presence, or saw him as a danger. No wonder he was livid with rage. How would he feel if he knew that his 'insurance policy' was safe in the hands of Sergeant Bottomley?

'You know perfectly well what I mean. I can

see from your face that you've read that damned letter, and drawn your own conclusions. You'd better give it to me, or it will be the worse for you.'

Caroline looked at the secretary's handsome face, and saw in his eyes not strength and determination, but weakness and fear. Fear, as she well knew, would be the end of *her* if she yielded to it, as this man was doing. Fear paralysed the power of reason.

It was a hot day, and the front door, she knew, would still be open to the garden. If she took Hayden by surprise, she would be out of the house in seconds. In less than a minute, she would be back on the bridge.

With a sudden movement Caroline sprang past Hayden to the door. She moved quickly, but had misjudged Hayden's agility. In a flash he had darted in front of her and barred her exit. He made as though to seize her and, in her panic, Caroline ran up the stairs. Somewhere, on one of the floors, there would surely be a servants' stair that would take her down to the basement area, where she could get out into the rear gardens of the house.

Her heart pounded, and the blood roared in her ears. She fled along the first-floor landing, and was amazed that, even in a moment of sheer terror, her curiosity made her glance at the pasha's clock in its alcove, noting that there were now only four statuettes. The fifth, the one stained with Dean Girdlestone's blood, lay buried in the garden.

She heard the clatter of Hayden's boots on the stairs, and the panting of his breath. She reached the second floor. Could she hide? No, because all the closed mahogany doors shielded mysteries. Sir Charles Blount himself might have been in any of the rooms behind them, waiting to pounce. She saw no sign of a servants' stair. She fled past the great, overblown painting of the Villa Paolo, watched by the grinning satyrs and fauns.

Hayden's pace quickened, and she could hear a horrible wheezing, rasping sound coming from his lungs that somehow made him even more frightening. Here he was, now! What should she do?

The observatory! She pulled open the narrow door in the panelling, and clattered up the uncarpeted stairs. In a moment she emerged into the empty, echoing chamber, glazed on all sides, that crowned the tower rising above the roof-line of Ladymead. Then, as Hayden began a laboured ascent of the steep staircase, she realized that there was no escape from the empty observatory, and so no escape from Blount's murderous secretary. She had boxed herself up in a trap.

Hayden appeared on the threshold, and walked slowly towards where she was standing. Far below her she could see a throng of people going about their daily business, and, in a far away land across the river, the tower of the ancient cathedral rising above the stately trees.

'You'd better tell me where it is, you know,' Hayden panted, 'otherwise I'll have to *make* you tell me. No one knows you're up here, but me.'

It was vital not to panic, not to show weakness. This man was essentially weak. Perhaps he could be defeated by a combination of moral strength and female ingenuity? It was vital for him to think that all she knew about was the two men's involvement in fraud. If she admitted that, it would lead his thoughts away from the possibility that she had overheard his conversation with Blount. If either man ever found out that she had been sitting at the Louis XIV desk while they were speaking of their murders, instead of at a desk in the extension, then she would be as good as dead.

'I'll tell you where it is, Mr Hayden. But first, it might be a good idea if you were to listen to what I have to say. Yes, I found that letter, which told me that Sir Charles had been involved in fraud. I knew your habits, and deduced that you'd thrust that letter into one of the drawers to use as a lever against Sir Charles if ever that became necessary—'

'Very clever of you, Miss Parrish. But you can cut short this account of your cleverness and tell me where the letter is. I want it, do you hear?'

He seized her wrist, and his strong hand felt

like a constricting manacle. His voice came in little shallow bursts, and his face was very pale, but his presence was frightening, and it was only with the greatest effort of will that she kept her voice steady. It was time to be inventive.

'I hid that letter in a cavity beneath one of the stalls in Ancaster Cathedral,' she said. 'And there, Mr Hayden, it stays! You want that letter to use as blackmail. I need it to guarantee my own safety. I came here to work for a titled gentleman and his secretary. I found that I was employed by a brace of rogues.'

Even in his furious anger, the gentlemanly Hayden blushed with shame. He released her wrist, and she immediately pressed home her advantage.

'Somebody else knows where I have hidden that letter,' she said. 'If anything happens to me, that person will take it to the police.'

Hayden rested one hand against the bare wall of the chamber. His chest heaved as he took great gulps of air. Was the man ill, or so enraged that he could not breathe? His eyes burned into hers, but she met them unflinchingly.

'I don't believe you,' he said.

Outside, people were crossing the elegant suspension bridge. They inhabited a different world. None of them could help her.

'I don't believe you,' Hayden repeated.

'Why not? Have you stopped to ask yourself why I didn't hand that letter to the police? The answer to that question, Mr Hayden, is that I feel great attachment to Sir Charles Blount, as you do, I expect. The monetary affairs of Ancaster Cathedral are no concern of mine. I had no intention of ever alluding to the matter, and if you hadn't behaved in this disgraceful manner this afternoon, the whole business of the fraud would have remained a fast secret.'

She saw the doubt and indecision in the secretary's eyes, and knew that she had won the battle for his belief. It was at that very moment that she heard the strong voice of Sir Charles Blount calling testily from the second-floor landing below.

'Hayden! Confound it, where are you, man? Come down, won't you? There's no time to be lost.'

For a moment she felt that she would collapse with fright. The two of them were still in the house! But then, her inventive intelligence reasserted itself.

'Your master's calling you, Mr Hayden,' said Caroline, smiling. 'He's *my* "insurance policy", you know. Think what he'd say if he knew that you'd kept that letter—and *why*!'

Hayden said nothing. He simply looked at Caroline with an expressionless face, turned away, and stumbled down the steep stairs. In a moment, the narrow door had closed behind him.

Caroline slid down to the floor in a dead faint.

CHAPTER FIFTEEN

A CRUISE TO NOWHERE

When Caroline came to herself, she realized that she must have lapsed into an exhausted sleep. She could sense that the sun had moved across the sky since her dramatic encounter with Hayden, and she was feeling both stiff and cold. She clambered to her feet, and made for the door. Were they waiting for her, hidden behind the many inscrutable doors on the landing below? She tiptoed down the steep wooden stair, and cautiously pushed open the narrow door. There was no one about. Glancing over the banisters, she looked down to the marble-floored hall below. Nothing. The house seemed eerily quiet.

She walked slowly down the stairs, glancing nervously to left and right. On the first-floor landing the pasha's clock showed her that it was nearly three o'clock. She had been asleep for something over half an hour. She reached the ground floor, and hurried along the hall towards the front door.

A man stood on the front step, his

motionless figure silhouetted against the frosted glass panel of the door. He was fumbling at the lock with a key. Her heart leapt with fear, and she darted into the empty drawing-room, and then through the arch into the picture gallery. She heard the front door open, and the sound of heavy footsteps on the hall tiles. She would shelter as best she could in the shadow of the great Louis XIV desk.

It was then that she realized somebody else was walking slowly towards her from the hidden extension. This time, there could be no escape . . . The man rounded the corner, and Caroline cried out in grateful relief. It was Sergeant Bottomley.

*   *   *

'We came especially to find you, Miss Parrish,' said Inspector Jackson, 'because our superintendent decided that it was too risky for you to remain here. We're sorry to have frightened you.'

They had left the gallery, and were sitting on one of the embroidered settees in the drawing-room of Ladymead.

'But how did you get in?' asked Caroline. 'It was you, wasn't it, Mr Jackson, whom I saw at the front door?'

'Yes, miss. The house was locked up, you see. I used a special instrument to open the front door. Sergeant Bottomley there would

310

have done the same for the rear entrance. What I don't understand, miss, is why *you* were in the house. Didn't Sir Charles know that you were here?'

Caroline told them her story. Jackson listened intently, and when she repeated the damning conversation between Sir Charles and Hayden, she saw how his eyes shone brightly with a kind of stern triumph. Sergeant Bottomley was writing rapidly in a little notebook.

When she had finished her story, the two men looked around them. Then Jackson treated Caroline to a kindly smile.

'One advantage of being in the police, Miss Parrish,' he said, 'is that you can look around a house without the owners making a fuss about it. Sergeant Bottomley and I are going to do a preliminary search now, while the house is empty. It won't take us long, because we'll only be looking for things that we know we'll find. Now, what would you like to do? Stay here until we're finished, or come with us?'

'I'll come with you, Inspector,' said Caroline quickly. 'One more scare here in Ladymead, and I'll go out of my wits!'

As Jackson had said, the search did not take long. She realized that the two detectives were ascertaining the layout of all the rooms on all three floors, only occasionally opening a drawer, or glancing into a closet. Clearly, they would return, armed with the necessary warrants, for more leisurely examination, with or without the owner's consent.

They ended their search in the basement area of the house, a range of cellars and kitchens with windows looking out on to a long, sunken yard. A stone-flagged passage between the cellars ended at a half-open door, from which exuded the unmistakable smell of coal. This was the fuel store for Ladymead's many fireplaces. A dust-smeared trail running from a glazed door leading in from the sunken yard led to the coal cellar. Jackson noticed it immediately.

'Sergeant,' he said in a low voice, nodding towards the half-open door, 'you'd better take a look in there.' Caroline gave a step forward, but the inspector restrained her. Bottomley disappeared into the cellar, and they heard his boots rasping on coal dust. Presently, there came the scrape of a match, and a flare of light appeared in the crack of the door. The light soon died out, and in a few moments' time Bottomley emerged from the dark cellar, wiping his hands on a handkerchief.

'Miss Parrish,' he said, 'if I was to stand beside you, would you be prepared to look at the man I've just found in that coal-hole?'

'A man . . .' Caroline's voice faltered.

'Yes, miss. I'm sure you'll know who he is, and it'll save us a lot of time if you were to have a look at him. He's quite decent and composed. He's dead, you know.'

312

A dead man! When would these horrors end? She had loved this high, bright house beyond the bridge, but now she hated and feared it. She would never enter it again. Soon, she would be safe in the comforting embrace of the Cathedral Church of the Holy Angels, and the adjacent redbrick mansions in Dean's Row—but not just yet. She steeled herself to do Bottomley's bidding.

Caroline took Bottomley's arm, and walked with him into the coal cellar. Jackson had followed closely behind, and it was he, this time, who struck a match. She saw the pale, handsome, dead face of Mr Hayden, the features calm, the eyes fast closed. The match went out.

*　　　*　　　*

Nicholas Arkwright uttered an involuntary cry of pleasure as Walter Parrish, looking very smart in morning coat and silk hat, came into the room at Primrose Street Police Station.

'My dear Canon,' he said, closing the large Bible that he had been reading, 'how very civil of you to call. Upon my word, I find myself in a very peculiar situation here. That man Bottomley came to see me, and convinced me that I was entirely innocent—'

'I assume he was speaking forensically, Mr Dean,' Parrish interrupted. 'Theologically, of course, you're *not* innocent. Not in the least.

313

How about the sin of Pride? How about your envy of poor Girdlestone? How about your determination to make a public show of yourself?'

Nicholas Arkwright sniffed in disapproval.

'You're very censorious today, Canon,' he said. 'I thought you were going to bring me a little cheer and goodwill. Perhaps that was too much to hope for.'

Canon Parrish glanced round the snug room, and then looked affectionately at his old friend. What an idiot he was! It was fear of losing self-esteem that was keeping him a prisoner in poor Traynor's night quarters.

'So this is where you're living now?' said Parrish. 'I must say, it's very comfortable. No wonder you won't come out. I was saying to Conrad only this morning—'

'How is the boy? He came here, you know, and made a fuss. I had to tell him all kinds of things to keep him quiet. Poor Mr Traynor mustn't be upset.'

'Conrad is very well, Mr Dean. Blooming, in fact. He's camping out in the Prebendary's House at present. He won't go back to Southampton until you're out of this place. He may have to accept demotion if he's absent much longer, he tells me.'

'Demotion? But—'

'Don't worry. I told him that his father's honour was much more important than mere employment. I'm sure he saw what I meant. I must go, now. I only came because that man Bottomley called round at Number 7 late this morning, and asked me to pay you a visit. Millie and I are very busy at the moment looking after Laura. After all,' he added, turning to the door, 'someone's got to look after her. It might as well be us.'

Nicholas Arkwright stood up. He looked the picture of guilt. 'Sergeant Bottomley assured me, Canon, that I was entirely innocent. Do you think—?'

'Yes, I do. You're just a man racked with guilt and shame because you hated someone who never did you any conscious harm in his life. You were jealous of him, while all the time he was envious of you. Well, poor Lawrence is dead. But Laura is alive, and waiting to be healed.'

Walter Parrish smiled, and threw open the door.

'Come on, Nicky,' he said, 'come home to dinner at Number 7. You're getting under Inspector Traynor's feet.'

*　　　*　　　*

Sir Charles Blount strolled out of the dining-saloon of the cruise liner *Queen of Persia,* entered the spacious smoking-room, and sank into an upholstered leather chair. It was just after nine o'clock, and the twinkling electric lights had been turned on. There were a few other men in the comfortable panelled room, but they had congregated in the central area, leaving him to sit alone by the fireplace.

He lit a cigar, and watched the smoke rise up towards the vaulted skylight. Beneath the conversation of his fellow smokers, he could hear the quiet and steady throbbing of the ship's engines as the vessel bore them nearer and nearer to Gibraltar, and the North African coast.

When his business affairs had lurched into crisis in mid-1892, he had considered various schemes for making good his losses and disappearing for ever from English life. Ladymead was heavily mortgaged, and he was in debt to certain sinister organizations in Sicily. The Villa San Paolo, and much of its contents, would have to be sold. Plundering the cathedral treasury had been an easy thing to do, but once it was put in train, it became necessary to plan a way of escape in case of emergency.

At first, he had considered a sudden flight to New York on board the *Majestic*, the magnificent White Star liner, but had decided against it. He had no base in America, no friends to tide him over a very bad patch. Then, when Girdlestone had begun his damned importunities, his busybody poking about in the cathedral accounts, he had determined to remove him. If the police came too close for comfort, then he would slip away, unseen, not to New York, but to the familiar haven of Tangier.

The swing doors opened, and a steward came into the room. Sir Charles beckoned to him, and he came smiling across to the fireplace.

'What can I get you, Mr Leverson?' he asked.

'I'd like a double brandy and soda, steward,' Sir Charles replied. 'A decent brandy, you know. Where are we now?'

The steward cradled his tray in his arms. Mr Leverson was a generous kind of man, free with the tips. There was always time for a few words with him.

'Well, sir, we're hugging the coast of Portugal, and just passing the mouth of the Tagus. We'll be off Cadiz by dawn. You've not travelled with us before, have you, sir?'

'No, this is my first cruise. I must say, this is a splendid ship.'

The steward glanced round the room, taking in the white and gold stucco, the panelling, and the oil paintings on the walls.

'Yes, Mr Leverson, they're all nice boats on the Queen Line. This is a favourite late summer cruise with our regular ladies and gentlemen, with generous stops at Tangier, with an excursion to Gibraltar for them that want it, then Tunis, Malta, and Crete—I'll get you that brandy, sir.'

Really, thought Sir Charles, he had been

very clever. He could have travelled by rail through Spain, taking ship from Barcelona in one of the tramp steamers that would call in at the windswept little harbour at Tarifa. There was a ferry of sorts from there to Tangier, a mere eight miles to the south. But he had adopted a very much safer course of action.

Months earlier, near the beginning of May, he had booked two berths on the cruise liner *Queen of Persia*, scheduled to sail from Southampton on 1 September. He had used the name Horace Leverson, and poor Hayden was to have been his nephew.

Sir Charles felt a sudden spasm of shock as he recalled what had happened to Hayden. Tears smarted his eyes, and he drew on his cigar as a kind of palliative. On the very day planned for their dramatic disappearance from Ancaster, his secretary had come running down the stairs in response to his ill-tempered calling. Poor man! He had looked pale and shaken, and had pointed up the stairs as though drawing his attention to some danger. But he had been entirely unable to speak, and the baronet, still annoyed, had turned abruptly away towards the basement stairs. They had agreed to slip out of the house through the rear garden, with its dense shrubbery, and make their way from there to a quiet suburban railway station. They were to take tickets to London, and once there, change trains immediately for Southampton.

As he had opened the glass door into the sunken yard, Hayden had dropped dead at his feet.

The steward returned, and served him his brandy. The smooth spirit cheered him, and he began to relax.

It had been a harrowing business, concealing poor Hayden's body in the coal cellar, and slipping out on his adventure alone. Hayden had been a staunch ally for a number of years, a man who had been gaoled for forging a previous employer's cheque for £100. It had been a gamble employing him, but the gamble had paid off. Gentlemanly and efficient, he had been profoundly grateful to Sir Charles for offering him a post as secretary, and had proved to be a genuine asset. His gratefulness had helped to make him a more than willing accomplice in the business of the cathedral treasury.

Well, poor Hayden, like dear old Ancaster, was a thing of the past. An uncertain, but exhilarating future beckoned. He had always found Tangier alluring. It was a magical sort of place, defying any attempt at categorization. Its varied population spoke French, but they were not Frenchmen. Its native people were Muslim, but seemed tolerant of all who came to it. The Phoenicians had been there, and the Romans, and the Byzantines. At present, the French and the Spanish conducted a more or less genteel squabble over who should exercise influence there. The Sultan listened, and bided his time.

Sir Charles Blount recalled that for a very brief period in the seventeenth century Tangier had been a British possession, part of Catherine of Braganza's dowry on her marriage to Charles II. What was it that Samuel Pepys had called it? 'The most considerable place the King of England hath in this world.' Well, perhaps he'd been right, but it was not British now, and there were no tiresome treaties of extradition to interfere with his liberty.

When the cruise line reached Tangier, Mr Horace Leverson would simply walk away from the ship and be seen no more. He had already arranged for his house in Lixus to be stocked and serviced in time for his arrival. The shipping line was welcome to the few necessities that he had taken on board the ship. It was almost certain that his absence would not be discovered until the *Queen of Persia* docked at Tunis. In any case, that would be their affair, not his.

Sir Charles had no doubt whatever that he would be welcome. He was a friend of the Sultan, and he would be bringing the considerable wreck of his wealth to Tangier. But if things proved too problematical—well, he could move south to Fez, and further than that, if the need arose.

But these things were mere shadows. All

was going well, and very soon he would leave the *Queen of Persia* and set foot on the elegant esplanade at Tangier. He would retreat to his house at Lixus, overlooking the Roman ruins. It was a beautiful spot, believed by some to have been the Garden of the Hesperides, from which Hercules removed the golden apples . . . Sir Charles Blount drained his glass, left the smoking saloon, and retired to his stateroom for the night.

*　　*　　*

Next morning, Mr Horace Leverson took breakfast in the dining-saloon, and then went up to the promenade deck. It was a glorious day, and there were quite a throng of passengers crowding the rails. To their left, across the blue-green waters of the Atlantic, the hills and coastal villages of southern Spain lay basking in the sun. Soon, they would be turning gently away from the approach to the Strait of Gibraltar, in order to make for the North African coast.

A naval vessel of some kind was approaching from the Strait, its Red Ensign and Union Jack fluttering from the mast. A light cruiser, by the look of it, one of the numerous ships of the British Mediterranean Fleet. It was a smart vessel, with two raked white funnels. Its decks were crowded with sailors.

As they watched, a string of coloured signal flags was run up on the foremast. After a few minutes, it was taken down, and replaced with another string. There came the unmistakable ring of the ship's telegraph to the engine room, and the *Queen of Persia* stopped engines. Blount glanced up beyond the liner's two red and black funnels, and saw an answering line of flags hoisted on the rear mast—gaily coloured, patterned, merrily flapping pennons, spelling out words that he hadn't the skill to read.

Oh God! It could only mean one thing. They were coming for him . . . Nonsense! How could they know that he was on this cruise liner? It was some naval affair, nothing to do with him.

The passengers were curious, excited. 'Why have we stopped, steward?' 'A visit from the Fleet, sir.' The cruiser was almost upon them, and they could see her name painted on the head of the forecastle: HMS *Hardy*. Soon, the two ships lay only fifty yards apart, and the liner's passengers watched as the naval vessel lowered a sleek launch carefully from the davits.

A man standing beside Blount on the promenade deck had a pair of binoculars glued to his eyes. 'Here's a naval officer and a bevy of sailors coming down the gangway! They're climbing into the launch—oh, look! It's propelled by oars. I thought it might be a steam-launch. I say! Here's a gaggle of civilians, men in bowler hats, you know, and a brace of villainous-looking policemen—'

'I wonder, sir,' said Blount, striving to control the tremor in his voice, 'whether you would kindly lend me your binoculars?'

'Certainly, certainly! This is really very thrilling, don't you think?'

For a fleeting moment Sir Charles Blount recalled the face of Caroline Parrish, and the quirky tones of Nicholas Arkwright, and experienced an almost unbearable yearning for the life that he had wilfully and wickedly forfeited. The images quickly disappeared, to be replaced by the face of the fearful present. He glanced up at the blue sky, where the seagulls were wheeling, and smelt the fresh breeze blowing from the sea—the scent of liberty. He put the binoculars to his eyes.

The launch was approaching steadily and unhurriedly, propelled by six sailors at the long oars. In the stern of the launch sat two officers in white uniform, and four civilians. Three of them were unknown to him. The fourth, a man in a brown tweed suit, with a gold watch-chain glinting in the sun, was Detective Inspector Jackson of the Warwickshire Constabulary.

CHAPTER SIXTEEN

THE DEMONS BANISHED

Deep in thought, Walter Parrish spread marmalade on a piece of toast, then glanced down the breakfast-table at his host and friend from Cambridge days, Augustus Morton. Gussie had aged very gracefully and gradually, managing his increased girth by resorting to a sympathetic tailor. He had inherited Vaux Hall well over twenty years previously. Despite the cunning stratagems of his parents, he had never married. His brother Tom, who had been Nicholas Arkwright's friend at Oxford, had died eight years earlier. Gussie was drinking coffee while reading *The Times*. He seemed to accept his four guests as though they had always been members of his family.

It was idle, thought Walter Parrish, to try and recall the past, but the last few days in the seclusion of Augustus Morton's remote wooded estate had done much to heal the wounds of the last month. Millie and Laura had spent a lot of time together, and Walter was sure that various confidences had passed between the two women that would help to forge anew the friendship that they had enjoyed thirty years earlier. They were all meeting as friends, not as Canons, Deans,

Prebendaries and their wives.

Augustus Morton stirred in his chair, and looked up from his paper.

'It says here that Charles Blount has been seized at sea by that policeman you were telling me about. Detective Inspector Jackson. Very unusual, I should have thought.'

'He's a very unusual man, Gussie,' said Walter Parrish. 'As for Blount—well, he deserves what's coming to him—hey, Nicholas?'

Nicholas Arkwright, Walter thought, was looking very dapper. He'd evidently bought himself a new suit of morning clothes, and even at breakfast he was sporting a rosebud in his buttonhole. He was sitting next to Laura Girdlestone, talking to her in low tones. Indeed, for most of the last week he had monopolized Laura, and she had raised not even the ghost of an objection.

'What?' said Nicholas. 'Oh, yes. Of course he does. Fancy an Ancaster man behaving like that! It seems that his whole life was a sham. Those two Titians he had in his gallery were worthless copies, I've been told. He'd long ago sold the originals to stave off his creditors. And yet . . . I could have sworn he was a true friend. He and I shared so many strongly held beliefs.'

'I know,' said Walter, 'and he was fully committed to his work as Hereditary Clerk. You couldn't fault him over that. People can

325

be very peculiar.'

Augustus Morton snorted impatiently and threw his paper down on the table.

'The fellow was a damned murdering scoundrel, and deserves what's coming to him. Well, I'm going out with the gun to look for a rabbit. You good folk do whatever you like.'

Walter stole a look at Millie. She rose from the table, and said, 'Walter, let us go into the small drawing-room. I want to talk to you about the girls.'

Walter and Millie left the room, leaving Nicholas and Laura alone. They sat in a kind of tense silence for what seemed like minutes. They looked at the debris of breakfast strewn across the table, and listened to the ticking of the dining-room clock. Nicholas glanced out of the French window at the sun-drenched terrace. The whole house seemed to be waiting for him to act.

'Laura,' he said, 'it's rather warm in here. Let us go for a stroll along the terrace.'

Laura Girdlestone said nothing, but she stood up and followed him out of the room and on to the terrace that bordered the gardens at the rear of Vaux Hall.

There was no romantic moonlight this time, just a steady, late summer sun, and the healing quiet of the countryside. They walked in silence the length of the terrace. Laura suddenly spoke, and her words seemed to annihilate the gulf of years separating them

326

both from their time of youth.

'I thought you were going to propose to me, Nicky. I'm talking about that night in 1868, when you asked me out here on to the terrace. I waited and waited, but you said nothing. So I told you that poor Lawrence had proposed to me already, and pretended that I'd accepted—'

'Pretended? You mean—'

'He had proposed to me, earlier that day, but I hadn't given him an answer. So when you said nothing, I decided to make you jealous—I wanted to spur you on to say something! And you did. You hoped we'd be very happy.'

A younger woman might have burst into tears. Laura Girdlestone merely smiled.

'And so I thought you'd changed your mind. I haven't just made up that bit about poor Lawrence. He really had proposed to me earlier that day, but I'd told him that I couldn't give him my answer directly. I was so confident, you see, that you were about to sweep me off my feet.'

'And I, simple, tongue-tied youth that I was, believed you. Well, it's all over now, Laura. You can't recall the past.'

'Oh, quite,' said Laura. A very faint smile hovered around her lips.

'But you can live in the present, can't you?' said Nicholas. 'If you want to, that is.'

He fumbled in the pocket of his morning coat, and produced a small jewel case. He heard Laura's sharp intake of breath, and

327

knew that she had realized what it contained. He was about to conclude the scene that had been interrupted a lifetime ago by their mutual misunderstandings. He opened the case, and removed the silver betrothal ring set with small diamonds that he had bought from a local jeweller in 1868.

'I have kept this ring ever since that day, Laura,' he said. 'If you accept it now, you will have consented to be my wife. As a clergyman, I feel obliged to remind you that in heaven they neither give, nor are given, in marriage. But it's different here on earth. If you take this ring, then I'm absolutely certain that Joanna and Lawrence will give us their joint blessings from above.'

'Oh, quite,' said Laura. Her face was grave, but her eyes sparkled. She took the ring from his hand, and placed it on her finger. Nicholas suddenly went down on one knee.

'Laura,' he said, 'I've made it sound so matter-of-fact, when it should have been wildly romantic! So now, I'll ask you straight out, and wait in fear and trembling for your answer. Will you marry me?'

Laura Girdlestone laughed, and the sound seemed to banish the shadows that had lowered over her for so long. She stood up, and offered Nicholas her hand.

'You silly boy!' she said. 'Get up, for goodness' sake! Bishop Grandison always said you were a self-dramatizer. You'll dirty the knee of those new trousers.' She helped him to his feet.

'Yes, I will marry you,' she said.

'You know that I'm an epileptic?'

'You know that I'm a demon when roused?'

'Well, my dear, Ancaster's full of demons. There's certainly room for one more. But I'll watch my step in future. You must remember that I've been accustomed to a quiet life for a very long time.'

They walked in silence back along the terrace, each speculating on what life was about to bestow on them. Laura thought: I will be a wife again, married to the man I've always treasured secretly in my heart. I will gain a son in Conrad, and if things go as Millie Parrish and I would like, I'd gain a daughter in Caroline. And Nicky is right: poor Lawrence will look down from heaven and bless this marriage.

'Laura,' said Nicholas, as they neared the French window, 'I know that you've hated living in Ancaster. When I carried you off to Arden Leigh, you rallied almost immediately. I want you to know that I'll live wherever you want. If you wish to go to London, I'll resign the Deanery, and seek a post there. You wouldn't, in any case, want me living in poor Lawrence's house—'

'Why not? That house is the Deanery, and yours by right of office. But it was also Lawrence's home, and part of him will always be there. His books are there, his awful cellar of choice wines is there. It was Lawrence who transformed the gardens from a wilderness to the lovely place you see now. He's left his stamp on the place in so many ways. So if you accept me, a widow, as your wife, you've got to accept that Lawrence will be there, too.'

'And as to London—'

Laura laid a hand on his sleeve. She smiled at him uncertainly.

'Leave the question of London open for a while, Nicky. When we return to Ancaster, I'll go to the Deanery, and you stay where you are at the Prebendary's House. Then we can think about our future, including where we should be married. I'd prefer a quiet wedding, perhaps at St Paul's, Knightsbridge. Or even that little church out at Arden Leigh. Anywhere, really, as long as it isn't Ancaster.'

'Oh, quite,' said Nicholas Arkwright.

* * *

Caroline Parrish opened the gate in the railings opposite Number 7, Dean's Row, and walked through into the cathedral precinct. Laura Girdlestone followed her. They had spent a busy hour in the Deanery with Ballard, discussing such mundane things as patterns of wallpaper, and the respective virtues of Axminster and Wilton carpets.

They had gone upstairs, and Caroline had

rather timidly suggested that Laura should abandon the confining suite of rooms at the end of the passage with the lockable door, and create a new, larger, sitting-room for herself at the rear of the house, overlooking the green expanse of garden, and the grounds of the Bishop's palace. Laura had enthusiastically agreed.

Now, at just after ten o'clock, they were approaching the north door of Ancaster Cathedral. It was Caroline's suggestion that they should make the visit, ostensibly to look at the monuments, but in reality to help Laura to lay the ghosts of her resentment. The last time she had entered the cathedral had been on the occasion of her husband's funeral.

As they turned the corner from the transept, the great west window burst upon their sight, glowing magically in the strong sunlight, as though celebrating the myriad colours of the spectrum. Laura stood for a moment transfixed, gazing at the brilliant array of apostles and martyrs, her black mourning dress transformed for a moment by the dancing reds, and golds, and blues, and the subtle greens of Master Geoffrey's great creation. Tears sprang to Laura's eyes, and she turned to Caroline.

'It's so beautiful, Caroline,' she whispered. 'Somehow, I never noticed it before. I resented this place, because it claimed so much of my husband's attention. I thought of

Ancaster Cathedral as an ogre—a brute beast, squatting in the sun. But it wasn't! I see that, now. It was all part of my resentment.'

Laura turned away from the window and walked slowly down the nave. The great carved reredos surrounding the high altar exhibited its array of saints, dwarfing the elaborately carved stalls of the choir.

'This is the place that Nicky loves best,' she said, 'and this is where we'll stay. That man— that cruel murderer—was instrumental in having Nicholas Arkwright made Acting Dean. Poor Lawrence would want him to keep the post.'

'So you'll stay in Ancaster?' asked Caroline.

'Yes. Somehow, I've lost all my feelings of frustration, my burning hatred for the place. I'm seeing it for the first time as it really is. Many years ago, my dear, I was confined to an asylum. I was suffering from a severe depression, so extreme, that I had to be restrained. That illness was cured, but I think some traces of it still lingered, which was why I behaved so badly over Lawrence's funeral. When I organized that frightful event, I was really and truly not myself.'

As Laura finished speaking, Dean Arkwright came into the nave from the north aisle. He was deep in conversation with old Bishop Grandison, who was walking very slowly, and leaning on Nicholas's arm. The Bishop's face lit up.

'My dear Laura!' he cried. 'How splendid to see you! You're looking very beautiful, if I may say so. Yes, indeed. This foolish fellow finally discharged himself from the police station, and has promised me that he'll behave more sensibly in future.'

The old Bishop dropped his voice to a confiding whisper.

'He was keeping bad company, you know. He was consorting with a very shady character who was actually living inside his head! Still, he was only a lodger, and Nicholas has sent him about his business. Now he can turn his attention to the things that really matter.'

Awful old man! thought Nicholas. What does he mean by that—'the things that really matter'? He's leading up to something, mark my words.

'So you're getting married?' the Bishop continued. 'I'm so very glad. Nicholas told me, you know, that he'd thought of proposing marriage to you before. I can't think why he didn't—'

'We'll allow a decent interval to elapse, My Lord,' said Nicholas, rather loudly, 'and then we'll be married quite quietly, and without fuss, in London. Probably at St Paul's, Knightsbridge.'

'A decent interval, you say? Why should you want to do that? And what's all this nonsense about London? Now, what I suggest is this. It's 5 September today. Let the wedding be in four weeks' time, and then you can both settle snugly into the Deanery before the exigencies of the Christmas season claim all our attention.'

'Four weeks? But—'

'Yes, Mr Dean. Four weeks. And the wedding will be here, at Ancaster Cathedral, as befits the Dean of Ancaster and his wife-to-be. I shall be delighted to marry you both myself, at the High Altar. Laura, you must tell me all that happened when you stayed at Vaux Hall. Nicholas's lips, apparently, are sealed.'

Nicholas Arkwright opened his mouth to protest, but the Bishop merely murmured 'God bless you!' gave his arm to Laura, and carried off his prize into the north transept. Awful old man!

'Speaking of blessings,' said Nicholas Arkwright to Caroline, 'you've proved yourself to be a blessing to me, personally—a Godsend, if that isn't being too profane. I know there's a great difference in our ages, Caroline, but I felt that you were a true friend to me from our first meeting on the platform at Ancaster Station. Yes, a true friend, and a brave one, from all I hear. Perhaps, one day, you'll be a daughter, too.'

Caroline felt the tears rush to her eyes. How she loved this dear, funny man! She suddenly threw decorum to the winds and gave him a nice, old-fashioned hug. Yes, she very much liked the idea of being Dean Arkwright's daughter, and not just because that would mean that Conrad was her husband.

'It's early days, yet, Mr Arkwright,' she said, 'but I really hope that one day, not too far in the future, Conrad will offer me his hand in marriage. But if he doesn't—well, I'm always here, with Uncle Walter and Aunt Millie at Number 7, or visiting those three girl cousins of mine whom I've never met—Helen, Emily, and Nancy. So I'll never be very far away.'

*   *   *

Saul Jackson and Sarah Brown stood in the dusty lane outside Jackson's cottage, talking to Herbert Bottomley. The sergeant had toiled up the steep road from Warwick to the hamlet, to leave a sheaf of documents with the inspector.

'I'll not stop, thank you, sir,' he said. 'The wife will have dinner waiting, and the girls will make a scene and a sulk if I'm late. They're always hungry—the little ones, at any rate.'

He turned his fine grey eyes thoughtfully on Sarah Brown, and his manner suddenly became grave and confiding.

'I'm glad to have seen you this evening, Mrs Brown,' he said, touching his hat. 'They told me about you at Arden Vale, when I was investigating there—what you'd suffered, and how highly you'd thought of poor Mr Girdlestone. Well, missus, that good man has been avenged, and his ghost can rest in peace. And maybe you can rest more contented, now, knowing that justice has been done.'

They watched Bottomley as he walked down the lane to the paddock. Presently, he emerged from the field, sitting high on his chestnut horse. He raised an arm briefly in greeting, and then cantered away in the direction of Thornton Heath.

'Mr Bottomley's a wonderful man,' said Sarah Brown, shading her eyes to watch him as he disappeared into the distance.

'He is,' said Jackson. 'He can read people like you and I read a book, and that's what makes him such a good detective. I honestly don't know what I'd do without him.'

'Will he not try for inspector one day, Saul?'

'No, Sarah. It's the drink, for one thing. I always turn a blind eye when he falls off his horse, but there's others that wouldn't. He's a first-rate sergeant, and that's what he'll remain.'

They went back into Jackson's cottage, and the inspector sat down in his cane-backed chair. He had been busy all that day, first at Ancaster, and then over at Copton Vale. When he returned to Meadow Cross Lane, he had found a welcome meal awaiting him. They had eaten plates of boiled gammon, with potatoes and cabbage, and had just finished some apple tart when Bottomley had knocked on the door.

The remains of the meal still lay on the table. Sarah Brown refilled their teacups, and sat down opposite Jackson. She asked him a question.

'What happened to Mr Hayden, Saul?'

'Well, Sarah, as I told you, we found him lying dead in the coal cellar at Ladymead. Dr Venner came, of course, and examined the body, and the upshot of it all was, that Hayden had died of natural causes. His heart had suddenly given away.'

Sarah shook her head. The gesture might have been one of sympathy, or of disbelief at the quirks of fate that could kill a young man in his prime.

'So that was one death that we couldn't blame Sir Charles Blount for,' Jackson continued. 'But he killed Mr Girdlestone, and he killed that wretched man Obadiah Syme. Stabbed him, you know, and then set fire to his room. He confessed all once I'd got him back to England.'

Sarah Brown put her cup and saucer down on the hearth.

'What I don't understand, Saul,' she said, 'is how you found out where he was. He'd just disappeared, hadn't he? And yet you found him, somewhere out near Gibraltar, wasn't it?'

'He'd been very clever, Sarah. He'd booked two places on a cruise liner, one for himself, and one for Hayden, using an assumed name. Horace Leverson, he called himself. Hayden was to be his nephew, John Leverson. Clever, but only up to a point. When it came to paying for those tickets at the shipping office in Southampton, he used a cheque drawn on one of a number of accounts he'd opened in false names to hide the proceeds of his robbery— the fifteen thousand pounds that poor Dean Girdlestone was accused of stealing.'

Jackson shook his head. He never ceased to be amazed at the arrogant certainties of amateur villains.

'Now, I'd already put out alerts to all the ports about Sir Charles Blount, as you can do in the police, and with each of those alerts I'd sent a list of all Blount's false accounts. Sure enough, a sharp-witted clerk at the Queen Line offices in Southampton noted that the booking for a certain Mr Leverson and his nephew had been paid for by a cheque drawn on one of those accounts. And that, you know, was the end of him.'

'And so you went after him? Really, Saul, I'm always amazed at the things you think of!'

Jackson laughed.

'Well, one thing I didn't think of was that he had fled from Ancaster on the very day that Sergeant Bottomley and I went to his house, and found Hayden's body. That was why he left the body practically where it had fallen. The first of September was the day his cruise began. By the time I'd grasped the situation, the *Queen of Persia* had already set sail, and had reached the north-west coast of Spain.'

'So what did you do?'

'I crossed France by railway, and joined a cargo ship at Marseilles, which took me to Gibraltar. This had all been arranged, you understand, by people at the Home Office. Arranged through the electric telegraph. Superintendent Mays has a lot of pull in that quarter. And then I was taken on board HMS *Hardy,* a fast naval cruiser, and we were able to intercept the *Queen of Persia* just as she was approaching the Strait of Gibraltar. And that was that.'

'You arrested him?'

'The captain of the liner arrested him, and delivered him to the captain of HMS *Hardy,* because at the time we were out of territorial waters. I formally arrested him on the strength of my British warrants once we'd docked in Gibraltar.'

Sarah Brown got up from her chair, and began to put the plates on to a tray. Jackson watched her, and wondered whether she would ever consider marrying again. She had lost husband and children through cholera. He had lost wife and child through fire. Perhaps, one day, she'd want to be a wife again.

'You know, Saul,' said Sarah, picking up the tray, 'the folk at Ancaster call those figures on the cathedral tower the Ancaster Guardians. Very proud of them, they are, and not very keen on outsiders turning up when they hold their precious Revel. But I was talking to an old man yesterday, one of those Methodists, he is, and he told me that the chapel folk call them the Ancaster Demons.'

Jackson stirred restlessly in his chair. He'd not much time for superstition.

'They're just old statues, Sarah, put up there centuries ago. They do no harm, and they do no good. They're just statues. But there *are* demons at Ancaster, and they're where you'll always find them—in people's hearts. Dean Girdlestone's demon was the conviction that he was always right. Poor Dean Arkwright's demon was good old-fashioned envy. He's a very decent man, and he had to struggle for a long time with that demon before he crushed it. And Sir Charles Blount's demon was covetousness. He wanted things that he couldn't afford, so first he stole, and then he murdered for them. Laura Girdlestone's demon—'

Sarah Brown laughed, and held up a hand to stop Jackson's speech in mid-flow.

'Hush, Saul! You'll frighten me to death with your demons, especially as dusk's falling. I'll just wash these things for you, and then be getting back home before the light fails.'

Saul Jackson rose, and lit his pipe. Yes, it was time to forget the demons. For the time being, at least, they'd all been laid. He stood at the open back door of his cottage, watching the last rays of the sun disappearing below the embracing circle of trees.

*   *   *

'I must say, Mr Dean,' said Canon Parrish, carefully lighting his pipe, 'that old Bishop Grandison surprised me this morning. It's not often these days that he leaves the palace. I think he made a special effort today to save you from yourself. He's afraid that you'll make some other fantastic gesture to draw attention to yourself. This idea of his that you should marry Laura shows how wise he is.'

Nicholas Arkwright, for once, refused to rise to the bait.

'I came here to Number 7, Walter,' he said, 'to thank you for the miracle that you wrought at Vaux Hall. While I was protecting my false self-esteem in Primrose Street Police Station, you looked after Laura at Arden Leigh, and then swept her off to Gussie Morton's place in Essex. Somehow, that made the past leap back to life. It was due entirely to you that I won Laura's hand at last.'

'One does what one can,' said Walter Parrish, drawing on his pipe. He spoke dismissively, but it was obvious that he was delighted with Nicholas's sincere compliment. 'Incidentally, talking of Bishop Grandison, he told me the other day that your permanent appointment as Dean of Ancaster is almost certain to be ratified by the Privy Council next month. He told *me*, not *you,* because you were too preoccupied languishing in gaol. As you know, the Bishop is usually right.'

The two men, who were sitting in Walter Parrish's little study, were silent for a few moments. Then Arkwright spoke.

'I always wanted it, you know. The Deanery, I mean. I still can't really believe that it's happened. I can't wait to vacate that dreary house at the bottom of the steps, and come up here, to dwell among the bigwigs.'

Walter Parrish laughed. The 'bigwigs', indeed. What an idiot Nicky was! He thought to himself: I've always looked after Nicholas. I expect I always shall.

'Well, the diocese must continue to be governed,' he continued, 'and the cathedral to be cosseted, despite all our tragedies and triumphs. There'll be the question of a new incumbent for your parish of St Mary in Campo. They'll be sorry to lose you there, but of course you can't hold a parish and be Dean at the same time. Then there's the business of the choir school—'

'Lawrence Girdlestone informed me,' Nicholas interrupted, 'that the Dean is really and truly master in his own house. The choir school will be built on that vacant plot in Fort Street, just across the road from the almshouses. Master Geoffrey's window will remain unblocked in perpetuity. I intend to get our lawyers to fix that—for a fee, of course.

Oh, and the Ancaster Guardians will stay where they are. While Solomon's working up there on the St Catherine Chapel roof, he can make them secure. I think all that will form the agenda of the next Chapter meeting.'

Canon Parrish smiled wryly, and knocked his pipe out on the hearth.

'Yes, Mr Dean,' he said.

We hope you have enjoyed this Large Print book. Other Chivers Press or Thorndike Press Large Print books are available at your library or directly from the publishers.

For more information about current and forthcoming titles, please call or write, without obligation, to:

Chivers Large Print
published by BBC Audiobooks Ltd
St James House, The Square
Lower Bristol Road
Bath BA2 3BH
UK
email: bbcaudiobooks@bbc.co.uk
www.bbcaudiobooks.co.uk

OR

Thorndike Press
295 Kennedy Memorial Drive
Waterville
Maine 04901
USA
www.gale.com/thorndike
www.gale.com/wheeler

All our Large Print titles are designed for easy reading, and all our books are made to last.